*It was at times like this that Jim Raynor,
former marine lance corporal, proud citizen of the
Confederacy, and erstwhile farm boy,
felt most alive.*

At the speed at which he was urging the vulture, the wind cooled his face so that the oppressive heat vanished. He felt like a wolf hunting down prey, except the purpose of today's adventure was not the death of a living being but the death of the empty state of Raynor's and Tychus's wallets. This was a cargo train, not a passenger train, and inside its silvery innards was—if Tychus's tip was right, and Jim had every reason to believe it would be—a very lovely, very large safe filled with Confederate credits.

"Why, it's a rescue mission, Jim," Tychus had rumbled, his blue eyes dancing with good humor as he had filled Raynor in on the plan. "Those poor creds—they'd just be condemned to lining the pockets of some Old Families who don't need any more money. Or else put to some nefarious scheme that could hurt somebody. It's our duty—hell, it's our *calling*—to liberate them creds to where they could do something that really mattered."

"Like buying us drinks, women, and steak dinners."

"That's a good start."

"You've got a heart of gold, Tychus. I've never met a m̲a̲n̲

tears

DON'T MISS THESE OTHER THRILLING TALES IN THE WORLDS OF

STARCRAFT II

DEVILS'
DUE

CHRISTIE GOLDEN

Based on the video game
from Blizzard Entertainment

POCKET STAR BOOKS

New York   London   Toronto   Sydney   New Delhi

Pocket Star Books
A Division of Simon & Schuster, Inc.
1230 Avenue of the Americas
New York, NY 10020

This book is a work of fiction. Names, characters, places, and incidents either are products of the author's imagination or are used fictitiously. Any resemblance to actual events or locales or persons, living or dead, is entirely coincidental.

First Pocket Star Books paperback edition April 2012

POCKET STAR and colophon are registered trademarks of Simon & Schuster, Inc.

For information about special discounts for bulk purchases, please contact Simon & Schuster Special Sales at 1-866-506-1949 or business@simonandschuster.com.

The Simon and Schuster Speakers Bureau can bring authors to your live event. For more information or to book an event contact the Simon & Schuster Speakers Bureau at 1-866-248-3049 or visit our website at www.simonspeakers.com.

Cover art by Glenn Rane.

Interior art by Paul Kwon (1), Gerald Brom (2), Paul Kwon (3), and John Polidora (4).

Manufactured in the United States of America

10 9 8 7 6 5 4 3 2 1

ISBN 978-1-4391-9664-9
ISBN 978-1-4391-7271-1 (ebook)

This book is dedicated to the legions of StarCraft fans, who waited so long and so patiently. I must also thank the wonderful folks at Blizzard with whom it is always a privilege to interact, my former editor Jamie Cerota Costas, and my current editor Ed Schlesinger. You are all fantastic! I look forward to many more projects.

And finally, it's dedicated to "Butch and Sundance," Paul Newman and Robert Redford, whose cheerful presences helped guide its writing. A special nod of thanks to Paul Newman, who led a life that serves as an inspiration: a life dedicated to his craft and to helping others. Thanks, Butch. We miss you.

CHAPTER ONE

BADLANDS, NEW SYDNEY
2494

The sun was a merciless yellow eye glaring down at a landscape of rock, hard-baked earth, the hardiest of scrub brush and the most stubborn of life-forms. There was not a single cloud in the fiercely blue sky to mitigate the intensity of its gaze, and the promise of relief in the form of nightfall was many hours away.

Movement cut through this barren desert; silvery and sleek, it looked almost like water flowing through a valley, but it was nothing so natural or pleasant. The swollen sun's rays glinted harshly on the metallic train as it twined, snake-like, soaring through the badlands toward its final destination, where it would disgorge its precious cargo.

Two men waited in the cool shelter of a cave, watching the silvery serpentine object. They were silent, but it was an easy silence, and the only sound was the inhalation of one of them as he sucked smoke from a glowing cigar one final time, dropped the stogie, and crushed it out with a single step from a massive boot.

"Let's go ride that pony," said Tychus Findlay. Next to him, not in any way a small man but looking comparatively tiny next to the giant that was Tychus, was a shaggy-haired, bearded man who was already sitting astride a vulture hoverbike. He gave his friend a wicked grin.

"Move your ass, then, slowpoke," he said, kicked the bike into life, and charged down the sloping ravine toward the maglev train. Tychus swore, jumped on his own bike, and took after Jim Raynor at a reckless speed.

It was at times like this that Jim Raynor, former marine lance corporal, proud citizen of the Confederacy, and erstwhile farm boy, felt most alive. At the speed at which he was urging the vulture, the wind cooled his face so that the oppressive heat vanished. He felt like a wolf hunting down his prey, except the purpose of today's adventure was not the death of a living being but the death of the empty state of Raynor's and Tychus's wallets. This was a cargo train, not a passenger train, and inside its silvery innards was—if Tychus's tip was right, and Jim had every reason to believe it would be—a very lovely, very large safe filled with Confederate credits.

"Why, it's a rescue mission, Jimmy," Tychus had rumbled, his blue eyes dancing with good humor as he had filled Raynor in on the plan. "Those poor creds—they'd just be condemned to lining the pockets of some Old Families who don't need any more money. Or else put to some nefarious scheme that could hurt somebody. It's our duty—hell, it's our *calling*—to liberate them creds to where they could do something that really mattered."

"Like buying us drinks, women, and steak dinners."

"That's a good start."

"You've got a heart of gold, Tychus. I've never met such an altruistic man in my life. I got goddamn tears in my eyes."

"It's a tough job, but somebody's got to do it."

Jim grinned as he recalled the conversation. He and Tychus were behind the train, catching up to it quickly. He stayed right and Tychus veered left. Tychus crossed over the maglev tracks, adjusting the magnetic frequency on his bike to compensate so that he, like the train itself, could cross easily. Jim increased his speed, moving alongside the maglev until the right car came

into view. He and Tychus had spent hours analyzing all kinds of transportation vessels over the
last few years, sometimes simply from blueprints
or images, but usually up close and personal, as
they were about to do now. They had "liberated"
other credits before—it seemed to them like hundreds of thousands over the years, although the
liberated credits never seemed to stay with them
very long. That was all right too. It was part of the
ride that life had become.

"Careful, boy. Don't move ahead too fast,"
came Tychus's gravelly voice in his ear. "I ain't
coming back for you if you drop in on the wrong
car."

Raynor grinned. "Right. You'd just take all
the creds and hightail it out to Wicked Wayne's."

"Damn straight. So hit the mark."

Timing was crucial. Raynor sped up even
more, glancing down at his controls to see the
small dot that represented Tychus doing the
same. He knew they were mirror images of each
other after doing this as often as they had over
the past five years.

"Upsy-daisy," Tychus said. In unison, they hit
the lifts and rose vertically so the vultures—cus-
tomized within an inch of their lives—were now
flying, if not as high as their namesakes, then
at least slightly higher than the train's roof. The
uniquely modified hoverbikes landed, bumped

the top of the train, landed again, and the two men had them clamped and locked down within half a second—the magnetic locks also custom-installed for exactly this purpose. They leaped off the bikes. Next step: getting to the back of the car, climbing down, opening the door, and seeing who comprised the welcoming committee.

At that precise instant, the train took a bend and brought them right into a crosscurrent of wind. The sudden sharp movement threw Raynor off balance. He fell hard and started sliding toward the edge. Tychus's gloved hand shot out and grabbed the neck of Raynor's vest while he threw himself down, reached up, and seized the secured vulture.

Raynor jolted to a halt. Adrenaline shot through him, but not fear. He'd done this before, too, and he was prepared. He took a second to get his bearings, then pointed. One hand on the bike, the other clutching Jim, the bigger man moved Raynor about a third of a meter until he was facing the end of the car rather than the side.

"Hold my legs!" Raynor shouted to Tychus. Tychus grunted, releasing the vest collar, then grabbing first Jim's belt and then his ankle as Raynor slid forward.

Raynor pressed a button and activated the powerful magnets embedded in his vest. Between these and Tychus's near-bone-crunching grip on his ankle, Raynor wasn't going anywhere. Normally he'd try to drop down on the small platform at the back of the car, but the train was still going through what seemed to be a damned wind tunnel, and time was of the essence once they'd landed with what had to have been an audible thump on the roof of the thing. Raynor stretched forward far enough so he could get one arm down and felt about quickly but blindly. There it was: the top of the door. Not the ideal place to plant the explosive, but it would have to do.

He fished out the small device from his pocket, tapped in the activation code, slapped it on the door as far down as he could put it, deactivated the mag grips, and yelled, "Pull back! Pull back!"

Tychus yanked him back so hard, Jim felt the exposed part of his arms burn from the friction. It wasn't comfortable, but he didn't mind too much, as he was safely away from the explosion, which shot black smoke and bits of debris in all directions.

"Don't suppose you got anything resembling a look-see?"

"Nope," Jim said. Still lying down, he grabbed his pistol from his holster, shot Tychus a grin, and said, "What? You scared of dropping in on a bunch of Confederate guards?"

"Not me, little girl," Tychus said. His own

weapon was strapped to his back. He reached and pulled it out: an AGR-14 that looked as mean as Tychus himself. "Let's go."

Tychus dropped to his belly beside Jim, and they let the very speed of the train move them forward. They slid to the edge, and at the last minute each man shot out a hand, gripped the top of the train, and flipped down, somersaulting into the cabin, ready to attack.

They were greeted by no one.

"Aw, shit, Jimmy," Tychus said. "This ain't the car with the safe!"

Indeed it was not. It was crammed to the brim with cargo: instruments, statuary, furniture, all carefully wrapped up and secured. No doubt there was a fortune here, but it was nothing they could do anything about.

Jim half expected Tychus to slap the back of his head, but the man was already moving forward to the end of the car. "You were supposed to have done your research," Tychus muttered.

"I did," Raynor said. "Seventeenth car. They must have changed—"

Raynor was following, pistol out but pointed down, when a curious shape caught his eye. Tychus was wrestling with the door, so he permitted himself to pull back the protective covering.

His eyes went wide.

"We're gonna have to blast this one too, looks like—Jimmy, what the hell are you doing back there?"

Raynor paid him no heed. He tugged more, and the covering slipped away.

"I think I'm in love," he breathed as his eyes took in the beauty of the antique in front of him.

"You say that every time we visit Wayne's," Tychus muttered, but swung his head back to see what had Jim so distracted. "What the hell is *that*?"

Jim felt as though he were having a religious experience, and indeed the item he was gazing at worshipfully reminded him of the old-style stained-glass windows he had seen images of. It was a piece of furniture, though, huge and solid and curved at the top, like a window. Glass of bright colors covered its front, and if it was what Raynor thought it was, those curving tubes of glass would light up when the thing was activated. And inside—oh, inside was where the treasures were.

"I'm not sure—I've never seen one before, but I think . . . I'm pretty sure it's a jukebox," Raynor said, reaching out a gloved hand to touch the curving metal and wood and glass construct.

"I am no more enlightened than I was before, Jimmy," Tychus growled, "and time is wasting."

"A jukebox is an old, old method of playing

music," Raynor explained. "Music used to be pressed into vinyl disks called records. There might be up to a thousand songs in here—songs that no one's heard in maybe a couple hundred years."

"You and your old-fashioned crap. First the Colt, now this." They had done one robbery, early on, of the summer home of one of the lesser Old Families of the Confederacy. The place had been oozing valuable antiques, and when Raynor had stumbled across a Colt Single Action Army revolver hundreds of years old, he'd had to have it. It went with him constantly, although he had more contemporary weapons as well. Getting bullets made for the antique was expensive, so he rarely fired the thing. He just liked the feel of it on his hip. Tychus had rolled his eyes then the same way he was rolling them now. "Nice history lesson, Professor. Now, let's get our asses outta here. We still got a safe to blow."

Tychus was right. Raynor gave the old machine a final pat and turned to follow Tychus.

Finally, with a muttered grunt and a well-placed heave of his shoulder, Findlay opened the door, stepped out, placed the second explosive device on the door of the car ahead of them, and then ducked back into the car with Jim. Both of them dove for cover as the device detonated.

Raynor grimaced, for two reasons. One,

they usually only brought four sets of explosive devices with them: one to blow the door, one to blow whatever safe they were trying to open, and two as backups. Which they had just used. There had better be only one last door between them and their goal, or else the Confederate credits would not get liberated after all. Two, they'd have to make a stand here, in this room, and the jukebox might get hit. He found he was unreasonably distressed by the thought.

Even before the smoke cleared, the first few rounds of gauss rifle fire came through the blown-open doors, spraying down the contents of the room. There was a clang as metal struck and pierced metal, and pieces of wood splintered and flew up in the air. Crouched down behind what seemed to be an upright piano, Raynor didn't dare raise his head to see if his jukebox had taken any damage. He'd find out soon enough.

Tychus, with a roar, rapidly closed the distance between himself and the guards and began slamming them with the butt of his rifle. They were taken completely off guard, having expected an in-kind firefight and not anticipated that they would be rushed by an apparent madman. At such close quarters, they couldn't fire lest they harm one another, and Tychus and Jim whooped as they either knocked the hapless fellows unconscious or tossed them off the train through the blown-open doors. Tychus kicked the rifle out of the final guard's hands, gave him two quick punches, one with each hand, and then picked up the large man and chucked him out. He turned back, grinning and exaggeratedly dusting off his hands. Jim shot him an answering grin, then looked about, making sure that—

It had survived unscathed. Raynor let out a breath of relief and then realized something. Something he was going to have to tell Tychus, and that his friend would definitely not like. But that was later.

Now they surged forward, stepping over bodies to jump into the next car. There it was: a huge safe, big as life, a gleaming metallic box that filled up half the car.

And in front of the car, his eyes wide, his arms spread out as if he could actually protect the thing with his skinny body, stood not a Confederate guard but a mousy man in a uniform that marked him as a government employee.

Tychus blinked, his weapon trained on the man as Raynor's was, but didn't fire. "Son," he said, transferring the rifle to one hand and reaching into his pocket, "would you mind telling me just what the hell you think you're doing standing there?"

The man was trembling so hard, Raynor marveled that he could even stand erect. "Sir," he said, his voice shaking, "I am a duly retained employee of the CBPMVI and I very, *very* much regret to inform you that I cannot permit you to take the contents of this safe."

Tychus paused, an unlit stogie halfway to his mouth. "That's a mouthful of letters. Son? You don't want to be fooling around with old Tychus Findlay."

The man went milk-pale. "Oh, dear," he managed. Clearly he knew the name. His watery blue eyes darted over to Raynor, then back to Tychus. He swallowed hard as Tychus put the stogie between his lips, lit it, and took a few puffs.

"Mr. Findlay, Mr. Raynor, sir—if this were *my* stack of Confederate credits, I can't tell you how honored I would feel if you were the ones to steal it from me. But this doesn't belong to me. It belongs to the government of the Confederacy of Man, and I am charged as an employee of the Confederate Bureau of Protection of Monies and Valuable Items with making sure it arrives safely at its destination."

Tychus stared, puffing. Raynor shifted, following Tychus's lead and also lowering his weapon. For a long moment, the only sound was the rumble of the train and Tychus's sucking on the stogie. Finally, Tychus laughed, a deep chuckle that started in his chest and finally exploded in a loud guffaw.

"Son, you got balls, I'll give you that. I ain't never seen anyone stand up to me like that, let alone someone so puny who don't even have a weapon. What's your name?"

"G-George Woodley," the man stammered, starting to look cautiously optimistic that he might actually survive the encounter.

"You married, George Woodley of the Confederate Bureau of Protection of Monies and Valuable Items? Got kids?"

"Y-yes, sir, to both. I got me a wonderful wife and two beautiful children."

"Well, George Woodley," Tychus said, "you just put me in a good mood. And I tend not to kill people who do that. So if you'll just step aside, we'll blow this safe, and the Confederate Bureau of Protection of Monies and Valuable Items won't have to send a sad letter to your wife and kids."

The man's thin, ferrety face fell. "Oh, dear," he said again. "I'm so sorry, but I just can't do that."

While Raynor admired the man for taking his job so seriously, this had gone far enough. He lifted his pistol. "Mr. Woodley, we've gone to an awful lot of trouble today to get these credits. I'm pretty sure that the CBP . . . whatever the hell the rest of the letters are, doesn't pay you enough to stand there and get shot defending credits that belong to rich people."

"Well, sir, that might be true, but you probably ought to know that Marshal Wilkes Butler has been notified of the attack on this train and should be here shortly to attempt to take the both of you into custody."

Tychus let out another guffaw. "We ain't scared of ol' Butler," he said. "You're gonna have to come up with a better bogeyman than him if you want to frighten us away."

Butler had been like a dog nipping at their heels for the last couple of years. Once or twice, Raynor had to admit, the marshal had almost gotten them. But with every "encounter," he and Tychus had been given the opportunity to study the man and observe his methods. While Wilkes Butler was no one's fool, he hadn't managed to nab them, and that last bit was all that Jim and Tychus cared about. As Tychus had once put it while smoking a cigar and fondling a buxom beauty perched on his lap, "Only thing that matters is where you end up. 'Almost,' 'coulda been's,' 'shoulda had's,' they don't mean jack shit."

Raynor put on a worried expression for Woodley's benefit. "I don't know, Tychus," he said. "If Marshal Butler and his men are on their way, maybe we should just leave while the gettin's good."

Tychus turned, brows drawing together in a

scowl that had frightened braver men than Woodley, who emitted a whimper and then clapped his
hands over his mouth.

"You're talking like a yellow coward there,
Jimmy," Tychus said. "But you got one thing
right. We *should* leave—but we're taking that
money with us. Just gotta get this little rodent
out of our way, and then we can go."

He lifted his rifle and pointed it at Woodley.
Raynor felt a twinge of pity for the brave but ultimately foolish government man as he closed his
eyes and awaited the attack.

It came.

CHAPTER TWO

Jim launched himself at Woodley and brought the pearl-handled butt of the Colt down on the man's temple. He crumpled quietly to the floor. He would have one hell of a headache when he awoke, but he'd be alive to tell the tale.

"Funny little man," Tychus said, then turned his attention to the safe. "Grab something to truss him up with, and I'll blow this thing."

Raynor went back to the previous car to find some rope. The jukebox was there in all its cathedral-like glory, and again he paused, enraptured. He gently unbound the ropes from the piano they had hidden behind. Tychus entered at that moment, George Woodley slung over his shoulder like a sack of potatoes. Findlay stepped over the fallen guards, then dumped his burden unceremoniously and ducked, with Jim, behind another pile of what were probably priceless antiques.

Another boom echoed as the safe blew. Jim turned Woodley over onto his front and began to tie his wrists and ankles. As Tychus rose to get their newly liberated credits, Raynor said, "I want to take the jukebox."

Tychus turned on him, frowning. "*That* thing? It must weigh a metric ton. You out of your fekking mind?"

Jim shook his head, inspected the knots, patted poor George gently, and rose. "Nope. I want it. It's beautiful, it's rare, and I just know that one day we're gonna be glad we have her."

"'Her'? Damn, boy, you need a good poke if you're calling pieces of furniture 'her.'"

"That might also be true, but it doesn't change the fact that I want it."

"We got Butler barreling down here to throw our asses into jail. Or have you already forgotten what Woodcock told us?"

"Woodley."

"Whatever the hell his name was."

Tychus was probably right. And yet, Raynor glanced again at the jukebox, that exquisite house of so much old music that probably hadn't been heard in centuries. He just couldn't leave her behind.

"We can handle Butler. How many times have you told me that?"

"Damn it," Tychus snapped. "Just once I wish you'd throw my words back at me when I agree with them. All right, we'll take your damned Lady Jukebox. But if it's a choice between it and me, I'm dropping it. Understood?"

"Deal," Jim said. He was surprised that Tychus had agreed at all, even with conditions. They moved back into the car, and the lovely sight of the safe with its door hanging from the single remaining hinge cheered him further. Each of them set to work stuffing credits into the collapsible packs they had brought with them. Not that long ago Tychus would have insisted on taking the extra time to divvy up the money equally. During one of their first jobs together, Jim was pretty sure that Tychus had taken a bit off the top. Another time, Tychus had all but accused Jim of the same thing. Now they just shoved the creds in until their packs were bulging. Over the years, the trust they had built up in each other had survived a lot of testing, regardless of what might or might not have happened in the earlier days, and things like this were nothing new. They didn't even know how much they were "liberating"; they knew only that it was quite a lot, and would buy alcohol and the prettiest girls at Wicked Wayne's for a good long time.

"Okay," Jim said as he closed his pack securely and fastened it around his waist. "Let's get the jukebox."

Tychus shook his head but followed. "So, how do you propose we get that thing outta here?" he asked as they stood again before the ancient machine.

Tychus was strong. Very, very strong. But even he wasn't as strong as a man in a combat suit. And, of course, they had come without their suits this time, on the theory that agility was more important in this particular heist than brute strength.

"There's got to be a way to move this thing," Jim said aloud, working the problem through as he spoke. "Some kind of dolly."

"Figure it out and hurry the hell up. I ain't getting any younger, and Butler ain't getting farther away." He stood back, folding his arms and watching Raynor poke around until Jim found what he was looking for. A hoverdolly, switched off and tucked back in a corner behind a ceramic elephant that somehow had managed to avoid all the gunfire. He eased it out and activated it. It hummed to life, lifting itself about a third of a meter off the ground. Raynor poked a button, and the dolly rose another third of a meter. He grinned in triumph.

It was going to be tricky, but it could work. "Okay. We get the thing on the dolly and lift it up onto the roof. From there we slide it onto the back of my vulture, and off we go."

"Mmm-hmm," Tychus said. "There are *people* I wouldn't do this for."

"People," Raynor said earnestly, "aren't jukeboxes."

"Got that right. Come on, crazy man. Let's get that thing on your vulture before Wilkes Butler surprises us and dies laughing."

"It's not gonna stay level," Tychus said about seven minutes later.

"Yeah, it will," Raynor said with more confidence than he actually felt. They had attached the hoverdolly to his vulture. While at ordinary speeds the hoverdolly might work as intended, Jim was having his own doubts about whether or not it would tip over at the speeds they would have to reach to escape from—

"Everyone's at the party. It's Butler," Tychus said.

Raynor craned his neck to see where his friend was looking and groaned inwardly. There were several small puffs of dust in the distance blurring into one large cloud, and the merciless sun glinted on metal.

"Damn it," Raynor said, and made a decision. With pursuit this close, there was no way he could go slowly enough to prevent the hoverdolly from jackknifing and destroying the beautiful jukebox. "Let's get it on my vulture."

"No. Leave the damn thing, Jimmy."

"Come on, we can slide it right off and tie it down."

Tychus sighed and expressed his displeasure by blowing a puff of cigar smoke in Jim's face. Nonetheless, he went to the dolly, steadied himself, and heaved.

Not for the first time, Jim was impressed by the sheer physical power of the man. The jukebox weighed three hundred pounds if it weighed an ounce. And while Tychus did break a sweat and the veins stood out on his neck as he lifted and pushed the huge piece of furniture, he nonetheless managed to move it slowly and steadily onto the back of Raynor's vulture. Jim would sit directly in front of it. Jim tried to help, but he did little more than guide the jukebox and quickly strap it down. Together, they heaved the now-useless dolly off the side.

Tychus stepped back. "First round of drinks at Wayne's is on you, buddy. Now let's haul ass."

With that, he mounted his own vulture. Raynor glanced back at the jukebox, marveled at his own stubborn foolishness, and followed.

The chase was old hat. But they had never let Butler and his posse get this close to them before, and Raynor had never had a three-hundred-plus-pound jukebox on his hoverbike before, and he was alarmed at how much it slowed him. Too, the credits strapped to his back made balance even more precarious. Findlay was already a rapidly disappearing speck in the distance. His voice crackled in Jim's ear over the comm.

"I said haul ass, not drag it."

"I am," Raynor replied.

Tychus said something that would blister paint off the wall, and Jim saw his friend curve to the right and come back. "I'm going to draw them off and give you a chance to get some distance, Grandma. What the hell are you going to do with that thing?"

"The cave," Jim said, referencing the place where they had first caught sight of the maglev. "It goes pretty deep, and it's in the middle of fekking nowhere."

"I'll meet you there. If that thing falls on you, though, I ain't coming back for you."

"Oh yes, you will," Raynor said. "I still got a shitload of Confederate credits on me."

Tychus chuckled and gave Jim a one-fingered

salute as he roared past him and in the direction
of Butler's posse. Raynor returned the salute and
headed off as fast as his overburdened vulture
would take him.

Tychus was not an incautious man. Even when
he seemed reckless to others, he knew exactly
what he was doing. But he also enjoyed having
a little fun with fate from time to time, and now
seemed to be a pretty good opportunity.

He grinned, imagining the confusion that was
going through Butler's mind as he headed *back* in
their direction, then veered sharply to the left.
And he laughed out loud as they all came to a
screeching halt and scrambled to change direction in order to follow him. He heard shots, but
they went wide; no one was going to be able to
aim for at least a few seconds, and by that point
he'd be leading them on a merry chase.

For all his joking with Jim about Wilkes Butler, Findlay knew the man was never to be taken
lightly. Once you started underestimating the
enemy, that was when he pulled something that
got you killed. One hoverbike had already recov-
ered and was barreling down at him. That was,
Tychus suspected, the good marshal himself.

Tychus and Raynor had scouted out this
locale for several kilometers around. While he
did not quite know it like the back of his hand,

Tychus suspected he was more familiar with it than Butler, and headed southwest to where he knew a nice little obstacle course would present itself.

Here in the New Sydney badlands, ravines, canyons, and the tower-like formations color-fully known as "hoodoos" were everywhere. The route Tychus took now was an alternate one he and Jim had scouted out and dismissed once they found the cave and the coolness it provided. It was twisted, convoluted, and dangerous—and therefore exactly what Tychus was looking for.

"Any sign of pursuit?" Tychus asked Jim.

"Nope," came Raynor's voice. "Looks like you got them all following you."

Tychus slowed down slightly, just enough to tease his pursuers with the hope that they might actually catch him, and then took them to an open area where dozens of long, jagged hoodoos erupted from the earth. He drove straight toward one, veering at the last second. Butler's men were good: they missed the stone pillar.

This time.

They weren't so lucky the third time Tychus made a seemingly suicidal run at one, veering at the last minute. Two of Butler's men were follow-ing too closely and collided spectacularly as they awkwardly attempted to avoid the rock. One of the bikes slid into the eons-old rock formation.

A huge chunk toppled free and a third hoverbike narrowly avoided it, only to lose control and go spinning into the dirt.

Four more were still coming. Tychus lost one of them zipping in and out among the columns, and another when he led them straight for a dramatic drop-off, swerving at the last minute. He took the curve too fast, however, and found himself staring at a sheer rock wall. Swearing, Tychus leaped off the vulture scant seconds before it slammed into the stone. He hit the sunbaked earth hard enough to have the wind knocked out of him, but not hard enough to injure himself or—perhaps more important— dislodge the credit-laden pack strapped onto his back, and came up with his AGR-14 in his hands.

Gunfire spattered erratically around him. Findlay dove for the cover offered by a huge boulder and fired the rifle, taking down one of the two remaining vultures. The man leaped out of harm's way but did not land as well as Tychus did, and as the final vulture came to a stop and there was a sudden silence in the hot air, Tychus heard the wounded man swearing.

"I wouldn't do that if I were you," Tychus warned as the man seated on the remaining intact vulture pointed a pistol at him.

"Tychus Findlay," said Marshal Wilkes Butler.

He didn't lower the weapon. Tychus didn't lower his. They stared at each other.

This was not the first time the two men had found themselves in this position. Wilkes Butler was in his early forties, of middling height and build. He was almost entirely ordinary looking except for a thick head of glossy black hair, a magnificent mustache that almost completely hid his mouth, and absolutely piercing blue eyes. Now he wore a helmet with a visor that hid both black hair and blue eyes, and the gun didn't waver.

"Wilkes Butler," Tychus rumbled in return.

"Where's your buddy?"

"Nowhere you need to worry about," Tychus replied. "I don't know about you, but I'm finding it mighty hot out here. I could use a shower and a woman or two and a cold beer or three. Maybe you can go rustle up some iced tea or something."

"You've stayed a step ahead of the law for too long," Butler said. "If you're so hot, I know a nice shady prison cell for you."

Tychus sighed, brought the rifle over toward the still-swearing but living man, and planted a single spike between his legs a scant two inches from his crotch. The man squealed and scooted backward, an action that simply produced more pain.

"I missed," Tychus said. "I won't miss again. You shoot me, my finger convulses—your man is dead. Or else without some equipment I think he'll miss right badly."

Tychus saw the muscles in Butler's jaw clench and could almost hear the man's teeth grinding together. After a moment, he lowered the gun. Tychus made a beckoning gesture, and the marshal tossed the gun—carefully—in Tychus's direction.

"I always said you was smarter than you looked," Tychus said. "Off the bike, and slowly. Mine seems to have met with a mishap."

Butler obeyed, his eyes looking daggers. With the rifle, Tychus waved him back to stand over near the wounded man, who, if he wasn't imagining things, looked grateful at having been spared death or a fate worse than.

"Thank you kindly, Marshal," Tychus said, straddling the vulture. "Nice bike you got here."

Without another word, Tychus roared off into the distance. A scant second later, he heard shots being fired, but they went wide. He grinned and turned the bike back toward the cave where he would rendezvous with Raynor.

"Busted your darling yet?" he asked Jim as he approached.

"Nope," came Jim's voice in his ear through

the link. "Waiting for you to unload it, you big ox. What's taking you so long?"

"Had to change bikes. You intent upon keeping that antiquated music box?"

"Hell yeah. I'm coming back for her. I got a feeling she's going to come in real handy one day."

"You know what's handy?" Tychus said. "A shitload of credits to buy beer, cigars, and women."

"You got me there."

CHAPTER THREE

TARSONIS CITY, TARSONIS

Tarsonis was the habitat of the rich and famous, of captains of industry, of scientific geniuses and political masterminds. The gleaming towers of its capital rose proudly, glittering structures whose lines were elegant and harmonious. They created an unparalleled skyline, representing the pinnacle of the Confederacy's technology: not just a city, but a super-city. This was where deals—of all varieties—were struck, and where someone emerged flush with victory and someone went home licking his wounds, only to come back for another round. Any new fashion, event, or technology was seen and applauded and courted first here by the Old Families of the Confederacy. Tarsonis in all its splendor was in its own way not quite real: a high-tech toyland where fortunes were lost and made daily and all could be mended with the right wine, or cigar, or drug, or whispered word. The very air of Tarsonis City—so unimaginatively named by the Old Families, who were not particularly imaginative themselves—capital of the planet, seemed to thrum with power and felt thick with intrigue.

There was, as was true of all things, a shadow side to the shining city. There were slums, and alleys, and people lying in them. Some were even alive. They had no beautiful homes with verandas, no servants. They did not dine on expensive imported food; sometimes they did not dine at all. In a place called the Gutter—a slum that ran beneath most of the shining city, even under the senate building, Nagglfar Hall, its marble-columned glory lit as brightly as if it were midday—there was filth, and death, and malice. Tarsonis was as ugly as it was glorious.

An elderly, white-haired man strode down the steps of Nagglfar Hall with a briskness that belied his years. Hale and tanned, with the practiced smile of the lifetime politician, Senator Westyn MacMasters emerged from its hallowed depths. He waved genially to the throngs assembled as if they were old friends, even though they were separated from him by lines of Special Service agents who wore expressions that indicated they didn't give a damn about the forthcoming speech, only about protecting their charge. As MacMasters approached the podium decorated with the crest of the stars and bars of the Terran Confederacy, there were still more lights: those of cameras filming the event. A band was playing the Confederate anthem, "To the Eternal Glory of the Confederacy," and doing so rather well. It finished to great applause, and MacMasters smiled out at the crowd before beginning his speech.

The man in the window of the building kitty-corner to the senate building knew Tarsonis City well. He had lived there until his late teens, viewing the city from a private terrace of a sixty-three-room mansion.

His name had once been Ark Bennet, son of Errol Bennet, of the Old Family Bennets, and he knew the man who was currently in his sights; had had dinner with him, played with his two sons. But the man in the window, who blinked steadily, regulated his breathing and practically his heartbeat as his world slowed down, was no longer that privileged, impossibly sheltered young man.

As a teenager, straining against the constrictions placed on him by the circumstances of his birth, he had slipped out while attending a conference with his father in the Hall of Reason. Wandering less than a mile from the safety of the university, Ark Bennet, scion of one of the Old Families, had been approached by an attractive young woman, drugged, and abducted, and had wound up conscripted into the military. At first, he had been frantic to alert his father about his situation. He had filed forms and affidavits again and again. It seemed to have no effect.

And then something happened. He found something he was good at—very, very good at.

Killing.

Ark had been the son of wealth and privilege, but there had always been something lacking in his life: a purpose, a direction. Something he could contribute. And in the military, this almost uncanny gift he had—he had heard it termed "the X factor," an ability to seemingly slow the passage of time as he took his shots—had helped win battles. Even more importantly, it had saved the lives of friends.

Ironically, it was when he had ceased to worry or wonder if he would ever have a chance to go home that two men from the Military Security Service had arrived. He had lied at first, saying that he had faked the claim about his true self. But they had confronted him with irrefutable proof as to his identity. It was then that he had pleaded with them—tried to explain as best he could what his new identity, his new role in the world and his ability to protect people he now thought of as family, meant to him. And they had understood, and at that moment Ark Bennet was dead, and Ryk Kydd was permitted to live on.

But things had happened. Bad things—things that shouldn't have happened. Some friends—many—had died, and he had parted ways with those who survived. Ryk Kydd was, and would always be, a sniper par excellence. Except now he wasn't doing it for the military: he was doing it for himself. He had become a hired killer. There was no noble cause now, just the cold action of pointing the rifle, squeezing the trigger, and collecting his pay.

Although he had once known the man lined up in his sights, Kydd felt nothing for him one way or the other. He didn't care about MacMasters's politics, or his family, or the ramifications of the action about to occur. All he cared about was doing this thing he was so good at, using the gift some hellish angel had blessed him with.

"Fellow Confederates, I cannot tell you what joy it brings me to see so many of you turned out here tonight."

Gently, like a lover caressing the object of his desire, Kydd placed his finger on the trigger. There was no computerized helmet to help him gauge the temperature, humidity, altitude, and barometric pressure. There were only slight modifications to the scope of the rifle itself. He had surpassed the need for most of that, experience and instinct coming together in a duet of death.

Carefully, Ryk started to squeeze the trigger.

"Not the best idea."

At once Kydd spun around, but the intruder was too fast. There was a blur of motion, a swirl of a long coat, and a kick too swift to see, and Kydd's rifle went flying out of his hands and clattered on the floor. Even as he lost his grip on it, Kydd was reaching for a dagger, which he brought down with all his strength on the arm clutching his coat.

It clanged on impact, the blade slipping off to the side uselessly. Startled, Kydd stared up at his attacker.

The man grinned wolfishly. "Cybernetic arm," he said.

Quick as a thought, Kydd shrugged out of the black coat caught in that mechanical grip, dropping and sliding, scissoring his legs to try to trip the man. He was rewarded by feeling the man's balance shift for an instant. His pleasure was short-lived, however, as the attacker kicked free, leaped straight up, and landed hard with one booted foot on Kydd's left hand. Kydd arched his back, his mouth open in a silent scream. The stranger sprang back into a martial arts stance.

"One down," the man said, grinning. His lean, angular face was decorated with a neatly trimmed goatee, and his teeth looked startlingly white. He licked his lips in anticipation. "Three to go."

". . . and their grievances are perfectly just. Shiloh and other worlds have tirelessly given of themselves to feed the Confederacy, particularly during wartime. Given to the point where many, busy producing food for others, have nothing to eat themselves. To go hungry when—"

Kydd bolted upright. His left hand was completely useless, but his right still clutched the dagger. He let his gaze flicker to the rifle, and as his adversary's eyes turned to follow his, he hurled the dagger straight and true, right for the man's turned, exposed neck.

The cybernetic hand whipped up faster than the eye could follow, and closed down on the blade.

"Nice try."

The next thing Kydd knew, white-hot pain seared his right hand, and he was lying on his back again. His own dagger had pinned his hand to the floorboards. He tried to pull free, to clasp the hilt, slippery with his own blood, with his smashed left hand, knowing that any second now the man would be on him to finish the job.

Except it didn't happen. His would-be killer hung back, his white teeth gleaming, his eyes bright as he watched Kydd struggle. He was . . . *enjoying* this. Kydd had faced death before. He had the natural fear of such a thing, but as he glanced up at his attacker and saw that grin, a new kind of fear, hot and electric, blossomed painfully in his heart. The man grinned more widely.

Furious and frightened, his broken hand unable to grip the hilt sufficiently, Kydd leaned over and fastened his teeth on it, tasting the metallic tang of blood. Clutching the hilt with his teeth and simultaneously *willing* himself to pull it free, he succeeded. But what could he do with two ruined hands?

The only thing he could do. He scrambled to his feet and leaped forward in a flying kick.

Kydd's feet met some sort of light armor, and even as the kick connected, the unknown man moved with the blow. Kydd fell hard on the floor.

"—to report that Farm Aid is doing exactly what it is supposed to: feed the loyal farmers whose sacrifices have placed them in this sad situation."

Cheers and applause greeted the statement, but Kydd did not hear them. All his attention was focused on the man now descending upon him, his fake arm shooting out to close on Kydd's throat so fast, it was a blur. The hand started squeezing, slowly, and with equal slowness the man lifted Kydd off the floor. His thin lips peeled back in a grin.

"Somebody wants you dead," the man continued in an almost conversational tone. "That's fine by me. But he didn't stipulate *how* you were to die. Nor how long it should take. That was left up to me to decide." And then the man actually winked. "And we got *all night.*"

Terror threatened to close in on Kydd, but he fought it back. With the cybernetic arm, his assailant could have snapped his neck instantly. Instead, he was choosing to kill slowly, and that gave Kydd a fighting chance. Using the arm that was choking him as a support, he pressed down on it with his lower arms, lifted his legs up, and kicked out as hard as he could. His attacker stumbled back a step or two, but the grip around Kydd's throat didn't loosen.

"How's it feel now, Ark? Having trouble getting air in? Feeling the blood pressure build up? Do you want to swallow?"

He couldn't break the man's grip, because it wasn't a man's grip—it was a cyborg's—and panic surged up into Kydd as he struggled. He tried to lift his legs for another attack—the only option available to him—but he didn't have much strength left, and they kicked ineffectively, swimming in the air until with his other arm the assailant almost casually slammed something hard against Kydd's kneecaps. Distantly Kydd realized it was his own rifle.

Kydd couldn't even howl in pain, the cry stifled by the implacable fingers closing, closing around him.

"—are honoring those Old Families who have seen the need and generously donated to those less fortunate than themselves, who might otherwise be too proud to ask for the help they so need. Those who would harm the Confederacy, such as the terrorist Sons of Korhal, who would take food from the mouths of—"

"Good," the man murmured. He tightened his grip slightly. Kydd's crippled hands flew to the false fingers, stupidly, uselessly trying to pry them from the slender human throat they were crushing. Blood thundered in his ears. His lungs labored to get something, anything—the merest puff of air—into them. Darkness started to melt in around his vision. He kept flailing, though, slapping his crippled hands against the metal substance of the human-looking arm. His legs moved ever more frantically, and he felt a warm wetness seeping into his crotch area.

The hand on his throat kept squeezing.

He felt heavy, too heavy to resist, to move. His eyes closed, and he felt himself being shaken, the grip loosening

"Damn it, not yet!" the man cried.

But it was too late. Kydd didn't hear it, nor the growing passion in the senator's speech, nor the wildly cheering crowd.

He didn't hear anything at all.

For a long moment, the murderer simply stood in the room, alone with the corpse that five minutes ago had been a living, breathing human being, and who had been so beautifully, gloriously afraid. Sighing, he relaxed his fingers and let the body thump to the floor.

It hadn't lasted nearly long enough. He gazed ruefully at his artificial hand, flexing and twiddling the fingers. "Don't know my own strength sometimes," he said. He picked up the rifle and took a moment more to caress it, thinking about how many times Kydd had held it, had fired it, had snuffed out a life in a heartbeat. Chances were the victim never knew it was coming.

Where was the fun in that?

He turned his attention to the body, got what he had come for, dropped it in a small satchel, and rose. He went to a corner of the room near the door and picked up a small device he had activated when he first entered, before he had revealed his presence to Kydd. His metallic hand closed about it protectively, and he smiled.

His job done, the killer turned and left.

"Let us not be dazzled by lies dressed up to look like truths. Let us remember that the Confederacy and the Old Families always—always— have our best interests at heart. Ladies and gentlemen . . . for freedom, for Farm Aid, and for the Confederacy!"

The bright lights from the rally spilled in through the window, casting their illumination on the floor and on what was left of Ryk Kydd, once known as Ark Bennet.

CHAPTER FOUR

**RED MESA, NEW SYDNEY
WICKED WAYNE'S**

The erratically blinking sign proclaimed the establishment to be Wicked Wayne's, although the "n" and the "e" kept shorting out so that it more often read as "Wicked Way's." When Raynor was drunk, which usually happened a couple hours into any visit here, he found this beyond hilarious.

Even now, the sight made him smile as he and Tychus entered, climbing up the familiarly creaking wooden steps into a bar/gambling house/"dance hall" that was raucous, smelly, and lively. Jim loved the energy of this place. Unlike some places he and Tychus had visited, it did not have any pall of despair hanging over it like a thick cloud. No one came here to drown their troubles. People came here to have fun. Big Eddie—Jim and Tychus had been coming here for years, and Raynor still didn't know the man's last name—had an eye for finding and removing not only belligerent and possibly violent customers, but morose and melancholy ones as well. Wayne, for whom the place was named, once said a sad drunk was just as bad as a mad one, and neither would be tolerated in his establishment.

"Evenin', Mr. Raynor, Mr. Findlay," Big Eddie said. Every bit as large as Tychus, he was much better weathered, lacking scars or a broken nose. "Welcome back."

"Hey, Eddie," Raynor said, and slipped him a handful of credits. "When you're off duty, enjoy yourself on me."

Eddie chuckled. "I will at that, Mr. Raynor. Thank you."

"Daisy working tonight?" asked Tychus.

Eddie's smile, wide as the sky, widened further, showing he still had all his teeth. "She most certainly is, but if she wasn't, I'm sure she'd come in special for you."

Tychus grinned.

Lots of people did things special for Jim and Tychus. They always spent their money freely and with good cheer, and Wayne, Eddie, Daisy, and the others looked out for them. Many a time had Butler and his deputies tried to surprise the two, and each time their plans had been foiled. Wicked Wayne's looked after two of its best clients in every way.

The music was loud, with a heavy thudding boom that Jim could feel in his bones. The air was thick and gray with smoke, and the laughter was raucous and frequent. Tychus took a deep breath.

"That's the smell of pleasure, Jim," he said. "Only a couple scents missing: the sweat of the man who's losing to you, and the perfume of the girl you're slamming."

"You're a poet, Tychus."

"Heh. Don't I know it. Ah, there's my girl."

The stage was in the center of the place, with the bar on the left side and a VRcade off to the right. Several gambling tables were set up in the back, near an easy exit. On the stage now, wearing luminescent jewelry and enough scanty pieces of clothing so that they'd actually have something to remove for the customers, were the girls—and boys—of Wicked Wayne's.

Tychus went right up to the chairs closest to the stage. He glared at the man currently seated within groping reach of the dancers. "You're in my seat," Tychus rumbled.

The man looked up at him. "Don't have your name on it."

"This does." Tychus made a fist with his left hand and brought it close enough to the man's face so that he could read the letters P-A-I-N—a letter tattooed on each finger.

Jim chuckled at just how fast the blood drained from the man's face as his eyes flickered from the word to Tychus's implacable expression. Without a word, he and his buddies picked up their drinks and relocated. Tychus settled into the chair, plopped his booted feet on another one, and grinned up at one of the gyrating dancers. Tall, red-haired, with legs up to *here* and breasts out to *there*, she wore infinitesimal scraps of fabric that barely concealed the gifts that nature and, Raynor always suspected, technology had given her. This was Daisy, Tychus's favorite of all the girls at Wicked Wayne's, and she gave him a big smile, a wink, and a shake of her finely curved behind as she continued to dance in heels so high and so spiked that Jim always thought they could be used as weapons.

Jim grinned and headed for the bar on the left. Misty was tending tonight, and he was delighted. While the dancers of both genders were permitted and, frankly, expected to give "private performances," the bartenders were under no such instructions. But Misty liked Jim, and he liked her, and if her shift ended on time, sometimes she'd serve him a drink upstairs.

"Jim!" Misty was adorable. Petite, impish, with pale blond hair, hazel eyes, and a body that had none of the outrageous curves of the dancers but was decidedly attractive, she was much more appealing, Jim thought, than any of the actual performers. "How you been? I see Tychus has found his usual seat."

Jim laughed. "Some things never change."

"Let's see, Scotty Bolger's Old No. 8 for the both of you, and beer chasers?"

"That doesn't change, either."

She winked. "Coming right up."

She moved to get two shot glasses and two beer steins. He watched her appreciatively for a moment, then turned his attention back to the dancers.

They were certainly worth paying attention to. One particularly striking "performer" removed what was left of her costume and tossed it at Tychus, then turned her dark head slightly to catch Jim's eye. He was glad he'd ordered drinks because his mouth was suddenly dry. The brunette beauty gave him a sultry wink and mimed a kiss, then continued performing.

"Her name's Evangelina," said a voice behind him, and he jumped, turning guiltily to Misty as she shoved the beverages at him. "She's new. Very popular."

Her voice held no trace of jealousy. Evangelina.

Jim had to smile a little. The unit to which he and Tychus had once belonged had gotten the nickname Heaven's Devils. Evangelina was an angelic name, and her face was indeed as lovely as any angel's he'd ever seen painted. But that body certainly promised devilish things.

"She busy tonight?"

Misty gave him an annoyed look. "Jim, I just take drink orders. Wayne handles everything else."

Properly chastened, Jim nodded. He leaned over and gave her a kiss on the cheek. She gave him a look. He gave her credits.

"That's better. Go have fun. I'm off later tonight if Evangelina's got no time for you."

He smiled at her and returned to the table, carrying all four drinks carefully, and set them down. Tychus handed him the still-warm brassiere Evangelina had removed. "Here."

"Uh, thanks," Jim said. He placed it down on the table slightly awkwardly and took a sip of Scotty Bolger's whiskey. He smiled at the familiar burn and looked around. This was home, such as it was, and had been for almost five years now. Wayne ran a good establishment: his dancers, bartenders, and dealers were paid well and liked working here. He and Tychus were always made welcome, and even though he suspected it was more because they usually showed up with fistfuls of credits rather than because they were just so inherently likable, it was a good feeling.

There had been camaraderie among the Heaven's Devils that Raynor found himself missing. He had some of it still with Tychus, but most of the Devils—red-haired, fire-tempered Hank Harnack; kindhearted Max Zander and Connor Ward; Tychus's onetime girlfriend Lisa "Doc" Cassidy—were dead now. Dead because of the treachery of their commanding officer, Colonel Javier Vanderspool—the one person they should have been able to trust. Ryk Kydd, the sniper who'd saved their asses more times than Raynor wanted to admit, had gone off on his own. They hadn't kept in touch. Most of the memories of those times were piecemeal and vague; Jim hadn't wanted to remember much about it.

But here, while this was hardly a familial establishment, there was a sense of family. Of belonging.

"It's good to feel . . ." Tychus frowned. "What's the word I'm looking for? That word when you don't have no more stress and tension and danger breathin' down your neck."

"Relaxed?" Jim offered.

"Yeah, that's it. It's good to feel relaxed for a while."

"You better not be spending all my credits.

You still owe me from that time you pocketed more than your fair share of the deal."

Tychus placed a huge hand to his heart, looking offended. "James Raynor, I ain't never done no such thing."

"Sure you didn't." Most of the time, this was just banter, as it was tonight. But sometimes Jim wondered. Tychus Findlay could be counted on to always look out for himself.

Jim took another sip and leaned back in his chair. His eyes wandered to sloe-eyed, red-lipped Evangelina. Again Jim swallowed hard.

"Tychus," he said, "I got a problem."

"Ain't never seen a problem enough creds can't fix, and we got ourselves a fekkload of creds," Tychus said, downing the whiskey in one quick motion and reaching for the beer. He gave Raynor an amused glance. "So, what's yours?"

"Evangelina," Jim said, nodding at the goddess parading about on the stage.

"I wouldn't call that a problem."

"Well, see. . . . Usually Misty and I sheet dance if she's free. And she's free tonight. But . . . Evangelina . . ."

"Is smoking hot," Tychus supplied helpfully. "Still ain't a problem." He winked at Jim and took a long pull on the dark amber beverage. "Have 'em both. Problem solved."

Jim supposed it was.

* * *

The fone had the most horrible noise in the world. Especially if you were dreadfully, agonizingly, and profoundly hungover.

Beep. Beep. Beep. Raynor felt as if his eyes were glued shut and his limbs weighed a thousand pounds each. Fifteen angry elephants were stampeding inside his skull. "Just shut up," he told the fone. What came out of his dry, foul-tasting mouth was "Uuhhnnggg . . ."

The girl lying beside him murmured something, shoved at his chest weakly, rolled over, and covered her head with a pillow. For a terrible moment, Raynor couldn't recall which one he had decided to take to bed. He wrested one eye open. Judging by the length of the female body under the covers, it was Misty.

Beep. Beep. Beep.

"Turn it off," snapped Misty, her voice slightly muffled. Jim moved his heavy-as-lead body toward the table and made an attempt to get the fone. He encountered his Colt first—as he should have—and shoved it aside. His fingers closed on the fone for an instant, fumbled, and succeeded only in knocking it off the table. He swore and leaned over to get it.

The blood rushing to his head only exacerbated what was vying for the Worst Hangover in the Universe title, and he almost threw up. With a heroic effort, his hand closed over the fone. He heaved himself back onto the bed and looked at the message, rubbing his bleary eyes with his free hand.

It was from one Myles Hammond. The message consisted only of a handful of coordinates.

Jim tossed the fone back onto the table. It made an incredibly loud clatter.

"Shit," Raynor said, and covered his face with the pillow.

PITT TOWN, NEW SYDNEY

The terrain was all but lifeless. Not quite the unforgiving emptiness of the badlands: there, people had never quite dwelt comfortably. Here, they once had thrived. And that made it feel all the more empty.

Once-hospitable land had been bombed into aridity. No grass, no trees. The only sign that life had once flourished here were the skeletons—though mercifully not of humans, not anymore. The skeletons that loomed on the horizons were those of bombed buildings. A wall here and there, or a pile of tumbled plascrete—sometimes an entire house missing only the roof and people to live in it—stood silent, accusatory sentinel over the area. These were stark reminders of what human beings could do to each other when one faction decided it didn't like another. The Guild Wars, the wars in which Raynor and Findlay and their other friends had fought, had seen to it that this was all that was left of Pitt Town. Jim would like to think that people wouldn't forget, that they would learn from it, but he knew better than that. There would be other bombed-out skeletons in other places, in other planets of the Confederacy. The only difference between wars was how long the lulls between them lasted. Once, he had been naïve enough to believe in things like a "cause" and "justice." And then he'd fought in the Guild Wars and seen, up close and very personal, that the only "causes," really, were those of the individual. With good people, there were good causes. With selfish, evil people—

Jim hadn't even left a note for Misty. He hoped to be back before she woke, and if not, he knew she'd simply shrug and get on with her day, with her life. The message from Myles Hammond had told him too little and too much, and both things had put him in a foul mood. And when he was in a foul mood, he tended to not want to be responsible. Besides, the wind in his hair felt good.

He veered to the left, to the remains of a building so nearly obliterated that it was impossible to tell what kind of function it had served in better times. It was large, so Raynor guessed it was a public building of some sort. Saloon, hotel, magistrate's office—all were hideously equal in the aftermath of a war.

He brought the vulture to a halt. He checked his fone. According to the navigation system on the vulture, the coordinates that his old friend Myles had sent him should be just a few steps ahead. Raynor trod carefully over the broken lumber and shattered plascrete. And there, partially obscured by the pile of rubble in which it had landed, was what he had expected to find.

The beacon was an older model, small and decidedly not sleek. But it served its function. Jim nudged it with his toe and debated with himself.

He didn't want to find out what it said. He really, really didn't want to. There was no way in hell that anything Myles had to say to him at this point in his life was going to be good news. His hangover was receding but still there, crouching in the back of his mind like some dark beast. He rubbed at his beard.

But he did have to find out what it said. He owed the man that much—he owed *himself* that much. Sighing, Raynor squatted down, pressed a button, and activated the beacon.

A holographic image of Myles Hammond appeared. Jim hadn't known Myles when he had hair, but the fringe that had encircled his head above the ears was now snowy-white rather than gray. He had always been lean, but now he looked even thinner. All in all, he looked older than Jim remembered him—older than a mere five years should have aged a man—but that was no surprise. War and time did that to people.

But Jim suspected mostly war.

"I've always been a blunt man," said Hammond's image, "and I don't beat around the bush. Jim, you need to come to Shiloh, and you need to come soon. There's issues with the money you been sending to your mom." The hologram sighed. "She ain't taking it, Jim. She's getting by, thanks to something called Farm Aid. By that I mean she's getting food and the basic comforts, but . . ." The image looked flustered. "I can't tell you what I need to this way. We need to talk in person. Come on back to Shiloh. Come on home."

The image flickered and disappeared.

Raynor stared at the spot where the image had been. What did Myles mean, "issues" with the money? Why wasn't his mother taking it? He couldn't go back to Shiloh. Myles knew that. What was going on? His mother needed that money. Had needed that money for a long time, since before his father had died. It was the reason he had joined the military in the first place—to help out with money back home—and now there were "issues" . . . ?

His eyes narrowed. Was what Myles had said really true? The whole thing was really kinda strange, when you thought about it.

Anger flooded him. He swung his leg back and was about to boot the beacon all the way to Shiloh. He gritted his teeth, turned, and kicked out at a rock instead. He wished he could tear this whole place down around him with his bare hands. He forced the anger down and ran a hand through his wind-tousled hair, then made his decision.

He knelt beside the beacon and erased the message on it. Thumbing a button, he heard it click and hum and come to life as it recorded.

"Can't come to Shiloh, and you know it. I got the heat all over me. And . , . tell Mom to take the damned money." *Somehow. Get her to take it, and you better not be touching one lousy credit yourself.* He thought of Karol Raynor, that steady, stable, wise woman, and swallowed. "I don't care how you do it; just *do* it. And don't contact me anymore unless you gotta."

And that was all he had to say, really. For all his comments about being a man who didn't beat around the bush, Myles was being very cryptic. Raynor ended the recording. He tapped in a few coordinates, flicked a button, and the beacon whirred and vibrated for a bit before retracting its landing legs and moving slowly skyward, hovering there for a moment before suddenly shooting straight up.

It was going home, to Shiloh.

Jim Raynor wasn't.

CHAPTER FIVE

TARSONIS CITY, TARSONIS

Ezekiel Daun's duster moved with him, billowing about his calves as he strode fluidly down the long, dim hallway. In one hand he carried a small satchel. His booted feet were muffled by carpeting as he was led through the building by a cheerful, smiling young man. The high-rise was a maze of corridors and elevators and secured rooms, most of which looked identical, so Daun supposed it was logical to assume he might get lost.

He knew, however, that such a concern was not the real reason for the guide. He had been examined—politely and courteously and with many apologies, but still frisked—when he had arrived. The guard had worn an expression similar to the white-clothed man who was leading him at the moment; apparently the boss man wanted all his employees to be resocialized. Daun imagined that made them easier to manage.

All his employees, of course, except those he had to go outside his little group to hire.

Like Daun.

"And these are the master's quarters," the resocialized servant, or resoc, said, stopping in front of a large door. In contrast to the sleek, modern, artistic feel of the rest of the high-rise, this door looked somber and forbidding. It would take a lot to break through the thick neosteel door, and the keypad on the right demanded not just a code, but fingerprint and retinal scans as well. Humming a little to himself, the resoc entered the code and submitted the other verifications of his identity. After a moment, with a groan of protest, the door slid open. It was even more dimly lit inside than in the corridor, and initially Daun could see nothing.

"He's expecting you," the resoc said. "Please go on in."

"Thanks," Daun said.

"I'll be waiting right outside to take you back when you're finished." The resoc beamed as if the prospect of this made him deliriously happy.

"Of course you will."

The attendant's smile never wavered as the door slowly closed.

Daun's eyes adjusted to the dim lighting. He wasn't sure what to expect, but this certainly wasn't it. There were various computer stations and other pieces of equipment in the room, outfitted with many blinking lights and operated by resocs who did not give Daun a second glance. But that was not what so intrigued Daun.

What intrigued him was a large metal coffin. Or at least, it looked like a coffin. Lights chased one another along the outside, and several tubes went in and out from small apertures. Another caretaker stood discreetly off to the side in front of a screen on which statistics rolled constantly, and a strange bellows-like contraption moved slowly overhead. There was a rhythmic noise, a sort of dull thunk, that occurred every few seconds.

There was one thing that made it significantly different from a coffin, however.

A head was sticking out at one end.

Daun smiled a little at the contraption. His smile widened at the sound of a voice, hollow and echoing and obviously artificially enhanced.

"Ezekiel Daun," the voice rumbled.

"The same," Daun said.

"I presume you have brought good news."

Ezekiel shrugged as he opened the satchel.

"Well, if you call this good news, then it'll make your day."

He reached into the satchel, grasped something, pulled it out, and tossed it in the direction of the iron lung.

Bouncing and rolling, the head of Ryk Kydd came to a stop and stared sightlessly back at Daun. His expression was frozen in stark, utter horror, the eyes shut, the mouth open.

"Bring it here," the voice ordered. "Let me see it. Quickly, you idiot!" One of the resocs stepped forward. His face betraying nothing but calmness, he grasped the severed head by its hair and lifted it up, showing it to the man in the iron coffin.

The only sound for a moment was the rhythm of the machine.

"It's a start, Mr. Daun." The resoc stepped back, casually holding the head as he awaited further instructions.

Daun narrowed his eyes.

"I believe you have two more left, don't you? Don't come back until your satchel bulges with two other trophies: Tychus Findlay and James Raynor."

Daun grinned. "Don't worry, old man. They're next." He inclined his head and went to the door. He rapped on it, and it opened. The resoc awaited him, smiling.

"Seems like you like your job an awful lot," Daun said to the resoc.

"Why, yes, sir, I do."

"So do I."

Tychus was very warm. It was because he had company.

Curled up spoon fashion in his arms was the lovely Daisy. She was sleeping soundly, snoring just a little bit. In Daisy's arms was Annabelle, also dead to the world. Behind Tychus, her arm draped over his waist, was Anna-Marie, and snuggled up with her was Evangelina.

"Mornin', sunshine."

The voice did not belong to any of the four beauties currently sharing his bed. Tychus opened one eye.

Staring down at him was what seemed like a walking cadaver. Impossibly lean and gaunt, with eyes that were large and intense, the man stood with his hands clasped behind his back.

Several responses went through Tychus's head, but all of them involved disturbing the ladies, who seemed quite comfy where they were, thank you very much. So he chose the one option that didn't disturb them. He blinked at the man, sighed, and languidly reached for a cigar and a lighter. Daisy and Annabelle shifted slightly but otherwise did not seem to be awake. Tychus blew a long stream of smoke upward.

"You got about two seconds to tell me who you are and what you want 'fore I get real nasty."

"Who I am is not important," Cadaver said in a thin, reedy voice. He did not appear at all intimidated. "I am in the employ of one Scutter O'Banon, and he sent me with a proposal."

Tychus continued puffing. The girls were starting to awaken but, taking their cue from him, merely stared at the newcomer.

"Friend of yours?" asked Daisy sleepily.

"Well, honey, that remains to be seen," Tychus said. "Tell me more about this proposal."

"You've caught Mr. O'Banon's attention, Mr. Findlay. You and your colleague, Mr. Raynor. You've managed to impress him, and he's not a man who impresses easily. He'd like for you to join his organization. He thinks you'd be very valuable assets, and he would treat you accordingly."

"Well," Tychus said, sitting up and letting the sheets fall around his waist. "That's a mighty flattering thing to say. Mr. O'Banon is quite the powerful fellow, ain't he?" He scratched his belly absently. "Now . . . I respect power. I really do. But you know what I respect more?" He waited.

The man gave an exaggerated sigh. "No, Mr. Findlay. What do you respect more?"

"Money."

Cadaver nodded. "Mr. O'Banon understands that sort of respect. He intends to give you quite a bit of money. *Quite* a bit."

"How much?"

"As I'm sure you can understand, I cannot reveal figures, because we do not know what sort of assignments Mr. O'Banon will have for you. Let me put it this way." He pointed at the girls, who were lazily listening to the exchange. "You could buy and sell these . . . floozies . . . two dozen times over."

The pretty faces were marred with frowns as the girls, sleepy as they were, realized they had just been insulted. Tychus patted Daisy's head and chuckled.

"Well, that sounds right fine, but I'll need to discuss it with my business partner before making any kind of commitment. I'm sure Mr. O'Banon will understand that. Now, you got about three seconds to get out."

The man looked confused. "I will relay your response, but why three seconds?"

"'Cause I need to pee about a liter's worth, son." Tychus made as if to move the sheet.

"Oh . . . of course. Please excuse me." Cadaver, his lips turned down in disgust and his pale cheeks coloring in embarrassment, turned and hastened for the door, Tychus's booming laughter following him down the hall.

* * *

Raynor was in a foul mood when he stomped up the stairs to Wicked Wayne's. He needed a drink, a woman, and entertainment, not necessarily in that order. The daytime bartender, Keifer Riley, glanced up and saw Jim's expression. A wise man, Keifer didn't even try to engage Raynor in conversation, just slid him a beer across the bar. Jim expressed his appreciation with a grunt and chugged half the beer immediately.

The place was oddly darker during the day than at night. Once the sun went down, spotlights on the dancers and the illumination of the several video games provided quite a bit of light. During the day the windows were shuttered, and the only light came through the thin slits in the blinds and from the small lamps at the gambling tables. Over in a corner, though, he saw movement, and a small glowing orange-red dot, and he knew before his friend spoke that Tychus had taken up residence there.

"Grab me one while you're up," Tychus said. Jim did so and plunked the amber bottle down in front of Findlay. Three dead soldiers were lined up beside the remains of a meal that would have fed any two other men. Tychus pushed the plate and the empty bottles aside when Jim sat down.

He blew out a long stream of smoke, then eyed Raynor. "Where you been?"

Jim scowled. "Personal business."

Tychus nodded and chewed on the stogie for a moment before continuing. "I had some business come my way this morning."

Jim had a dim memory of Tychus leading—could it really have been four?—women upstairs sometime last night. "Personal business?"

"Well, one might say it was, considering the man came into my room while I was surrounded by lovelies," Tychus said, feigning thoughtfulness.

"Holy shit, really?"

"Yep." Tychus took another drag, and the ember glowed like an orange eye. "Man's got balls, that's for sure."

Jim was forced to agree. "So, what did he want?"

Tychus's eyes crinkled in a grin. "Us, Jimmy boy. Apparently our fame is beginning to spread. Not that that surprises me none. You knew somebody'd be hollering like a little girl after we liberated those creds."

Jim grinned, remembering the rabbity Woodley. "Have a lead on a job for us?"

"Not . . . exactly. Fellow didn't give his name, but he told me who he works for. Says his boss is mighty interested in forming a mutually beneficial relationship. Promised it'd pay well. Very well."

Jim's eyes narrowed. "Tychus, after the day

I've had, I'm really not interested in hearing about being somebody's puppet."

"Aw, hell, Jim, I ain't even named the guy."

"So name him already."

Tychus leaned forward. Raynor did as well. Tychus brought his mouth close to Jim's ear and whispered, "Scutter O'Banon."

Jim gave his friend an incredulous look. "Fekk that. You know what kind of a reputation that man has?"

Tychus nodded.

"Well, then, you know my answer. That man—" Jim realized his voice had risen and brought it back down. "That man deals in the worst kind of shit. The things connected with his organization—hits, drug running—Tychus, there are predatory animals that ain't that vicious. It ain't just stealing or even killing."

Tychus rumbled noncommittally, his eyes still fastened on Jim. "So?"

"So I don't want to get mixed up in that. We danced close enough to that edge when we went AWOL. This guy sounds like Vanderspool, only about six hundred times worse. The bastard's . . . I don't know, Tychus . . . *evil*. I didn't get into this to work for some thug, or to become a criminal."

Tychus ground out his cigar and laughed, long and low. He reached for his beer. "Hell, Jimmy, what the fekk do you think you *are*?"

For an instant, Jim almost lost it. His teeth clenched and, unbidden, his hands curled into fists. Tychus eyed him steadily. Jim thought of his mother's tired but sweet face. His father's innate decency.

Those memories were chased away when Jim thought about how he, Tychus, and the rest of the Devils had been slated for resocialization by their unit commander, Colonel Javier Vanderspool. The once-elite and valued unit was, in the end, used as cannon fodder, chewed up and spat out. Betrayed. But then he thought about how much sheer fun he and Tychus had had over these last few years. He thought about the Colt and the jukebox, and his lips twitched with an unbidden grin.

"Yeah, I guess you're right," he said.

"Fekk yeah, I'm right."

"Well, then"—Raynor lifted his half-finished beer—"to criminals . . . who work on their own."

"To criminals who don't need a space mob." Tychus clinked his bottle of beer against Raynor's and then drained it down. "So, if we're not throwing in with Scutter's merry band, I got an idea of what we should be doing next."

Jim sighed inwardly. "You spent your share already? We just got the creds!"

Tychus shrugged his massive shoulders. "Settling old debts, taking care of four girls for several days, and lubricatin' all of Wicked Wayne's adds up, Jim," he said with mock seriousness. Jim grinned and shook his head.

"Daisy says you still ain't paid her," he said.

"Daisy always says that. But yeah, I'm getting low. You know I hate being in one place too long, and besides, ol' Butler is gonna come sniffing around here eventually. He always does."

They differed on that. Jim cast a longing look around the bar/dance hall/gaming establishment/pleasure pit that was Wicked Wayne's. This place was oddly comforting to him. It was home when he was on this planet, and he preferred it to most other comparable places he'd visited. He'd be happy to hang out here for much longer than another night or two. But Tychus was right about one thing: Marshal Butler usually checked out Wayne's every time Jim and Tychus pulled something on New Sydney. No one had ever ratted them out, and they'd either been tipped off that the marshal was coming or had the blind luck to just not be here.

"All right," Jim sighed. "What's your plan?"

"Got a lead that Barton Station is going to be getting a shipment of crystals in later this evening." Tychus had leads everywhere. When Jim commented on the astounding number of contacts the man had—and that he'd yet to see any of them turn on him—Tychus had rumbled, "You forget, Jimmy, I been at this for a lot longer than you have. I got the nose for 'em. You'll get it too."

Raynor wasn't so sure.

"Well, that's mighty fine, Tychus, but the fact that it's the damned Horley Barton *Space Station* would kinda indicate that it's *in space*. And you and I don't have a ship to get into space."

"Not yet we don't. But I know where to find two little planet-hoppers just begging to be liberated."

"Planet-hopper" was the term for a short-range spacecraft. That would work well enough, Jim thought. "Oh?" he asked Tychus. "Who is keeping them prisoner?"

"Marshal Wilkes Butler and his buddies."

Jim stared, then threw back his dark head and laughed. "You embarrassed poor old Butler pretty good just a few days ago," he said. "This is really gonna ruffle his feathers."

Tychus grinned. "But ain't that fun?"

Jim pretended to consider, then drawled, "Well, I reckon it is."

CHAPTER SIX

RED MESA, NEW SYDNEY
RED MESA COUNTY MUNICIPAL
ENFORCEMENT DEPARTMENT

It had not been the best of weeks for Marshal Wilkes Butler.

New Sydney was, if not exactly a hive of criminal activity, certainly a fringe world that was known to be friendly to those who were not necessarily on the right side of the law. Butler and his men were therefore kept busy. He had been offered a transfer to Tarsonis two years ago and had turned it down on the belief that he could make more of a difference here. Crime in a place like Tarsonis was much different than here on a fringe world, on the outer edge of the reach of government and politics. There were fewer . . . entanglements. Butler was a man who liked things as clear as possible. He preferred to be unencumbered by shades of gray. He did what he did, and did it well, and, while having no trouble reporting to the sector's magistrate as was his duty, preferred to have no master other than the law itself in his day-to-day activities. In Tarsonis, nearly everyone had his fingers in someone else's pie. There were deals, and payoffs, and looking the other way.

Butler never looked the other way. There was keeping to the law, and there was breaking it, and heaven help any lawbreakers who happened to take their activities within his jurisdiction.

The wall in the entryway to the Red Mesa County Municipal Enforcement Department had been plastered with wanted posters when Butler first arrived. Now large patches of the wall were bare, save for pushpins trapping small bits of paper. He paused and glanced briefly at the faces. He knew them all: names, ages, criminal records, contacts, bounty fees. His eyes narrowed as they fell on two in particular.

The blunt, ugly mug of Tychus Findlay stared out at him with squinty eyes. The same eyes that had squinted at Butler while Findlay had deliberately shot at an injured man. Beside Tychus was Jim Raynor. This man did not look like a criminal, but his record gave the lie to his otherwise genial appearance. Butler did not know which one was the brains of the outfit, though obviously

Findlay was the brawn. He imagined Raynor, but Tychus Findlay was no stereotypical stupid thug, either. Butler suspected both of them were highly intelligent, even if they tended to take outrageous risks. That made his job all the harder.

He thought back to the chase Findlay had led him on a few days ago. They had been seven against two at the outset, then Findlay had too neatly gotten them going after him alone. Seven. One by one they had fallen, victims of the chase through the treacherous badlands. Three of the men were still in the hospital; one of them had just come out of a brief coma. The rest were in various stages of being walking wounded, and only two had come back to even shortened shifts. He was grateful Findlay and Raynor had not added murder to their already-existing charges of theft and manslaughter. It was a lucky break—for them.

Butler passed a hand over his face, his spirits briefly lifted as he rubbed his thick mustache. Rumor had it they were still planetside. He didn't think they had any vessels. Sooner or later they would be too cocky, or forget about some key element, or trust the wrong person.

And then he would have them.

He opened the door to his office and blinked in surprise. A woman was standing there, her back to him, silhouetted by the window. It was an enticing silhouette: she had a perfect hour-glass figure, a short skirt, and long legs. As she heard the door open, she turned around and stepped away from the window.

Butler swallowed hard. Her face was exquisite, with pale skin, high cheekbones, and green eyes. Red hair tumbled down her shoulders. Her breasts strained against the buttons of her dress as if the fabric were a hated jailer. Her legs seemed to go on forever and ended in dainty feet in stiletto heels. She smiled at him, full red lips parting to reveal even white teeth.

"Uh . . . ," he managed, "may I help you, miss?"

The smile widened. She put her purse on the desk, moved over toward him with the grace of a big cat, and closed the door.

"I don't—"

She turned around and draped her arms about his neck, smiling up at him. Her perfume made him slightly giddy.

"My name's Daisy," she said, in a sultry voice, "and I am here all morning because those two fine, upstanding gentlemen, Tychus Findlay and James Raynor, felt that you should have some kind of . . . recompense . . . for your stolen little ships."

Butler swore, firmly removed her hands from his shoulders, and pushed her away as he raced for his desk. He slammed a hand down on the intercom, and his cultured voice was heard throughout the station.

"This is Marshal Butler. All officers available, to the depot. Now."

Daisy sighed as he raced past her out the door. Halfway out, Butler paused, stuck his head back in, and fixed her with an intense gaze.

"Stay right here." Her knowing laughter followed him out. He ignored her.

Raynor and Findlay. Damn their eyes.

By the time he got there and had hopped off his hoverbike, all the officers in the area had been alerted and had arrived. The building's alarms were wailing, and the poor fellow whose job it was to open up in the morning looked like he was waiting to be shot in the head.

Butler would have liked to have obliged, but he wanted to shoot Raynor and Findlay even more. Besides, on this planet, men who were willing to work on the right side of the law for the paltry sum of credits the government parsimoniously doled out were few and far between. He couldn't lose any of them—not even the idiots.

He didn't waste time with "What happened here?" or even "How did they get in?" The answer to the first he already knew, and the answer to the second was irrelevant at the moment. Instead he asked, "What did they get?"

"Two planet-hoppers, sir," the man said. He looked slightly less nervous, but only slightly.

"Damn it." Now they *did* have ships.

"Any leads, sir?" asked his deputy, Rett Coolidge. Rett had the distinction of being the last one Findlay had injured in the recent chase and had come perilously close to losing a certain part of his anatomy that most males were extremely partial to.

Butler smiled bitterly beneath his mustache. "Tychus Findlay and Jim Raynor," he said.

Rett swore violently. "What makes you say that? Not that I don't believe it."

"They had the audacity to send a girl to serve as 'recompense.'" It was really too bad he couldn't have the girl arrested. While prostitution—at least by that name—wasn't legal on New Sydney, exotic dancing, right down to performing buck naked, was. And she hadn't said that she was offering her body. She likely would, when questioned, say that Jim and Tychus had hired her to go "dance" for the good marshal. But she'd have to be one hell of a dancer for her performance to pay for two planet-hoppers.

"Go to my office," he told Rett. "Hopefully there's a woman still there."

Rett raised an eyebrow, and Butler scowled at him. "Come on, Rett, she's one of Findlay's and Raynor's girls. Find out what she knows. We can hold her on associating with known criminals if we have to."

"Yes, sir."

"Sir!" It was the security chief of the depot, and his face looked considerably brighter than it had a few minutes ago. "The transponders affixed to every government vehicle are still working. Looks like they couldn't disable them."

Hope flickered in Butler's heart. "Well, cough it up, son. Where are they?"

"They're about forty kilometers due west of here. They're not moving."

Butler frowned beneath his mustache. Why steal planet-hoppers if you were just going to stay stationary planetside? The hope died back down but did not vanish altogether.

"They could be loading cargo," he said. "All units, let's go."

Marshal Wilkes Butler and his entire staff, save for a skeleton crew left behind, arrived a few moments later at the location the transponders indicated. He sat on his bike for a full minute, digesting what he saw.

Of course, there were no planet-hoppers, with Jim and Tychus busily loading cargo.

There were two vultures. And that was it. No one said anything. There was only the tick-tick of engines cooling and the sound of a wind kicking up. One of the bikes fell over.

"They switched the transponders," said Butler, with unnatural calm. "They broke into a marshal's depot. Stole two spaceworthy vehicles. Switched the transponders and had time to hire a girl to come make sure our faces were rubbed in it."

His men glanced at one another uneasily but wisely stayed silent.

Butler dismounted and walked to the remaining standing vulture and glared at it, his hands on his hips. His eyes narrowed, and he reached down and plucked out a tiny microphone.

"Findlay? Raynor? Listen and listen well. You think you're so clever. I make you a promise, boys. You come on my world again, and I will have your asses thrown in jail so fast, it'll take an hour for your heads to catch up with them. You got that?"

And he threw the tiny mic down on the rocky soil, crushing it beneath his boot heel with more savage energy than any of his men had seen in him before.

Safely out of reach, Tychus Findlay and James Raynor were laughing so hard, they couldn't talk.

"Oh, man," breathed Jim, "that was too much. I couldn't fly straight there for a moment."

"Hell, Jimmy, you couldn't fly straight if you

were sober as a preacher and had nothing else on your mind."

"I ain't been drinking!" Jim retorted.

"Maybe you should be," Tychus replied. "Might help you straighten out."

Tychus was right. Their current careers necessitated that they become jacks-of-all-trades. They'd flown a lot of vehicles in their day, and so could manage an attempt at almost anything. Just not very well. It would probably have made their departure from New Sydney quite comical to watch, if anyone had been watching. They'd opted to take two, just in case the law got onto them and they had to split up. Such a tactic had often worked well for them. Now, though, Jim wondered if maybe they should have just picked one: perhaps both of them in a single vessel might have made for one good pilot.

Jim glanced at the viewscreen to see the other small vessel ahead and slightly to the right. He snorted; Tychus was still weaving.

"You're one to talk. I've seen four-year-old girls who were better pilots than you."

"Maybe we should enlist them into our gang, then. We could use a decent pilot."

Jim laughed. "Speaking of girls," he said, "although a bit older—how the hell did you talk Daisy into going in to see ol' Butler?"

"Girl's sweet on me. She'll do anything I ask."

"And anything for money," Jim added. "Sweet or not, girl's got a lockbox for a heart. All of Wayne's girls do. How much did it set you back?"

"Not a single cred."

Jim was so surprised, he found himself drifting, and pulled on the yoke to resume a straight course. "Really?"

"Mmm-hmmm. Told her I'd pay her when I got back."

"And she agreed to that?" Jim was surprised. *"Again?"*

"Told ya, Jimmy boy. Tychus Findlay has charm."

"Well, then you better be putting it to good use, because we're going to need to get permission to land."

"Don't need charm, Jimmy. Daisy did a bit more than delay ol' Butler. I told her exactly how to disable a certain part of their communication grid while she was waiting for him. It's gonna take them a while to figure it out and then replace it. Until then, no official messages going out, and in the meantime, we got us two official law enforcement vehicles. Watch this."

Tychus's voice took on a calm tone. "Horley Barton Space Station, this is Officer Tyler Whitley and my partner, Officer John Tanner. Here for the routine inspection. Requesting permission to dock."

"You guys are early. Hasn't been a full month since last time."

"Vacation time coming up," Tychus said.

An understanding chuckle. "I understand, sir. We are ready to receive code."

Code?

Shit . . .

Tychus's voice came over the private channel. "You better rustle up a code, Jimmy, or we need to beat one hasty retreat. . . ."

Frantically Jim started searching the planet-hopper's computer. A disturbing number of codes began to scroll across the viewscreen. Jim cross-referenced them with the name of the station.

"Any time now, Jimmy," came Tychus's laconic voice.

"I am going as fast as I can," snarled Jim.

"Officer Whitley? Is there a problem?"

"Not at all," Tychus said, his voice smooth and calm.

Jim's heart was racing. There. That one looked promising, and he stabbed a finger down to transmit it to the station.

There was a long pause.

Jim blinked. "They gotta be onto us. I told you we shouldn't have sent Daisy in. Butler's probably already notified them."

"Keep your panties on, Jimmy. Butler's fast, but he ain't that fast. And sometimes the easiest way to get into a place is just to walk through the front door. These are legit planet-hoppers. The numbers checked out just fine."

"Yeah, *hot* legitimate planet-hoppers. They're going to be reported as stolen within ten seconds if this code doesn't—"

"Transit beta four-zero-five-two, you're clear to dock, Officers. Please proceed to docking bay 39, ports A and B. Enjoy your stay."

Jim closed his eyes and exhaled in relief.

"Thank you kindly," Tychus said, as if there never had been any doubt of anything at all.

Jim flanked Tychus as they headed for the space station. He could see docking bay 39 and ports A and B directly ahead, on the second tier of the slowly spinning station. There certainly didn't seem to be anything amiss.

"So far, so good," Jim remarked.

"That's true enough. But within about five minutes, you and I will be mixing with the populace of the station and heading for our freighter loaded down with crystals," Tychus pointed out.

Jim relaxed. It wasn't like they'd never done things like this before. They'd just never done it in stolen law-enforcement vessels. A furrow creased his brow for a moment as the thought came, unbidden, of the one-way conversation with Myles. About how his mother wouldn't accept her son's money because of where it had come from. She would have a few choice words, he was sure, about him being in a stolen law-enforcement vehicle.

Raynor punched a couple of buttons with unnecessary vigor before he found the right one and a map of the station appeared. It was extremely basic, laid out on an easy-to-follow circular grid. Public docking bays formed the outer, widest layer, C. As Raynor maneuvered the small vessel, doing his utmost to fly casually, he could see that all kinds of ships were docked there in ports of varying sizes, from small one-person ships to several extremely large ones. Most of them looked as if they'd seen better days.

The second level, B, the one to which he and Tychus had been directed, seemed to have more workmanlike vessels. This layer was designated "Station/Governmental Vessels." A, the top layer, had fewer docking bays, and they were much larger. This level obviously catered to VIPs, either actual ones or those who had enough money to be regarded as very important personages.

"Our freighter's going to be on C," Raynor said to Tychus. "Looks like there are about two dozen landing areas large enough to accommodate it." He touched the screen and found the stairs. "Man, this is gonna be cake."

"Providing we can actually land these babies," Tychus said.

"Yeah, it would kind of blow our cover to crash as we dock," Jim said.

"Then straighten up and fly right."

The Horley Barton Space Station, as befitted such an out-of-the-way place, was more than a little run-down, outdated, and lax in security. After Raynor had landed and figured out which door opened the hatch of the small vessel, he was greeted by a bored worker with a data log—a device that enabled him to read data chips and most likely gave him access to information about all the ships on the station. The worker was clad in dark-blue overalls with a patch that proclaimed his name as Crawford. He had at least a day's growth of stubble and vacant eyes, and was chewing something with more enthusiasm than he had displayed while checking out Raynor's falsified credentials.

"Yep, Officer Tanner, you've got the run of the station," Crawford said, turning his head to spit with a pinging sound into a metal urn of some sort. He took a square piece of plastic, stuck it into the slot of a machine on the side of the wall, and sat back for a moment while it hummed and clicked, then spat out the plastic square.

"My partner, Officer Whitley, and I need to investigate this freighter," Jim said, handing Crawford a data chip with the ID of the desired vessel on it. "And we'll need the area cleared out. We think it might be stolen."

Vague interest flickered in the man's hazel eyes before subsiding. "Stolen, huh? Let me see that." Crawford read the information and tapped in a number on his data log.

"Okay . . . that baby's gonna be in docking bay 22, port C. Let me notify security and send you in with some backup." He turned to do so.

Jim lifted a hand, projecting calm certainty. "No, thank you, that won't be necessary. The quieter this job is, the better. No need to start a panic. Officer Whitley and I simply need the area unobtrusively cleared out."

Crawford eyed him. "You sure?"

"Absolutely. The Red Mesa County Municipal Enforcement Department will offer a sizable reward to station staff members who cooperate and who are directly responsible for the apprehension of the criminals." Which was sort of true. Of course, Jim was talking about the reward that applied to him and Tychus, who were about to be the thieves he was claiming to chase.

That got Crawford's attention. "Really?"

Jim smiled and fished in his pocket, counting out a not-inconsiderable number of credits. "In fact," he said, "I've been authorized to pay particularly helpful individuals in advance. There should be more upon completion of the operation," he added, handing them over to Crawford.

"I see," Crawford said, pocketing the credits after counting them quickly. "Jax Crawford at your service, Officer. I've given orders to security to clear out the area around docking bay 22, port C, and to leave you and Officer Whitley to do your thing."

He smiled a little, and Raynor realized that Jax Crawford wasn't quite as stupid as he had seemed. He was, however, as greedy as Jim had hoped. Raynor stuck out his hand, and Crawford shook it heartily.

Raynor stepped out into the corridor, speaking quickly and quietly into a small handheld personal comm link. "Docking bay 22, port C, got it all cleared out for you."

"Already there, and it's nice and quiet. Get your ass up here 'fore someone decides it's too quiet."

Raynor picked up his pace. Fortunately, it seemed as if everyone on the station were in a hurry to be somewhere other than where he was; as long as he didn't adopt an out-and-out run, Jim knew he would be fine. He saw Tychus up ahead, trying to look as unobtrusive as possible. Which, being Tychus, wasn't very. He nodded at his friend and they met at the door to 22C. Jim inserted the key the helpfully bribed Jax Crawford had given him, and the door slid open. They stepped inside, closed the door, and locked it.

The freighter was nothing remarkable. A few years old and a type of vessel as common as dirt, it had seen a lot of use. Neither Jim nor Tychus much cared for the ship itself, only what it contained in the hold. Quickly they got inside and headed back. Here, too, there was nothing that announced the bounty the ship contained. Simply standard large storage containers.

"We can't open them," Raynor said.

"We don't need to worry about that," Tychus replied. "That is the problem of whoever takes them off our hands."

That still left the question of verification. And then Jim saw the data log resting on top of one of the crates. He thumbed it quickly and grinned.

"By virtue of our brilliance, balls, and outrageous good looks," he said to Findlay, "we are now the proud, if not exactly legal, owners of exactly fifteen storage crates of crystals."

Tychus grinned back. He reached into his jacket pocket, fished out a stogie, lit it up, and blew smoke into the air. "Well, ain't we just the finest pair of gentlemen on this station?"

"Now let's be the finest pair of gentlemen *off* the station," Jim suggested, heading back toward the cockpit. "I assume your contact specified a site?"

"He did. We're to meet on Hermes."

Hermes was one of three moons that lit up the night skies of New Sydney. Something about the name was familiar, and Raynor suddenly laughed.

"What's so funny?"

"I just remembered a class from my childhood. Hermes was an Old Earth mythological god."

"Yeah? So what?"

"He was the god of merchants. *And thieves.*"

Tychus chuckled around his glowing cigar. "Plays both sides, then. Think I like this god."

CHAPTER SEVEN

HERMES

As a vacation spot, rather like the planet it orbited, Hermes left a great deal to be desired. And yet, it seemed to attract quite a lot of visitors. It was spartan, enclosed, and while the atmosphere was breathable, for the right amount of money it could be doctored so that one would be better able to enjoy one's stay. Bars served intoxicants of all varieties, inhaled, injected, and in liquid form. Jim was somewhat surprised when they entered a particularly dark establishment called, quite aptly, The Pit, and Tychus steered him not toward the wall of alcohol guarded by a very muscular, scarred bartender but to another area where various-sized tanks were suspended. They ranged from about the size of Tychus's fist to the size of his arm.

"I'm in the mood for a drink, not a puff, at least not without knowing what's in there," Jim said, frowning.

"Ah, Jimmy, trust ol' Tychus Findlay," the larger man rumbled. He plopped down a handful of credits. "Keep it coming all night," he told the attractive, tattooed young woman. "For me and my innocent young friend here."

She grinned, pulled down the larger-sized tank, and attached a hose to it, then repeated the gesture for Jim's benefit. He still had no idea what was in the tanks, but he shrugged mentally. There were times, he knew, when he just had to jump and trust that Tychus knew what he was doing.

Of course, sometimes he didn't.

The woman—the tank-tender? He wondered what you called someone in this profession— glanced back at Tychus. "You want it here, or you want to take it with you? You'll have to pay a deposit if you take it."

"Sounds fine, honey. I want to be able to move tonight, if you know what I mean."

He gave her a broad wink. By this point Jim was utterly confused. She reached below the counter and brought out two harnesses.

"Didn't know you were into that sort of thing, Tychus," Jim said blandly.

Tychus laughed. "Not *that* kind of harness," he said. And sure enough, Jim realized that it meant that they could simply carry the canisters with them. Tychus needed an extra large one; Jim was equipped with a medium. They strapped the contraptions on, shifting so the canisters lay comfortably on their backs and fastening buckles around chest and waist, and Jim felt slightly better to see that they weren't the only ones wearing them.

"Take a puff," Tychus urged, inserting the nose plug into his right nostril and inhaling. Tentatively, Jim did the same. And then laughed.

"It's air!" he said.

"Oxygen, more precisely," Tychus confirmed. He took another deep inhalation.

"How come?"

"Jimmy," said Tychus, clapping his friend on the shoulder, "what do you like to do most?"

"Sleep with women."

"Besides that."

"Drink."

"Exactly. Because of the composition of Hermes's atmosphere, you'd be under the table if you had three normal drinks. With this harness on, you can drink maybe even more than normal. Life is good."

"Tychus, you're a genius."

"Hell yeah," Tychus said. He let out a

melodramatic sigh. "Sometimes it's hard, Jimmy boy. Damned hard."

While a staggering variety of characters who could charitably be described as "colorful" and more accurately described as "unsavory" made their way into and out of The Pit, Jim knew instantly when their contacts wandered in about an hour later.

There were five of them: three men and two women. One of the men was tall, with black skin that gleamed as if oiled in the dim, smoky light of The Pit. He had one golden hoop in his ear, as did most of the others. The other two men had skin that was almost ghostly pale, as if they seldom troubled to venture forth into actual sunlight. They looked hard and worn and ready for anything.

The women were similar: well-muscled, as the men were, with a few more piercings and almost as many tattoos. One of them was smaller, with dark-blond hair. The other was almost warrior-womanesque in her proportions, with black hair, blue eyes, and, yes, bones in her nose and ears. All of them wore sleeveless shirts or vests

They were greeted with raucous whooping from some other patrons and with enthusiasm from the bartender. The five of them swaggered in as if they owned the place, and for all Raynor knew, they did.

Among the five was a man about ten years older than Tychus. He was sharp-featured and thin but ropy with muscle. He hung back slightly as the other members of his crew grabbed drinks or old friends. Small eyes that missed nothing scanned the room and then settled on Tychus. Thin lips parted in a grin, showing a gold tooth. He walked over to Jim and Tychus with the glide of a predatory cat.

"You must be Tychus Findlay," the man said, in a voice that was deep as a crater and smooth as oil.

"That I am," Tychus replied, puffing on the air tank as if he were puffing on his more familiar stogie. "This here's my partner, Jim Raynor. And you have just got to be Declan Moore of the Screaming Skulls."

The gold-tooth grin widened. "We don't take pains to hide our identity, not here," he said. "I understand you have a freighter full of shinies for us."

Tychus glanced around. "Let's drink first and discuss business later."

"I told you, we don't take pains to hide our identity here, Findlay."

"Yeah? Well, I do."

There was a tense moment while the two men sized each other up. Tychus could obviously snap Declan's neck with one meaty hand. But Raynor had seen enough to know that the skinny pirate leader probably had a trick or forty-seven to counter with, and knew Tychus knew it too.

Finally Declan shrugged. "There's a back room, for just such occasions."

"Sounds just about right."

A few moments later, they had been ushered into a particularly dark and not particularly fragrant area of The Pit. The room was quite small; Tychus practically filled it himself. Every member of the Screaming Skulls had piled in for the conversation, and the small table did not have an inch of space to spare once everyone's drinks, ashtrays, and other items had been piled atop it. It was further crowded because, like Tychus, all the others wore harnesses with oxygen so that they could extend their enjoyment of the alcohol.

But apparently none of the Skulls seemed to mind. They were the most—Jim groped for the word—*cheerful* band of murderers and cutthroats he had ever seen. There was much laughter, spilling of beverages, bawdy talk, and generally good-natured camaraderie.

Declan made sure everyone was settled, then he turned to Jim and Tychus from a distance of about eight inches away.

"Now," he said, his whiskey-scented breath bathing them, "shinies."

Tychus had the warrior woman in his lap—her name was Elli, or Ella, or Alli; Jim hadn't caught it clearly in the hubbub of the bar—and had to maneuver around her in order to fish out the crystal he'd brought as proof of his and Jim's good faith. Alli/Ella/Elli didn't seem to mind, chuckling throatily as she shifted on his lap.

Tychus placed the crystal on the table. "One of an entire freighter full," he said. "Ought to fetch you a real nice price."

"Ought to indeed," Declan said. He reached out a hand for it, fingering it with the expertise of someone who knew what he was looking for. His eyes narrowed as he perused it.

Jim realized that, while not exactly an act, the happy-go-lucky, wild playfulness Declan and the others cultivated was far from all of what they were. There was a blade in the colorful, over-the-top sheath—a cutlass, no doubt—and that blade was very, very sharp indeed. He was suddenly quite glad he was doing business with the Screaming Skulls, not competing or in conflict with them.

"Decent-quality crystals," Declan said. He reached over to Alli/Ella/Elli's ample bosom and tucked the crystal snugly between her breasts. She gave him a wink. "We'll give you a decent price."

He put a pile of credits on the table. It wasn't

as large as Jim had fantasized about, but it was damned fair. He nodded to himself. They liked booze and fellowship, and they paid pretty well for work. Something cold splashed on his neck, and he jumped.

"Damn, sorry about that. Let me clean it up," came a soft female voice. It was the other woman, the small blonde, and an instant later he felt a warm tongue licking up the trickle of alcohol.

Oh yeah. He liked the Screaming Skulls.

Talk of business was suspended for a while, during which time the party spilled out of the small back room into The Pit proper. Jack, the large black man who was apparently Declan's second in command, was sent to confirm that the freight was indeed as laden with crystals as Jim and Tychus had promised. He returned with a large smile. More rounds of drinks were ordered, and some strange little snack that was deliciously and addictively salty. Jim was certain he didn't want to know what it was.

At some point, the warrior woman detached herself and stumbled up to the bar. She was passed a mic by the grinning bartender. Finding one of the tables that had only a few drinks on it, she stood on it, tossed her black hair, arched her back, exposing her pierced midriff, and began to sing. Surprisingly well.

"Alli's good," Declan said, accepting a cigar

from Tychus and permitting the bigger man to light it for him. "At a hell of a lot of things."

Jim wondered if Declan meant what he thought he meant.

"No shit," said the dark-skinned man. "She fillets better'n anyone I ever seen. Gets them screaming within three minutes, don't finish 'em off until three hours." He shook his head in admiration. "One hell of a woman."

Jim settled back carefully in his chair.

"Got another job for you, if you want to take it," Declan said, taking another puff. The tip of his cigar glowed orange. "We'd do it ourselves, but we ain't got the time. Gotta pace yourselves, you know? Don't want to miss the opportunity, but don't want to burn out."

"One must pause to enjoy the little things in life," Tychus agreed, puffing on his own stogie.

"You impressed us with the freighter," Declan said. "So we'll share the profits with you. Generously."

"Define 'generous,'" Jim said.

"Seventy-thirty. And you get the seventy."

Jim's eyes went wide: it was one hell of an offer—they must have made a mighty fine impression—but Tychus had the better poker face.

"Let's say twenty-eighty. Us."

A murmur went around the table, and the conviviality dropped several notches.

"I mean, after all, we're the ones out there risking our necks. Taking all the chances. You just got the info."

"Twenty-five–seventy-five," offered Declan.

Tychus rubbed his chin, apparently contemplating whether or not the stubble warranted a shave. "I reckon that is acceptable."

At once glasses were clinked and alcohol was sloshed. Jim grinned and took another hit of oxygen before ordering another round.

Life was good.

An hour later, the plans having been discussed, staggering a little despite the oxygen they had inhaled as a precaution, Jim and Tychus were aboard the Screaming Skulls' vessel, the *Privateer*. She was medium-sized, older, but with a lot of personalized touches. The slightly weather-beaten interior seemed to suit the cheerful group that piled in, heading, predictably, for a cabinet that housed a particularly rare vintage of something golden and strong-smelling.

Declan poured drinks all-round. Jim felt he could almost get drunk off the smell of the amber liquor. He swirled it around in the small glass, mesmerized by the thick flow.

"To new partnerships!" announced Declan, and he knocked his back.

It was the best thing Jim had ever tasted—strong like a good punch, smooth like a long, slow kiss. It burned a fiery trail down to his stomach, and he took another sip.

"If the partnership starts this way," said Tychus, "I think we might be doing business together for quite some time."

"Where can we drop you off, boys?"

There was only one place that Jim and Tychus particularly felt like spending the Skulls' money.

CHAPTER EIGHT

NEW SYDNEY
WICKED WAYNE'S

Raynor inhaled the smell of tobacco, other smokes, and spilled alcohol as if it were a fine perfume. This was the smell of Wicked Wayne's, and it always made him smile. Big Eddie beamed and ushered them in, cheerfully accepting his tip, and Jim felt a smile stretching his own face as he looked around.

If there was anyplace in this sector he felt he could call home, this was it. Peace settled on him as he and Tychus entered, placed their drink orders with the ever-efficient and lovely Misty, and took their usual seats. Over in a corner, a live band was performing tonight.

"Where's Daisy?" Jim asked as he lifted his drink in salute to Evangelina, who was currently undulating on the stage in next to nothing.

"She's busy. Guess I gotta find my own amusement," Tychus said. They sat and watched the girls perform and drained their whiskeys in a comfortable silence.

Every time Jim saw Evangelina, he found her more striking. He kept looking for a physical flaw. He found one: a tiny little mole near her right eyebrow. And that was it. It astonished him. He'd yet to get her to bed—usually she was booked several weeks in advance—but she kept assuring him that just as soon as she had a break in her schedule, she'd be all his.

Tychus slammed his glass down with a grunt. "Time to go liberate some credits from some poor unfortunate souls," he said. "You care to join me, Jim?"

Jim was pretty comfortable right where he was, but the idea did have merit. He had learned to play poker in the military, with Tychus and the rest of the Heaven's Devils. Or rather, he had learned initially how to lose every payday. But by observing his compatriots, he'd learned to recognize "tells." And by stubbornly refusing to quit, he'd learned the game well.

Evangelina was going to be onstage for a while. Why not accompany Tychus in the meantime? "Sure," Jim said, rising and grinning at his friend.

Four games later, there were three faces at the table that registered varying expressions of glum, sullen, and pissed off, and two that were rather pleased-looking. Tychus's pile was a bit larger than Jim's, but the former farm boy had done pretty well for himself. And the night was young.

Tychus ground out his stogie and grinned wolfishly at the three losers. "Who's up for another game?"

One of them, an older man with graying hair, simply shook his head, pushed his chair back, and went to the bar, presumably to see if Misty was in the mood to extend credit, as Jim was pretty sure they'd cleaned him out. The other two nodded.

"I want to get that money back," said one.

"I don't know how you cheated, but I'm sure you did," growled the other.

Tychus just grinned. The funny thing about all this was, surprisingly enough, Tychus actually didn't cheat. He just knew how to read people very, very well.

"I think," came a feminine voice, "that Mr. Findlay is going to have to sit this hand out. And maybe a few more after that."

Jim and Tychus glanced up to see Daisy slipping her arms over Tychus's shoulders. "That does sound mighty tempting," Tychus drawled, "but I'm on a winning streak right now, honey."

"That you are," Daisy replied. "Wait till you see what I got in store for you."

Tychus searched her eyes for a moment, then grinned. "Wouldn't be a man if I turned that down," he said, shoving his pile over to Jim. "Here you go, Jimmy. Try not to lose it all on the first hand, all right?"

"I'll do the best I can, Tychus," Jim promised.

Daisy was not a small girl, but compared to Tychus, giantesses would look petite. Her hand was completely engulfed in his larger one as she led him up the stairs, glancing back down at him with a half smile and smoldering eyes that promised the world and more.

"Everybody's talking about how stupid Butler and his posse looked," Tychus said, "and that's all due to you, sweetheart."

Her half smile widened. "I had fun," she said. "You know he's come sniffing around Wayne's before. I had myself a good laugh, watching them scramble around, trying to find you."

Tychus chuckled. "I reckon you did. Jimmy and I had a laugh just imagining it. They weren't too hard on you, were they, darlin'?"

Daisy rolled her eyes and waved her free hand in a dismissive gesture. "That delicate flower of a marshal? Not likely. That deputy of his just kept turning redder and redder trying to ask me about my profession."

Tychus guffawed at that and squeezed her hand. "Thought you were usually booked tonight."

"I am," she said, winking. "I made a special exception just for you, baby. You usually don't stick around here too long."

"I always come back, though, and I always ask for you," he reminded her.

"That you do. And that's why I wanted to do something . . . well . . . special for you tonight."

Tychus raised an eyebrow in anticipation. "Special, eh?"

She grinned and tugged on his hand. "Special. Come on."

They ran up the rest of the stairs, and Tychus automatically headed to the room Daisy shared with three other girls. She shook her red head. "Not tonight," she said. "I told you: special."

She led him to a door on the far end of the hall, to a room he'd never visited before. She fished for the key, unlocked it, and pushed open the door.

The room was lavish, painted in dark, soothing colors, and Tychus whistled softly, impressed. Art hung on the walls, and the furnishings appeared to be genuine antiques. In one corner was a large claw-foot tub with gleaming gold fixtures.

But the centerpiece of the room was the bed. Huge, canopied, large enough for more than two, it had a frame of heavy cast iron and was probably hand-made. Fanciful creatures twined their way around the bed frame, culminating with two gargoyles perched on small golden orbs on each corner. The sheets were red and satiny-looking.

"My, my, girlie, you pull out all the stops when you say 'special,' don't you?"

"I most certainly do!" laughed Daisy, throwing her arms around him and kissing him. His massive arms went around her and he lifted her off her feet, kissing her back and then moving toward the bed. Daisy pulled free of the kiss and slapped playfully and utterly ineffectively at the broad shoulders.

"Hey, now, this is my surprise! Don't you go rushing and spoiling things!"

Tychus obediently set her down on the bed and grinned at her. "All right, darlin', you're running this show, and so far I like what I see."

Her gaze flickered down to his crotch. "So do I," she said. "Now, you gotta do just as I say."

He placed a hand to his heart and bowed mockingly. "I am your obedient servant, madam."

Still fully clothed, she kicked off her boots and scooted back on the enormous bed, her eyes bright with mischief. "Very good. Now. First of all, take off your boots."

He obeyed as she instructed him to divest himself of boots, shirt, weapons, and pants until he stood proudly naked before her. She patted the pillow.

"Now, stretch out here for me," she invited. He did so, appreciating the fact that the bed was large enough so he could fully stretch out. Daisy leaned over and kissed him, lingeringly and passionately. She trailed her fingers over his huge chest, then up one of his arms, and then—

Tychus laughed as a handcuff snapped into place around his wrist, securing him to the iron bed frame. He stared at the gleaming metal for a moment, then a huge grin split his face.

"Oh, darlin' Daisy," he said, warmth in his voice, "I didn't know you was into this sort of thing, or we'd have been playing games like this long before now."

"Well, I think tonight's the perfect time to start," Daisy replied, leaning forward to kiss his nose before snapping the second restraint around his wrist. Tychus tugged experimentally. These were the genuine articles, not play toys. It would seem Miss Daisy was more hard-core than he had imagined. It was a wonderful thought. Tychus made himself comfortable on the pillows, letting his arms relax in the handcuffs, and smiled as he anticipated the delights to come.

Daisy slipped off the bed and flounced to a

large dresser with several drawers and cabinets. She opened a drawer and withdrew something she playfully hid behind her as she approached the bed.

"Whatcha got there, darlin'?" he asked, waggling his eyebrows.

Her smile grew, became one of triumph. She took her hand from behind her back and showed him.

In her painted and manicured fingers was a hypo.

"You should have paid me two months ago when I asked, Tychus Findlay," she said.

All the heat that had been rushing to his groin dissipated, as if he had just had cold water thrown on him. He felt armor going up around his soul just as it did when he had put on the hardskin back in his army days. It was the oldest trick in the book, and he'd fallen for it. The thought infuriated him. He gave her a little smile.

"Aw, honey, that was a nice night. I thought that was a freebie," he drawled.

She laughed harshly. "You ain't that pretty, Tychus."

"Honey, that wounds me right to the core, that does. Hurts my ego."

Daisy was done bantering. She continued in a hard voice. "And that nonsense, sending me like a damn calling card to Marshal Butler when you and Jim made off with those planet-hoppers.

Also an unpaid job, I might add. Well, I told him quite a few things he was mighty interested in hearing. He and his boys are going to be here in just a few minutes. And when they get here, I'm going to be one rich woman off that bounty that's on your head."

"I think you get more if I'm alive," he reminded her as she scooted over to him on the bed, bringing the needle closer to his neck. "Last time I checked, anyway."

"You afraid of dying, Tychus Findlay?" she scoffed. "Course I get more money if you're alive. This is just enough sedatives to knock out a horse. Which should take care of you. You hold still, and this doesn't have to hurt any more than—"

He had been lying quietly, channeling his rage, controlling it. Now, as a teased animal kept in a cage might do, he flung open the door to his fury. Tychus directed his rage into his right hand, willing it to pull against the chain that imprisoned him, demanding that it break. It did, with a loud crack.

Daisy's eyes widened to the size of credit chips. An instant later his fist, his wrist still encircled by metal and trailing the snapped chain, was in her face. She flew across the bed and collapsed like a rag doll in the corner.

He let out a bellow of fury, using the sound to

focus his strength, and snapped the chain on the left handcuff. His feet hit the floor with a thump, and a heartbeat later Tychus Findlay was racing down the stairs, shouting for Jim at the top of his lungs.

It had been a good evening for Jim Raynor.

He had been enjoying himself, as he always did here, even before Daisy had sidled up to Tychus and stolen him away for the rest of the evening. With Tychus out of the game, Jim's luck had continued to improve, and he'd won three out of the last five hands. The alcohol had been doing its happy job, and he had grinned cheerfully at the glowering men whose chips he had gathered to himself lovingly. When in his unsteadiness a few had fallen to the floor, he had yelled, "Hey! Misty! Those are for you!"

"Jim, honey, you're a doll," she'd shouted back across the noisy room.

Jim went to the cashier's table, dribbling chips along the way and not caring because it was a drop in the bucket. He exchanged the colorful chips for credits and, feeling generous, bought the table of losers he'd left a round of drinks.

He made his way, carefully, to the dance stage and gazed up raptly at Evangelina. She gave him a big smile and a wink, and licked her lips.

Oh, yes, Jim thought as he settled in with a

beer and a goofy smile. This night was shaping up to be among the best he'd spent here.

And that was when he heard the bellowing.

"Jimmy! Jimmy, goddamn it, where the fekk are you?"

There was only one person who could yell so loudly. Jim turned, surprised, to the stairwell and blinked at what he saw there.

Tychus Findlay, in all his unclothed glory, filled the door frame. Even in the dim, smoky lighting, Jim could see the fury on his face. The faint illumination glinted off something metallic around his wrists.

The band fell silent and the crowd alternately gasped and laughed. The girls, pausing in their dancing routine, made approving whooping noises and applauded. Tychus ignored them all, marching through the room as the crowd hastened to part for him. He grabbed Jim by his shirtfront.

"Let's go! Now! Butler's on his way."

"Whoa, Butler? What happened? Where's Daisy? And how come you're na—"

Tychus shoved his face to within a half a centimeter of Jim's. "NOW!" He did not give Raynor an option. He slipped his hand around to the back of Jim's dark head, tangled his fingers in his friend's hair, and began to pull as he ran to the door.

"Ow! Hey!" Jim tugged free and cast an apologetic glance over his shoulder at Evangelina, who was laughing as hard as the rest of the girls and who blew him a kiss.

"What about your clothes?" Jim asked as he followed Tychus, deliberately not looking at anything but the other man's face.

"Ain't got time!" Tychus shouted. "Daisy turned me in, the bitch. They're gonna be here any minute now."

Tychus's lack of apparel continued to cause a bit of a stir as the two bulled their way through the gambling hall area to mingled exclamations of irritation, offense, amusement, and, from some of the female patrons, appreciation. Tychus almost didn't bother opening the back door as he kept going.

"Damn," Tychus said. "Left my keys in my pocket."

"Come on, then," Jim said. "I probably shouldn't be driving, but this is an emergency. Sit behind me. But not too close, okay?"

Tychus laughed. They headed for the new vulture Raynor had purchased and jumped on. Tychus grunted a little; the seat was no doubt cold and uncomfortable. Jim couldn't help it. He started to laugh, and once he'd started, he couldn't stop. As he gunned the engines and the responsive bike surged forward despite the extra weight, he could see several lights approaching Wicked Wayne's.

"Damn," Tychus muttered.

"What?"

"Left my smokes in my pocket too."

Jim laughed, then pointed. "See those lights over there? That's Butler and his buddies. They are going to be so pissed off."

"Makes me wanna stay just so I can see their faces."

They were already several hundred yards away, fleeing to—

"Uh, Tychus? Where the hell are we going?"

"Away from Butler, capture, and deceitful women, Jimmy. And that's really all we need to know, ain't it?"

"You know," Jim said as he turned toward nature's stone sculptures that were the badlands, "I reckon it is."

Dawn was spectacular as it spread languidly and in startling shades of color over the badlands. It looked to Jim, as he stood in the mouth of the cave, sipping a cup of powdered coffee heated with water boiled over a campfire, as if someone had poured pink and gold and lavender over the red stone.

"That's mighty pretty," he said.

From the depths of the cave, Tychus gave a grunt. "Sure is."

Jim turned from the painting coming to life before his eyes to glance at his friend. He could see Tychus only by the light of the glowing ember of a cigar he'd bummed off Jim.

They had managed to swipe some clothes after giving Butler the slip, but they fitted Tychus poorly. The shirt didn't button across the chest—hell, it was a good three inches shy of even closing—and already one of the thighs of the trousers had split. Findlay was lying on the stone floor, chewing his stogie, eyes catching its orange gleam. On one side of him was a sack containing various items they'd stashed here for just such an emergency: extra smokes, coffee, and a few credits. On Tychus's other side was the jukebox they had stolen from the maglev train. Jim sighed inwardly as he looked at "her." One of these days, they'd need to get her someplace where they could juice her up. She'd look like a stained-glass window and sound like a church choir.

Silence. Jim lit a cigar of his own and swirled the muddy coffee around in the canteen. He took another swig and grimaced. The fire crackled, burning cheerfully and adding some warmth to the cold stone cave.

"This is bucolic, ain't it, Jimmy?"

"Yep."

Another silence. Tychus sat up, ripping another seam, strode to the campfire, and tossed the cigar butt in.

"I hate bucolic."

Jim sighed. "We gotta give things a little time to cool down," he said.

"We need to get away from this whole damn planet," Tychus said. "Let things *really* cool down. I gotta tell you, after Miss Daisy's deception, I ain't very partial to Wicked Wayne's no more."

Jim said nothing. He, too, had been shocked by Daisy's betrayal. He thought of Evangelina, whom he never did get to take to bed, and Misty, who had been his bed partner frequently, and whom he found his thoughts lingering on. But Tychus was right. The whole thing had left a bad taste in their mouths. New Sydney didn't feel like their world anymore. Time to leave it to Butler and let the marshal think he'd won.

"Yeah," Jim said finally. He tossed his butt into the fire as well. "We do the Skulls' mission and then find a new planet."

"Someplace a little less . . . sandy. And rocky," said Tychus. He cast a sidelong look at his friend. "You know," he said casually, "I hear that O'Banon gives his top people pretty nice apartments, sometimes right on Tarsonis. Nice beds, baths—one of them copper jobs. Beds even come with women."

Jim shot him a look. "No," he said sharply. "I ain't hanging with O'Banon and his type. We work for ourselves."

Tychus snorted. "We're working for the Screaming Skulls right now, Jimmy boy."

"That's different and you know it. The Skulls are like us. They got their jobs and they do them, and when they can't, they get people they like and trust and cut 'em in for a piece of the action. That's decent business. But O'Banon . . ." His eyes hardened. "Ain't nothing decent about him and what he does."

Tychus blew out a thoughtful breath. "All right, Jim. We'll stick with the Skulls and our own judgment for now." He held out his hand, and Jim handed him another cigar. Tychus bent to the fire, popping another seam, and shoved his face within a few inches of it without flinching. The cigar sputtered to life. He puffed on it and then joined Jim at the mouth of the cave, staring into the new morning.

"Crap coffee, too-small clothes, no real direction, and a gorgeous sunrise," he said, blowing out a stream of smoke. He grinned fiercely. "Man, this life is fun!"

CHAPTER NINE

OUTSIDE CONFEDERATE–CONTROLLED SPACE, KOPRULU SECTOR

Jim was not a little worried that the ancient freighter the Skulls had delivered to them might not survive the journey.

"At least it's a model that's got two seats," Tychus said, lounging in the copilot's chair, which had more than a few rivets missing. "Besides, our cover is we're junk dealers, Jimmy. And this boat is certainly junk."

"Yeah, but we're supposed to be *carrying* junk, not flying it," Jim said. "I'm all for a convincing story, but missions are risky enough without factoring in our own cover as a hazard."

"Hell, Jimmy, what's life without a little risk?"

"Safer."

The unusual reply caused Tychus to shoot

his friend a searching look. Jim let himself grin.
"And more boring," he was forced to admit.

"Damn straight."

The ship's metal groaned as if in protest of the
assessment. Jim found himself unconsciously
patting the armrest of the chair, as if the freighter
Linda Lou were an agitated pet. They'd both
flown freighters before. If the ships were nothing
to write home about, at least they were uncom-
plicated to maneuver.

Fortunately, the ship did not have to make
a long space flight. The orbital scrap yard the
Skulls had directed them to was the proverbial
hop, skip, and jump away; in actual terms, it was
a mere half an orbit.

He and Tychus were no strangers to scrap
yards. They had found them ideal spots for several things: ditching hot ships and acquiring new
ones (temporarily—usually the "new" vessels
were on their last legs and good only for quickly
getting to where they could find superior ones);
scavenging parts for hasty repairs; and sometimes simply hiding for a while. Some had better security than others. This one was classified
as "moderate" by the Screaming Skulls, but that
was irrelevant. Their cover would allow them to
approach openly, as they were doing now.

Jim magnified the image on the screen. "Yep,"
he said, looking over the slowly turning debris

that littered space for several hundred kilometers. "It's a scrap yard."

The console beeped harshly, and a bright light flashed. "Refurbish and Recovery Station 5034 to approaching vessel. State your name and business."

Jim pressed a button. "Refurbish and Recovery Station 5034, this is Captain Jeffrey Ulysses Nathanial Kincaid of the *Linda Lou*."

Tychus snorted at the acronym. Jim gave him a huge grin and continued: "We've got some cargo to drop off."

"You bet, *Linda Lou*. Your admittance code is 3857-J. Give it to everyone you deal with: It's good for the next six hours."

"Thanks, roger that."

"Piece of cake," Tychus said. "We could do this with our eyes closed."

"We haven't done anything yet." The mission was not to dock, have a chat with a purchasing agent at the control center, and sell the items they were carrying. The mission was just a bit more complicated than that. They needed to get on board, get access to the private offices, and steal the junker logs. The logs dated back years and were scrupulous records of every piece of junk that had been delivered and sold during that time. Including the names of those who had dropped off debris and those who had purchased it from the scrap yard.

Apparently, according to Declan, there were people out there—people overburdened with creds—who would be thrilled to pieces to get their hands on this sort of information. And the Skulls had been contacted by a wealthy buyer who was one of those tragically overburdened people.

Took all kinds, Jim supposed.

He was maneuvering the ship in past the first field of debris when his fone beeped. He scowled. "Take her in, Tychus. I need a minute here."

"Sure," Tychus drawled, putting out his cigar on the metal flooring. He glanced over at Jim, but Raynor was entirely focused on his fone.

It displayed another set of coordinates back on New Sydney. Jim swore softly, then put the fone away. What the hell was going on? Why was Myles bugging him? Would his mom still not take the money?

"Your mama calling to ask why you were late coming home from school?"

"Shut up," said Jim. The joke hit uncomfortably close to home, and he was in no mood to discuss it.

Tychus peered at him for a moment, then shrugged. "Fine by me. Here, you take the controls. I need to use the head." He transferred control of navigation back to Jim, rose, stretched, and left the bridge. Jim was so distracted, he narrowly missed a large piece of debris and had to swerve sharply. He heard Tychus cursing from the head, and his spirits lifted a little.

When Tychus came back and plopped down in his chair, he asked, "What? You ain't broken in, beat the security sensors, found the logs, and hightailed it out of here in the time it takes me to take a leak? You're slipping, Jimmy."

Jim snorted and grinned.

A short distance in, there was a platform that was quite obviously not debris. This would be the check-in station, but not their eventual goal. Jim maneuvered into position. Someone in an exo-suit came out to meet them, a data log in hand. Even in the vacuum of space, Jim mused, there was red tape. Jim gave the man the code; he nodded disinterestedly and gave them a thumbs-up.

Tychus and Jim threw on out-of-date hardskins and stepped out to unload the fake cargo. It was, quite literally, junk. Jim thought that the Skulls had probably had a grand time assembling all this as props for the mission. Of course, it seemed to him that the Skulls probably had a grand time doing anything.

Fifteen minutes later, after all the various gears, drives, metal plates, sexbot heads— Tychus paused and had to consider a moment before throwing those in—and other detritus had been cataloged, numbered, sorted, and placed in various areas of the platform, the bored-looking scrap yard employee handed them a data log.

"There's your case number, itemized list, and estimated payment amount," said the man, who called himself Fitzgerald, his voice sounding even more flat and metallic than it should have coming out of a hardskin. "Also enclosed are the coordinates of your docking bay at the station proper. Show them this data log, tell them your code, and they'll give you your credits. And don't worry if you can't raise them right away. Comm's been on the fritz for the last half hour."

Jim frowned slightly. In his line of work, it paid to be suspicious. "Really? That unusual?"

Fitz-something—Jim had already forgotten his name—blinked at him for a moment. "This is a scrap yard. What do *you* think?"

The man had a point, and Jim relaxed, amused. "Thanks," said Jim. "So we should just head on in, and we'll find someone there who can give us authorization to collect scrap materials?"

"Of course. You'll want to speak with the Office of Material Acquisitions. They'll give you a registration number that you can use any time you return to make future purchases. Thank you for bringing your business to Refurbish and Recovery Station 5034. We know you have a choice of scrap yards to—"

"Yeah, save it," said Tychus bluntly. He turned

and jumped lightly from the platform, pulling himself along the tether to the *Linda Lou*.

Jim turned and smiled. "Thanks again," he said to Fitzgerald, then followed Tychus.

He was beginning to think his friend was right: this *was* a piece of cake. As he and Tychus entered the ship, closed the door, and removed their hardskins, Jim remarked, "We might have to take more jobs from the Screaming Skulls. This is easy."

"Not too many," Tychus said. "Easy ain't fun."

"Forty-eight hours ago you were running out of Wicked Wayne's, naked as the day you were born, in an effort to escape the due process of law. This is a definite change."

"And so you make my point for me."

They maneuvered through the junk field to what was vaguely its center. The station itself was surprisingly well kept up. It was a slowly turning sphere. There were several oval viewing stations interspersed with cranes. All the cranes were folded up tightly against the station, giving it the appearance of a particularly fat metallic spider. There were no other ships docked, and they went to their appointed bay with no challenges from the station. Apparently the communications were still, as Fitz had put it, "on the fritz." They brought the rickety freighter into the bay. The door to space irised shut behind them.

They'd visited plenty of scrap yards. Usually there was someone who had been alerted to their arrival who would come to officially check them in. However, there was no one waiting in the bay, and the door to the corridor that connected them to the station slid open as soon as the space door was closed.

Jim frowned and glanced at Tychus. "That's strange," he said.

"Could be SOP with this place. Automatically programmed. You saw how interested in personal contact the last fellow was," Tychus said.

Jim nodded. "Yeah. Still, Fitz-whatshisname said someone was supposed to check us in."

"If the comm is still down, then whoever it was probably doesn't know he's supposed to meet us yet. Or he could just be using the head."

Jim chuckled. Sometimes, the simplest explanation was the best. "Probably. Come on, let's go see if we can find him—or at least somebody."

They stepped out of the frigate and headed through the door. They hadn't gone two steps before it slammed shut behind them and the lights went out.

This is a scrap yard. What do you *think?*

Jim swore and drew his slugthrower, immediately backing up against a wall. Tychus did likewise. There was only the faintest blue emergency lighting here and there, and their eyes weren't adjusting fast enough.

"Any way we can open that door?" Tychus asked, his voice soft.

Jim shook his head. He'd spent some time examining the station just in case something went wrong. Something, oh, like maybe doors slamming shut behind them and lights going out.

"From this side? Not without the key code or an override command. We've got to get to the main control center and reactivate things from there," he said, keeping his voice equally low. In the near darkness, his eyes and ears strained for information. "Might as well head that way. I think I can get us there from here." Tychus used to tease him about the hours he would spend poring over maps. Jim had always said it would come in handy, and it seemed that now was that time.

"Besides," he added, "we'll need to get there anyway to find out where the logs are. Might as well complete the mission while we're—"

Tychus chuckled, a low, somehow angry sound that made the hairs on the back of Jim's neck stand up, even though he was Tychus's best friend.

"Oh, Jimmy, you're still so naïve. I don't rightly know who sprung the trap—we've pissed a lot of people off—but I can tell you who baited it."

And Jim realized he was right. "The Screaming Skulls set us up," he said sickly. "Damn it. *Damn* it!"

"Seems to be a fine time for betrayal," Tychus said. "Happened to us twice already. I hope our paths cross again. Soon."

"First we've got to get out of here. Come on."

"Wait," Tychus said. "Whoever sprung this trap has us right where he—or she—wants us. We can't go back to the bay, and we're in a nice, tight little corridor. There's going to be something, or more likely someone—probably several someones—waiting for us up ahead. We're doing exactly what they want."

"I'm open to suggestions."

Tychus paused. "Got none. Let's go."

They moved slowly along the dimly lit corridor. They were as quiet as possible, although they both knew that whoever had trapped them so neatly knew exactly where they were. As they continued, Jim racked his brain, wondering who the hell it had been, anyway.

Not Butler, that much was for certain. He might have shaken down the Skulls for information, but he wouldn't go in for something this dramatic. No, if he were behind this, the door would have been closed, and as soon as they'd opened it, he and Tychus would have been staring at a face full of weapons, all cocked and ready to be fired. Simple, forthright, lawful. No slamming doors, no darkened lights.

He couldn't think of anyone they had robbed, cheated, swindled, or attacked who would do something this elaborate. So it had to be someone they didn't know. The relative of a dead colleague or enemy, for instance. There were likely plenty of those around.

They had reached the end of the corridor. The station was circular, and Jim recalled that each narrow passage that led from the bay to the center of the station opened onto a broader walkway that circumnavigated the main area. Below them were two floors. On one were offices, break rooms, and living quarters for the staff. The control rooms and access to the inner workings of the station were on the floor below that. Everything was on emergency lighting, and even that appeared to have been tinkered with. It was not completely dark—just dark enough.

"Jimmy, ain't nobody here," Tychus said quietly.

Jim was beginning to think Tychus was right. There should have been fifteen people living on the station, including Fitz-something, whom they had spoken with earlier. The place . . . *felt* empty. His own breathing, and his increased heart rate, suddenly seemed very loud in his own ears.

"Yeah," he said. "Nobody but whoever trapped us. Come on."

He was certain they were being watched, and he knew Tychus knew it too. And he was equally certain that whoever was watching them knew exactly where they were going. But it was the only thing they could do. Without overriding the power, nothing in this place was going to open so they could escape. Jim felt like a rat being put through its paces in a maze, but there was no alternative.

He led the way, the slugthrower reassuringly solid in one hand as he reached out with the other, patting the walls to make sure of where he was. There should be a stairway up ahead that would take them to—

He tripped and flailed. Tychus's strong arm shot out and clamped down on his collar, keeping him from falling. Jim looked down at what had tripped him.

It was a body. Male. Even in the dim lighting, Jim could make out the wide eyes, the gaping mouth. And he could make out the darker stain against the lighter color of the man's shirt.

And the very large hole in the chest.

Someone—or some*thing*—had ripped the man's heart out.

"Holy *shit*, Tychus . . . ," he whispered.

Suddenly, in the silence, a hollow, echoing

voice filled the air: "No, please don't!" It was male, but it was pitched slightly higher than a normal masculine voice, and it was higher even than that due to utter terror.

He knew that voice, but for a wild second his mind couldn't remember whose it was.

And then Jim felt as if he'd just been punched in the gut.

He remembered. Even if he'd tried to forget the voice, and the man it belonged to, and the memories it dredged up. Even if he'd tried to forget a lot. Higher-pitched, yes, but not as high as a child's, nor with the timbre of a woman's. They'd only ever met one person who spoke like that. Now, stunned and shocked to the core, they exchanged alarmed glances. Tychus voiced what Jim didn't want to acknowledge but had to.

"The bastard's got Hiram!"

Hiram Feek was not a member of the Heaven's Devils officially. He was a civilian, the designer of the CMC-230-XE suit. He was fiercely intelligent and good-humored, and he had proved his loyalty repeatedly to the unit that had unofficially adopted him. As far as Tychus and Jim were concerned, the "little person," as he preferred to be called, with the large brain was as much a Devil as anyone who had been officially in the unit.

And he was being held by the person—or people—who wanted Jim and Tychus.

Jim opened his mouth to say something—what, he wasn't sure. Probably to stupidly repeat what they both knew, perhaps somehow to negate it. Tychus clamped a meaty hand over Jim's mouth. "Do not say a word," he hissed. He removed his hand.

"They've got—"

"I know, Jimmy boy, I know."

Hiram's voice came again. This time in a shrill shriek of torment. Jim winced. Tychus muttered something inaudible under his breath.

"We gotta do something. He saved our lives— more than once!"

With an almost physical pain, Jim recalled when the diminutive engineer had visited him while Jim sat in a military stockade for a month, serving time for assaulting a noncommissioned officer. Feek had quietly informed him that Colonel Vanderspool had sabotaged the Devils' hardskins. He had installed a "kill switch" in the Devils' CMC-300 armor. At any point, if he found the Devils too troublesome, Vanderspool could press a button and trigger the emergency lockdown mechanism. The suit would freeze in its tracks, along with the soldier inside it. Feek had discovered the lethal switches and unobtrusively deactivated them. White-hot anger surged up at the recollection. Vanderspool had earned—more than earned—what had happened to him. What Jim Raynor had done to him.

He'd killed Vanderspool himself.

"We gotta help Feek," he repeated, his voice shaking, his skin clammy with sweat. "He saved us, Tychus."

Tychus hesitated, then nodded. Jim knew that he, too, was remembering Feek, and that sickening revelation about the depths of Vanderspool's inhumanity.

"I—I know he did, Jimmy. It sounded like it came from below us."

Slowly they stepped over the body. Jim's boot slipped a little on the puddle of blood. It was only starting to congeal. The murder had been recent.

They made their way to the stairwell. They would be vulnerable here, more so than when they had been pressing against the wall, but there was nothing they could do about it. Quickly they descended, Jim wincing at the noise their boots made on the metal.

There was light up ahead. Hiram Feek was sobbing. Jim's gut twisted at the sound. Feek might have been an egghead, but he had courage. What was going on? What were they *doing* to him?

The sound abruptly ceased.

"I didn't break in a prison camp," came a weary female voice. "I won't break for you, you bas—*uhhnnnghh!*"

Who was this? Terror pulsed through Jim

with each heartbeat as his brain struggled to link this voice with a name, a face. Prison camp . . . who had they known who—

"Oh, God," Jim whispered. "Hobarth. Captain Clair Hobarth."

They hadn't known her well—not like they had known Feek—but she had played a pivotal role in their lives and military careers.

They had last seen her emaciated and weak, an escapee of Kel-Morian Internment Camp-36. She had brought with her intel that enabled the 321st Colonial Rangers Battalion to infiltrate the camp and liberate the POWs. Raynor had been so inspired by her that he had spearheaded the attempt—and been captured in the process. This gutsy woman had given them their name: the Heaven's Devils.

And now she, like Hiram Feek, was here. Being tortured by an unseen captor. Why? What had she done? There had to be a connection, but Jim's mind was like a numb hand trying to grasp it. It wasn't clicking.

"This is personal," Tychus rumbled, cold anger in his voice. "Two people we knew and liked. That can't be pure coincidence. And it's *really* starting to piss me off."

Hobarth started to moan, low and deep, the gut-wrenching sound of mortal pain. It rose to a sudden, sharp scream.

Jim held his slugthrower in both hands, pointing the muzzle down. Tychus emulated him. Jim jerked his head; they were just about to come out into the area where Feek and Hobarth were being kept.

Were being tortured.

"Fellow Confederates, I cannot tell you what joy it brings me to see so many of you turning out here tonight."

What the hell . . . ? That sounded like a politician's speech. Both men frowned, puzzled and alert.

"Not the best idea."

It was not the voice of anyone they recognized, but Jim took an instinctive dislike to it. It was . . . cold. Oily. Superior.

They heard the scrambling of feet, the clatter of something landing on the floor, and a strange-sounding clang, as if metal were striking metal.

"Cybernetic arm," came the speaker's voice.

Recognition flickered over Tychus's face. The big man went pale. His eyes widened and his lips pressed together tightly. Jim was as shaken by his friend's reaction to the words as he was by the whole situation.

"You know this guy?"

"I sure as hell hope I don't," was Tychus's cryptic reply.

"Ready?"

Still pale, sweat gleaming on his forehead, Tychus nodded.

"One, two—"

With perfect timing born of long experience, both men leaped around the corner . . .

. . . and saw not two living men engaged in hand-to-hand combat, but a hologram of the fight.

A man clad in a long duster leaped up and landed heavily on his victim's left hand.

He didn't want to remember the poor bastard getting attacked. Thoughts of Feek and Hobarth hammering in his head, he recognized this man, too, and his heart spasmed as memories— unwanted and unwelcome—slammed down on him.

"It's Ryk," whispered Jim.

Ryk Kydd. The only one besides the two of them who had survived; the rich kid who had become an assassin but somehow had never lost a sense of innate decency. Feek, they cared about; Hobarth, they knew; but Kydd had been one of *them*. Now they stared, watching sickly as Kydd's face contorted in agony. The attacker sprang back, lithe as a cat.

"One down," the man said, grinning. Now Jim could see his face clearly: lean, angular, a thin, cruel mouth framed by a trimmed goatee. "Three to go."

"Jimmy?" The voice belonged to Tychus. It was trembling, uncertain, and the sound of it issuing from Tychus's throat shocked Jim to his core. He kept the slugthrower raised, but despite the danger, he couldn't help but glance over at Tychus. His gut clenched at what he saw.

Tychus Findlay was utterly terrified. He turned a face greasy with sweat to Jim and swallowed hard.

"Jimmy . . . w-we're in trouble."

CHAPTER TEN

"I see you recognize me." It was the same voice as in the hologram—the hologram that was currently pinning the holographic Ryk Kydd to the floor with a dagger through the hand.

Jim whirled, the slugthrower out in front of him, trying to figure out where the voice was coming from. To Jim's unspeakable relief, Tychus appeared to have gotten his terror under control—for the moment at least.

Who the hell *was* this guy, who could rattle the normally unflappable Tychus Findlay so badly?

"Maybe. One thing's clear: you're one sick puppy." Tychus's voice betrayed none of the fear Jim knew he was experiencing.

"And you're not? The pot is, I believe, calling the kettle black. Your reputation precedes you, Tychus Findlay—as, obviously, does mine."

The two people in the hologram continued to struggle. By now their comrade in arms was being forced to fight with two ruined hands. But he was not giving up.

Jim knew what he was watching. And knew why the stranger wanted them to watch it.

He wanted them to see Ryk Kydd's murder.

He gritted his teeth, closing his hands more tightly around the gun to steady their shaking. He didn't want to watch, to give this bastard the satisfaction of knowing that his sadistic little light show had gotten to them. The voice seemed to come from different places. It was hard to get a bead on him, and the flickering light of the hologram kept drawing his eye back.

"Who is this guy, Tychus?"

For a moment Tychus didn't reply. Jim risked a quick glance, saw the big man close his eyes and swallow. "Goes by the name of Ezekiel Daun."

"Well, we're gonna kick Ezekiel Daun's ass," Jim said with assurance he did not feel.

The holographic Daun now had his implacable cybernetic hand clamped around Kydd's throat and was lifting him off the floor. Kydd's feet kicked frantically as he slapped ruined hands futilely against the cybernetic arm. Daun was grinning. Enjoying killing Ryk, as he was enjoying watching Jim and Tychus witness the murder.

"Somebody wants you dead," Daun said. "That's fine by me. But he didn't stipulate *how* you were to die. Nor how long it should take. That was left up to me to decide. And we got *all night*."

Tune it out, Jimmy, Raynor told himself. *Focus. Where is he? How's Tychus handling this?*

The latter question at least had an answer. Tychus was still afraid, but he wasn't letting it get in the way of escaping.

"He's set this all up very carefully," Tychus muttered to Jim, a hint of his old self creeping into his voice. Jim felt a brush of relief as his friend continued to regain control. "Which means that he's going to want us to watch it all. Bet those voices of Feek and Hobarth also came from a hologram of their . . . murders."

Jim swallowed.

"He won't do anything until he shows us that Ryk's dead, and maybe not until he forces us to watch him kill Feek and Hobarth too. Still, we'd best haul ass. Where is the central control area?"

"If we're at six, then it's at eleven," Jim replied, using antiquated references that were still useful for military purposes, if not their original.

"What's at the other hours?"

Jim tried to think, tried to shut out the sound of his friend being strangled.

"How's it feel now, Ark? Having trouble getting air in? Feeling the blood pressure build up? Do you want to swallow?"

"Nothing at seven," Jim continued, forcing the words out, clinging to the calmness thinking provided him. "Eight is the crane-operating station."

"Those manually controlled?"

"Usually, unless specifically set otherwise. At two, we've got—"

"That's enough hours in my day. We need a distraction. I got an idea."

They moved quickly, Jim's shoulders itching, expecting at any moment to feel a bullet or a metal spike between them. But he believed that Tychus was onto something. This Daun wouldn't have set up such a complex little display if he hadn't wanted them to appreciate all the effort he'd gone to. They had time. The question was: how much? And if it would be enough.

They approached the crane-operating station. In the center, Jim watched, sick to his stomach, as Ryk Kydd struggled, then went limp.

"Damn it, not yet!" cried the holographic Daun.

"Tychus? Whatever you're gonna do, do it fast, because I think we just ran outta time."

"Already on it." Tychus, his face close to the controls, was trying to figure out which was which. Then he muttered, "Hell, let's just do this thing," and punched one.

The station shuddered. Jim almost lost his footing, staying erect only by grabbing on to the console as Tychus was doing. The hologram, mercifully, winked out; its holoprojector had probably toppled over.

There was an angry cry from above them, and the sound of bullets firing. Tychus hit another control, and another, grabbing a joystick and yanking it about wildly in various directions. Then Jim realized what he was doing: he was using the cranes to slam into the station. As distractions went, it seemed to be working.

Unless, of course, one of the cranes actually broke through a bulkhead of the station, and all the air ran out.

The shots went wild, then stopped. Daun was trying to get to a better position.

Jim turned and bolted for the main override control panel. As such an important part of the station, it had more blue emergency lights activated than most of what they had seen until now. Jim perused it quickly. As the seconds ticked by, his tension rose. Doors, where were the doors? They—

"Damn it!" He pounded his fist on the console in fury and frustration.

"For fekk's sake, what now?" shouted Tychus from across the room.

"He took the master key. Nothing can be overridden without that. Nothing!"

A pause. "Oh."

Jim knew he was perilously close to losing it. The unexpected betrayal of the Skulls; Tychus's sudden, almost overwhelming terror; being forced to watch the torture and murder of a man he had cared about, who was a brother in arms, a *friend*, damn it; and this horrible sensation of feeling like a trapped animal—

"We can't get out! Don't you get that, Tychus?" he said, his voice rising in panic.

"I certainly do," came Daun's voice. Another crane slammed into the station, rocking it hard. There were groaning and crashing sounds as pieces of equipment came loose and toppled over. Tychus turned toward the sound of the voice and fired repeatedly.

Daun's laughter came, echoing and triumphant. "Nowhere for the Heaven's Devils to flee or fly," he said mockingly. "Your friends suffered. And so will you."

Jim, too, turned, firing and reloading. He ran out of ammo for the slugthrower and quickly switched to his beloved Colt. Though he used the revolver only rarely, simply firing the thing heartened him. It was a lucky weapon for him, and a smile tugged at his mouth as he took aim and fired.

The station was filled with the sounds of gunfire and laughter. Something on the other side of the level caught fire and added a glowing orange flicker to the blue emergency lighting. Sparks hissed and sizzled, and acrid smoke started to fill the air.

Click click click.

The sound of a Colt out of ammunition.

Jim lowered it, sickened.

Was this how it was to be? What a rip-off. Betrayed, trapped, and gunned down by a lunatic. It was such . . . a stupid, anticlimactic end.

His duster flying out like wings on either side, Ezekiel Daun dropped down from a catwalk. He landed beautifully, in a crouch, smoke swirling about him, and rose slowly. He had been intimidating in the hologram. But now, with orange and blue light dancing about his tall frame and catching the gleam of both the metallic hand and the metallic gun, he looked to Jim like an incarnation of Death. He kept the pistol trained on them, and they raised their hands slowly. Jim realized that both he and Tychus were shaking.

In his cybernetic hand, Daun held the

controller of a hologram. "You're being recorded, Mr. Findlay, Mr. Raynor. I have crafted an extensive library of my work, so I am able to sit down and watch whenever I feel like walking down memory lane. So far, this has been quite the little cinematic presentation. Feek was the only other who gave me a worthy show, I think. Hobarth was weak from her old wounds and Ryk Kydd went too fast to be properly appreciated."

Anger cut through the fear as Jim envisioned this man torturing Hiram Feek and Clair Hobarth. He clung to the anger. It cleared his mind of the crippling sensation of mindless terror.

"But I think I'd like to see a bit more from the two of you before I close the curtain," Daun said. "Maybe a little . . . dance routine?" He aimed the gun at Tychus's feet.

"Who the hell are you, and why are you letting our own cranes attack the station?"

The voice came from directly above them, and it belonged to the formerly highly bored Fitz-something. Now he sounded angry and not a little frightened. Jim realized that Daun had not factored the tech into his plans. He had killed everyone on the station, but he had not expected Fitz—who would, of course, have an override key—to leave his post. Daun had likely been tripped up by the very "comm problems" he had created.

Daun snarled bestially and lifted the gun. Two

shots rang out, and Fitz's lifeless body toppled down, landing with limbs askew, right at Jim's and Tychus's feet.

They acted as one.

Jim and Tychus sprang to either side of the still-twitching corpse, quickly holstering their guns. They grabbed Fitz's body, lifted it up in front of them, and charged Daun. The enemy fired at the center of Fitz's body. Jim and Tychus were behind the corpse but slightly to either side. The bullets passed between them.

They were on him now. Daun kept firing, but the shots went wild. Snarling, he dropped the gun, drew back his gleaming metallic arm, made a fist, and swung it at them. He punched directly through Fitz's sternum. The bloody silver fist protruded, covered in gore, from the tech's back. Still Jim and Tychus kept coming, using their momentum to push Daun's arm through even farther and trap it there. The bloody metallic limb still clutched and reached ineffectively as Daun went down under them.

Tychus raised a fist and slammed it down, but somehow Daun jerked to the side just in time. Tychus grunted as his knuckles met metal flooring. He drew his fist back for another punch. Meanwhile, Jim was fumbling beneath the corpse, praying that his hunch was right, when his hands closed on what he wanted.

He had the key.

He leaped up and sprinted to the far console, shoving the key in and twisting it hard. The station hummed to life, the relative brightness of the normal lighting harsh after he had been so long in the dark.

Tychus and Daun were struggling, the body of the hapless Fitz a barrier between them—one that Tychus was exploiting. It made for a ghoulish sight, and Jim felt bile rise in his throat. Tychus was pummeling the man hard, but Daun was still struggling to pull his arm free of its flesh prison. And Jim saw, as Tychus did not, that he was starting to succeed.

"Tychus! Let's go! *Now!*"

Tychus looked up, and for a moment Jim saw not his friend but something very dark and dangerous. Then it was gone. Tychus knew and trusted Jim well enough to obey when Jim started barking orders in that tone of voice. With a final savage punch that jerked Daun's already battered head brutally to the side, he threw both bounty hunter and corpse into a console. Daun's eyes closed and his body went as limp as Fitz's. Tychus nodded, then joined Jim as he raced for the stairs.

Their relief was short-lived. As they headed up the corridor at a dead run, bullets slammed into the bulkhead behind them. The shut and locked door would delay Daun only for a few moments.

"Thought I'd killed that bastard," Tychus muttered, unusually pale. On the other side of the door Daun raged, his cybernetic hand punching dents in the thick metal.

"You pieces of shit! You think you can escape me? No one escapes Ezekiel Daun! Do you hear me? No one! You'll die in agony, you—"

Jim tuned out the madman's rantings and concentrated on the door and the rickety freighter docked there. They'd have to ditch the ship as soon as possible, of course. The Skulls knew it, and now so did Daun. They dove into the cockpit and then turned to each other.

"Door ain't opening," Tychus said.

"Because someone's gotta open it, and Daun ain't gonna oblige," Jim said.

"You said there was a manual override for both doors from the bay," Tychus said.

"There is, over there. Next to the door to the—"

Suddenly there came a pounding. Daun had reached the door to the bay and was attacking it. They could hear his voice shouting. They couldn't understand his words, but they didn't need to.

"—corridor," Jim said.

"Good to go," Tychus said. "Keep this door open for me and hang on tight."

"What? Tychus—"

Before Jim could protest, Tychus had already slid from the cockpit and was at the manual override. What was he thinking? He was opening the docking bay door into space! Without a hard-skin or at the very least something to hang on to, Tychus Findlay was going to get blown right out.

Jim frantically prepped the freighter for launch, glancing worriedly at Tychus as the bigger man slammed down the release lever and the door started to iris open.

"Come on, come on, *hurry*!" cried Jim.

Tychus did. The second the lever had clanged down, Tychus Findlay had turned and was covering the space in long strides. The door was opening slowly. Tychus hurled himself toward the open freighter door, big hands clamping down hard as the vacuum of space hungrily sought to pull him out into its embrace.

Jim raced from the cockpit to the door, leaning over as far as he could, trying to pull Tychus in. Findlay's muscles strained and quivered, and Jim swore as he saw Tychus's thick legs being *lifted up*. Tychus bellowed in anger and, with a last powerful tug, maneuvered himself into the freighter. Few other men could have done it, and even Tychus was red-faced from the brief exposure to the vacuum of space. He was sweating and shaking.

But he was inside. Jim pressed a button and the freighter doors slammed shut.

The docking bay door was fully open now. Jim threw himself into the pilot's seat and frantically slammed buttons. The freighter rose, and Jim tried to get it out as fast as possible.

They shot forward, the drifting debris suddenly becoming an obstacle course they took at high speed. Jim was afraid they'd fly the old vessel apart, but he wanted to get away—*now*.

Beside him, Tychus Findlay whooped. "Even if Daun had gotten to us, last we'd see of him would be him dangling like a damned marionette!" he said, wiping his eyes. He flapped his arms disjointedly and mimed choking, his tongue sticking out.

Jim started to laugh too. It wasn't that funny, actually, and he knew hysteria when he felt it. But the high-pitched peals of laughter rolling off him released the fear and adrenaline. He felt his whole body shaking, and it was better to laugh at Daun than to feel that sick horror.

"Yeah," he said. "Guess we've seen the last of him."

Tychus sobered slightly. "I wouldn't be too sure about that, Jimmy. I'd like to think that, but I think I'll live longer if I don't. My one sole desire right now, other than to drink an obscene amount of alcohol, is to get the fekk out of this star system."

Jim was quiet for a moment. "I can't do that. I gotta get back to New Sydney."

"What?" Tychus's bellow nearly deafened Jim. "Madman like that is on our tail, and you want to head right back to where he knows he can find us?"

"I got a message and—"

"*I* got one for you, and that is that Daun is bad news of the absolute worst kind. You hear me?"

"Who the hell is he, anyway?"

Tychus folded his arms and sat silently angry for a while. Jim knew him well enough to know that the anger was not directed at him.

When Tychus spoke, his voice was low and very, very carefully controlled. "I don't know much for sure, and I thank whatever grace there might be in this universe for that. The rumors and what we just saw are bad enough."

"Tychus . . . ," Jim began. "You know how reliable rumors are. They—"

"I know my sources, too, Jimmy," Tychus snapped. "And when I say the rumors I hear would make you crap your pants if I told you half of 'em, you can believe it."

Jim did. Nonetheless, he had to know, and Tychus knew it.

The bigger man ran a hand through his short hair. "He don't just kill. He drags it out. Likes to torture his victims in every way possible afore he kills 'em. He knows just where and how to hurt. There was one man I heard tell of . . . Daun didn't have a deadline on the bounty, so he took his time. Got the man, and his wife. Weren't no bounty on her, but Daun got her just to play with. Flayed the skin off her first, right in front of the poor son of a bitch. Then did the same to him. Some versions of the stories say he brought a few kilos of salt with him and tried to—"

"Okay," Jim snapped. "Enough."

Tychus grinned, but it was a sham. "Suffice to say, he's a bounty hunter. With, from what I understand, a damn good track record."

Jim looked bleakly ahead. "Yeah. I got that much. Feek, Hobarth, Kydd . . ."

Tychus nodded, not looking at Jim. "Normally I'd say it's a good thing when a man likes his job, but . . . Daun likes it too much. I'm right glad we didn't see what he did to Hobarth and Feek, Jimmy. I will tell you that with my whole heart. What he did to Kydd was bad enough."

Jim listened. He had seen enough as well. Daun *recorded* his kills. Used them to terrify others he planned to kill, watched them alone at home and relived the moment, just like he said he did. Sick bastard.

"We just got away from him. We must've had angels on our shoulders."

"No we didn't." Jim's voice was bitter and hard and came from a place of pain and impotent anger. "We had a sap named Fitz-something who was in the wrong place at the wrong time. That poor fellow saved our lives and lost his."

"Better him than us," Tychus said bluntly, then added, "and better he died the way he did than the way the other souls on that station probably died."

That, Jim had no answer for.

Tychus grunted, rubbed his face, and sat up, looking more like his old self again. "Now we gotta ditch this ship and acquire another one, and we need to do it fast. Deadman's Port is just a jump away. I say we go there."

Jim was silent.

Tychus continued. "Deadman's Port is—"

"I know what it is," Jim snapped. "And I know who runs it."

He was pissed, and for a lot of reasons, not just because Tychus thought he didn't know about the place. Everyone knew about Deadman's Port. It had been around for a long time, in one incarnation or another, but always it had been a place for hiding out, conducting dark business, and watching your back even when you were with your friends.

Deadman's Port was a major city—if you could call it that—located on the planet known as, logically enough, Deadman's Rock. The place was a dumping ground and scrap yard that made the one they had just left look like a fine town house in Tarsonis City. Bars, gambling halls, brothels, and drug dens had sprung up among the rusting metal husks of long-abandoned ships and vehicles, like vermin finding hidey-holes in humanity's litter. Little was permanent, except the fact that wherever you went on the place, you could find something illegal, illicit, ill-gotten, or ill-advised.

And the man who ran it was the king of slimeballs.

Scutter O'Banon.

He thought longingly of Wicked Wayne's, of Misty and of Evangelina, of the good booze and cheerful laughter and comfortable beds. He wondered if it would ever be safe for him to return.

"Jimmy, we got Ezekiel Daun on our tail," Tychus said with exaggerated patience, interrupting Jim's brooding. "I know you ain't too keen on O'Banon, and I know my bringing it up makes you sore and all, but the man does have a very wide sphere of influence. I'd go a long way and do a great many things to have Daun quit sniffing around for me. And if you don't agree after what you saw back there"—he jerked a thumb

over his shoulder in a quick, harsh gesture—
"then you are just plumb crazy."

Jim thought about it. Getting another message from Myles had made him uneasy. He didn't
much care for the idea of not finding out at least
what the situation was.

And then in his mind's eye he saw Daun in
his duster, white teeth grinning through his goatee, cybernetic arm catching the light. He saw
the hologram of his friend getting strangled and
a bloody, silvery hand punching through a man's
chest.

A shudder shivered through him. Tychus
was right: if Myles really needed him, he'd send
another message on the fone, and Jim would
know it was truly urgent.

Until then . . .

"Tell me the coordinates for Deadman's Port."
Jim sighed.

CHAPTER ELEVEN

DEADMAN'S PORT, DEADMAN'S ROCK

It was, quite possibly, the single ugliest place Jim had ever seen. A sickly gray haze hung over everything, raw and malodorous and thick. The "port," as it were, was little more than a cleared-off area. Dull-eyed men let them land and not very subtly examined the freighter. Tychus indicated that said freighter might just be for sale. An offensively low offer was made. Tychus stated that the men had prostitutes for mothers and suggested a much higher price. Another slightly less offensive offer was made. Tychus and Jim shrugged, took the credits, and off they went.

Whereas most planets had trees, this place had rusted-out ships dotting the "landscape," with venues for traffic haphazardly weaving in and out of them. Vermin, animal and human, scuttled about furtively. Prostitutes made lewd propositions. They looked canny and hungry and dangerous, and once again Jim thought longingly of Wicked Wayne's, of the laughter and sense of fellowship and play. There was a reek about this place that had nothing to do with the pollution or the smells of unwashed bodies or waste matter in the streets. It was the reek of hopelessness, of coming to the end of the line. This might indeed be where people went to remake themselves, but not in any positive way. If this was what flourished with Scutter O'Banon at the helm, it only reinforced Jim's idea that he didn't want anything to do with the man.

And then he thought of Ezekiel Daun.

"Can't swing a cat without hitting a whore," Tychus said, approval in his voice. "And a bar every other place. I think I like this town, Jimmy."

They moved on, and Jim felt the back of his neck prickling. Casually, he looked over his shoulder. The streets were lively, certainly, but there were a couple of men who seemed to have more purposeful strides than most.

"Can you spare some food or change?" came a small voice down in the vicinity of his knee. The child was pale and dirty, his face pinched, his eyes too large for his small face. But even on that young visage was a look of craftiness, and Jim pulled back. Others appeared out of nowhere, converging upon him and Tychus with gripping little hands and words professing hunger and cold and need.

Jim frowned and tried to push the children off. "Get off me afore I drop-kick your tiny asses into the next star system," Tychus growled, much less restrained with the little gaggle of pests.

Before Jim realized what was happening, the throng of kids had deftly steered him and Tychus off the main street area into what passed in this place for an alleyway. Alarm shot through him and he pushed harder at the children, who now, as if responding to some unheard signal, scuttled back.

Four large men filled the entryway. Jim recognized two of them. They were the men who had bought the freighter.

"What's the matter, boys?" Tychus drawled lazily. "I ain't never before seen men scared enough to let children do their dirty work."

The men sneered. "Seems you tried to pass a piece of junk off on us," one of them said. "We don't much care for that."

"The money you gave us wouldn't buy a shot of whiskey on a backwater planet," Jim said. "Seems to me you looked it over and were just fine a few minutes ago. If anything, you got the better deal. We ain't looking for trouble."

"Oh, but we are." The men drew pistols and advanced. Jim and Tychus had theirs in their hands instantly.

"I'd say you found it," came a voice.

A man had entered the alley. He was tall and painfully thin, looking like a corpse come to life. There was the unmistakable sound of weapons being cocked, and then at least half a dozen armed and armored men crowded out most of what illumination came in through the alley entrance. The kids scattered like insects when a rock is overturned, and Jim and Tychus's rescuers let them go. The adults, however, slowly put down their weapons and placed their hands behind their heads.

"Cadaver," said Tychus bluffly. "Damn good timing."

"Hello again, Mr. Findlay," said the man Tychus had aptly nicknamed Cadaver. "I think you gentlemen should apologize to Mr. Findlay and Mr. Raynor here. Also . . . I thought you were limited to working in Paradise and not permitted here in Deadman's Port. I'm certain that was the understanding we reached."

The men immediately began uttering all kinds of remorseful words, quite literally begging for forgiveness. Their voices were shaking. Jim was thoroughly confused. Tychus obviously recognized the man, and—

And then he understood.

"Shall I let them go, Mr. Findlay?" asked Cadaver. "I'm quite sure they'll never trouble you or Mr. Raynor again during your stay here."

"What do you think, Jimmy?" asked Tychus. He was obviously enjoying himself a great deal. "Were the apologies enough, or shall we have my friend here dispose of these troublemakers?"

Jim regarded the men again. They looked terrified. "Seems to me like there's enough litter in this place that we shouldn't go making more things to stink it up," said Jim. "I say let them go."

"Today's your lucky day, gentlemen," said Cadaver. "Leave your weapons and any cash you have, though, all right? Let us know you're sincere in your repentance."

The men scrambled to obey, dropping surprising quantities and varieties of weapons and money. At Cadaver's nod, they fled. There was no other word to describe it. Tychus laughed.

"A fella could get used to this. We're royalty here, Jimmy, as long as we're with O'Banon. Told you it wouldn't be so bad."

Jim gave him a smile he didn't feel. "That was mighty fine timing, Mr. . . . ?"

"Baines. Edward Baines."

"I like Cadaver better," Tychus said bluntly. "I'll just keep calling you that."

Baines shrugged. "As you wish, Mr. Findlay.

I'm guessing that right now might be a good time for you to meet Mr. O'Banon?"

"I don't think we have any other pressing engagements," said Tychus. "Lead on."

Cadaver did. The six armed escorts accompanied them through the seedy streets to a different section of the port. Here, a sleek little system runner that had room for four was waiting for them. It was plush and comfortable inside and, to Tychus's amusement and approval, had a minibar. Jim and Tychus sipped some extremely fine whiskey while being granted a pleasantly distant view of the city. The pilot kept his helmet on and said very few words; Jim would likely never recognize the man if he saw him again.

They left the filthy city behind, and Jim realized that it wasn't quite the entire planet that was covered in derelict hulks—just most of it. The sea of metal thinned out, becoming, if not lush forested paradise, at least areas of dirt and grass and what looked like actual bodies of water.

"I'll be damned," Tychus said. "Looks like a whole other planet out here."

"It is," Cadaver answered. "This is Scutter O'Banon's world now."

Jim shook his head slowly, watching this "new world" unfold below him. Up ahead was what seemed at first glance to be a small corporate town. He realized quickly that all this indeed belonged to one man: Scutter O'Banon. It was his personal, heavily secured complex, with nearly a dozen buildings, laser-activated security measures, private swimming pools—plural— and even what looked to be a lavish garden and orchard. At the center of the sprawling complex was a house, if you could call something that mammoth by so humble a name. Jim quickly amended it to "mansion" and then wondered if there was anything more elaborate than that. His friend—his late friend—Ryk Kydd had once described one of the homes he used to live in. Jim felt that six of Kydd's mansions on various planets could easily fit under the roof of this one.

He thought of the children—thieves, doubtless, but probably also hungry—and of the terrible living conditions endured by those in Deadman's Port and in the ironically named Paradise he had heard tell of. All this wealth . . . for one man's pleasure.

There was, of course, a private landing field and, of course, about ten thousand uniformed security men and women awaiting their arrival. Cadaver whisked them through the process quickly. A small, old-fashioned groundcar then took them on the last leg to the mansion itself.

The driver took them and Cadaver along a long, well-paved drive through dozens of tall, meticulously pruned trees that swayed in the gentle wind. At last they pulled up in front of the mansion. An actual butler arrived, dressed in formal attire, to greet them. He seemed to be in his early to mid-fifties. He did not have a single hair—black, turning to what would eventually become iron gray—out of place. Jim felt very grubby as he exited the vehicle. Pale but sharp blue eyes looked him up and down, and the man's lips barely moved as he greeted them.

"Welcome, Mr. Findlay. Mr. Raynor. My name is Phillip Randall. Mr. O'Banon anticipated that you might enjoy a nice hot bath or shower and a change of clothes, and has prepared for your arrival. Please, follow me."

Jim and Tychus exchanged glances, then followed Randall into the yawning entry hall. Old wood gleamed, and trophy heads of various kinds of wildlife stared down at them with baleful, glassy eyes. They didn't recognize some of the kills, but they did see the distinctive gray, purple-spotted, feline face of a bengalaas and the black-tusked head of an ursadon. Someone had gone hunting on several planets.

They walked for what seemed at least a mile until they reached a curving staircase, then walked another mile until they came to two adjoining rooms.

Randall unlocked the door to the first one

with an old skeleton key. "I hope it is to your liking."

"Sweet mother of mercy," Tychus muttered at one point. The room was fully as big as any three rooms at Wicked Wayne's. Afternoon light slanted in thick as honey, illuminating a lavish bedroom with a canopied bed and gorgeous furnishings. There was an adjoining sitting room with a sofa and a cheerfully burning fire.

"There is fresh fruit, mineral water, and spirits available for your consumption," Randall said, indicating a sideboard.

Tychus looked at the bed. "Bed looks kinda empty. No one in it?"

Randall didn't bat an eye. "Mr. O'Banon was uncertain as to your tastes in that department, Mr. Findlay. Once you have let him know such, I am sure arrangements will be made promptly."

"Fekk, I like this, Jimmy," Tychus said. "How about smokes?"

"There is a humidor next to the bed," Randall said. "I am certain you will find something there to your liking."

"So am I, Randall, my good man," Tychus said.

"The bathing area is on the far side of the sitting room," Randall continued. "The closets have a selection of clothing that should be sized to fit. Mr. Findlay, this is your room. Mr. Raynor, accompany me, please. Someone will be checking in with you in about an hour. Please ring the bell by the bed if you require anything else, Mr. Findlay."

"Yeah, one blonde, one brunette, one redhead," Tychus laughed.

"That might take more than an hour."

Tychus lightly punched the smaller man in the arm. "I was just kidding with you."

Randall met his gaze evenly. "I wasn't, sir. If you'll excuse me, I should like to get Mr. Raynor properly settled."

"Go for it," Tychus said, already turning away and starting to tug off his dirty, sweaty, bloodstained shirt as Randall pulled the heavy wooden door closed behind him.

As Jim stepped into the shower in his own luxurious bathroom, turning on gold-plated faucets and feeling the most heavenly hot water cascading down on him from several different directions, he found himself analyzing Scutter O'Banon's home. Gorgeous, yes. Filled with antiques, yes. But there was—it was hard to put his finger on it—something . . . excessive about it. It was too much. Several antiques where one elegant one would have done. Dozens of alcoholic beverages to choose from instead of one or two specifically selected ones.

His parents had had a name for such people: "quick-made." People who got too much money too fast, usually from illicit and shadowy activities. They had more credits than taste, and felt a need to show it off so that others would be intimidated. His family was poor but honest, and everything they had, they had earned quite literally by the sweat of their brows.

Raynor thought of the coordinates on his fone and wished that he had had a chance to find out what Myles wanted. But right now, staying alive was more important. And he had to admit, enjoying a hot shower and fine liquor while doing so didn't hurt anything.

It felt better than he had imagined, and he realized just how sweaty, dirty, and beaten up he had been in the encounter. And then the image of Ryk Kydd, held aloft by a cybernetic hand crushing his throat, slammed into his mind.

Raynor's hands crept up to his temples, pressing hard, as if he could squeeze the memories out of his mind like he thought he had done. Prior to the recent disturbing events, he hadn't thought about Ryk, or Harnack, or any of the old Heaven's Devils in much detail for years. Life had moved too fast for memories. But the brutal encounter with Ryk Kydd's killer had hauled the recollections up out of the deep pool in which they had lain sunken.

It was funny how a spoiled, if decent-natured, kid from an Old Family had become a sniper. And even stranger, why. Kydd had been drugged and essentially sold into the military. At first he'd tried so hard to get out. Jim remembered his earnestness. He wanted to go home, and who could blame him? But then things had started to change.

Kydd had had a gift. He could shoot and kill beautifully. It had been almost—artistic. And in killing the enemy, he had saved his friends. Death had brought life for those Ryk cared for.

And now, he, too, was dead. Not of old age or accident, but at the hands of a—

Jim Raynor was forced to lean against the ceramic tile walls and let the hot water beat down on him for a long time.

Jim and Tychus knew the name of Scutter O'Banon, but they had never seen the man before. All the same, Jim had a good idea of what to expect, judging from the man's house, and he wasn't disappointed. Randall showed them into a parlor where there was another small table crowded with delicacies, alcohol, and fine cigars. Jim sat down in one of the chairs and found he had to perch close to the edge or risk being swallowed by maroon upholstery.

They waited for several minutes, an old

chrono ticking and Tychus's puffing on the cigar the only sounds. Jim was not in the mood for any more liquor or food, and simply sat, trying and failing not to clasp and unclasp his hands nervously.

"Gentlemen, such a *pleasure* to finally make your acquaintance," said a voice.

It was oily, and calculating, and drawling, and smug; Jim disliked it upon hearing it. Nonetheless, his mom had drilled courtesy into him, and he rose and turned to greet his host.

And had to look down.

Scutter O'Banon was not quite a "little person," as their late friend Hiram Feek had been, but Jim didn't think he was much over five feet. He had black hair, slicked back and slightly perfumed, and a round face with small, sharp, deep-set eyes. A red mouth topped by a pencil-line mustache was currently holding a thin cigar that Tychus would have called "girlie." Jim suspected, however, that Tychus probably would *not* opt to call it "girlie" to O'Banon's face, given the situation.

O'Banon stuck out his hand. Jim shook it. The handshake was surprisingly firm, although the hand itself was soft and utterly lacking calluses.

"Good to meet you, too, Mr. O'Banon," Jim said politely.

Tychus towered over the man as they shook

hands. "Your fellow Cad—er, Baines certainly does have mighty fine timing. I appreciate his help and yours, and your fine hospitality."

"You're most welcome, Mr. Findlay."

"Please—I tend to let people who've saved my hide call me Tychus. And this here's Jimmy."

"As you wish. You may call me Scutter, if you like. We're all friends here."

No we're not, Jim thought but did not say. He shifted his seat slightly. Hot shower, nice clothes, good food, alcohol, and stogies aside, he wanted to be out of here as quickly as possible.

"Mighty kind of you," Tychus continued. "I have to say, I was wondering just how it came to be that Baines was so quick to find us when we landed on your planet."

Jim's lips thinned at the phrase, but it was correct: this place *was* Scutter's planet.

"Quite simple, really. Very few people have turned down the chance to do business with me and survived," O'Banon said in that unctuous voice that made Jim's skin crawl. It was not a threat; it was the truth, and Jim knew it. "I was sufficiently intrigued that I had sent word out among my people that if you ever landed at Deadman's Port, I was to be notified immediately. I wanted to make sure you knew you were welcome."

Suddenly Jim wondered what would have

happened if they had told Cadaver they still weren't interested. It wasn't a pleasant thought.

"I have been a longtime admirer of your work from afar, gentlemen," O'Banon continued, gesturing to Randall to pour them all something rich and dark and tasty-looking.

"Well, that puts a smile on my face," Tychus said. "We do take pride in that work."

"As I have said before, I'd like for that fine work ethic to benefit us both. You've got a fair taste of the sort of thing I can offer you, and I know what you can do. I assume that since you have so kindly decided to call upon me, you are interested in pooling our resources."

"That we are," Tychus said.

"Why, I am so pleased to hear that." He lifted his shot glass in salute.

Jim lifted his glass as well, taking a sip of something strong and thick and syrupy. It could, he thought, be a metaphor for their host. He didn't much care for the stuff, whatever it was, and had to force himself to take another sip.

"I'm sure you have questions for me," O'Banon said next.

Tychus downed the liquor in a single gulp, leaned back in the chair, and puffed on the cigar. "I do have one particular question, and it's pressing on me mighty hard," he said.

"Fire away."

"We have ourselves a very nasty dog on our tails," Tychus explained. "Hard to shake him. Was wondering if you might be able to do that for us. It would certainly free our minds to concentrate on doing a better job for you if we didn't have a bounty hunter taking potshots at us."

O'Banon's red mouth pursed over his thin cigar. "Many of my employees come to me with tales of woe similar to yours. I'm sure we can throw this hound off your scent. Do you have any idea as to his identity?"

"Ezekiel Daun."

O'Banon went very still. The room's silence pressed in on them, and the ticking chrono sounded more like a ticking bomb to Jim.

"My, my, you do seem to have enemies in high places," O'Banon said at last. He blew out a thin stream of smoke, fixing his gaze thoughtfully on a corner of the room, and rolled the tiny cigar in his blunt fingers. "No offense, but while your work is artful, it is hardly on the sort of scale that warrants such retaliation. Who could possibly want you dead enough to spend the type of money needed to get Daun?"

Things had happened so fast and so brutally that Jim realized he hadn't even had a chance to think about that. Tychus glanced over at him and Jim saw that the thought was only now occurring to him as well. He couldn't think of anybody, and judging by Tychus's expression, the bigger man couldn't, either.

"Well, Scutter, you ask a mighty good question there. As we only recently found out that he was even interested in us, we haven't had much time to think about who the hound master might be."

"I see." O'Banon tapped the ash off his cigar and took another sip of the sweet liquor. "I'm sure that you must understand that this changes the nature of our relationship somewhat. The situation has . . . *evolved*."

Here we go, thought Jim.

"You don't want to just come work for Scutter O'Banon. You need my protection. That's something quite different. Our split is going to have to change slightly." He took another puff. "In my favor."

Tychus looked over at Jim, who shrugged. They were hip-deep in this now. The second that Daun's name had come up, O'Banon knew he had them by the short-and-curlies, and that was that. They needed him, and he knew it, and that gave him the upper hand.

He tuned out the details, listening with only half an ear as Tychus and Scutter O'Banon hammered out the deal. Tychus was better at this stuff, anyway, and the whole thing had been his idea.

No, rather than listen to the finer points of

negotiating, Jim found his mind focusing on one thing, and one thing only.

The question that Scutter O'Banon had asked . . . the question for which he and Tychus had no answer.

Who had hired Ezekiel Daun?

The holoprojector was enormous and required a rather burly man to maneuver it into the dimly lit room where their employer resided. The hover-dolly had small lights so they could see where they were going. Grunting with effort, the resoc eased the holoprojector off so that it would project its image directly in front of the huge metal box that surrounded their boss's body except for his head, which was now wreathed in shadow, illuminated only sporadically by the brief flash of lights that chased each other along the metal enclosure.

"You'll wake the dead with that clatter," the protruding head was saying, his voice husky and echoing in the room. "Hurry, hurry, I want to see this now, not tomorrow!"

"Of course, sir," the resocialized servant said nervously. "We understand completely, and we're almost ready."

"Almost, almost . . . ," the shadowed man growled.

There was the flick of a switch. The figure of a tall, well-built man in a long duster with a neatly trimmed goatee stood large as life in front of the metal coffin.

"Are they dead, Daun? Are they dead?" The raspy hollow voice was filled with anticipation.

"Not yet."

A shriek of raw fury rent the tension-filled air in the room, and the resocs paled and began to sweat.

"What? *What?* You useless sack of dog shit! You're supposed to be the finest bounty hunter in the sector, and you still have not produced your main targets! I do not tolerate failure, Daun, I do *not*!"

Daun's brows drew together. When he spoke, his voice was calm and even. "I'd advise you to watch your tone and remember who you're speakin' to," he said with a slight smile. "Sometimes killin' ain't just about money. Sometimes, and in fact quite a lot of the time, killin's about a man's honor. You wouldn't want to step on ol' Daun's *honor*, now, would you?"

There was a silence. The head protruding from the blinking casket turned away.

"No. I wouldn't." A pause. "You are the best in the business, and I'm sure you will succeed. Please let me know when the mission is accomplished."

"Of course," Daun replied. His goatee parted in a smile. "I'll show you."

And without another word, the hologram faded away.

"Get it out!" the man screamed. "Get it out of here now! *Now!*"

Instantly the muscular resoc sprang into action, loading the holoprojector back on the dolly and removing the offending item from his master's presence. As the one maneuvering the dolly stepped through the door that opened for him, another one entered. The newcomer stepped to the side of the coffin, monitoring the statistics that continuously rolled along a screen.

"You too," snarled the man. "I want to be alone. Get out of here!"

"Yes, Colonel Vanderspool."

CHAPTER TWELVE

They had become gods.

There really was no other way to put it. Word apparently spread fast in Deadman's Port that James Raynor and Tychus Findlay were under Scutter O'Banon's protection, and over the next few weeks the two former marines fought back grins as crowds often literally parted for them. They were able to belly up to any bar and get top-shelf drinks for the regular price, and sometimes on the house. The top gambling dens seemed to have a seat for them, and every "show" saw them at the best seats. Quieter offers were made, too, for more private shows.

There was one particularly notable incident that Jim knew he would remember for a long,

long time. Tychus had had more to drink than any man ought to be able to stomach and survive. Even so, to the eyes of those who didn't know him well, he seemed little affected by the liquor. Jim knew better, and when Tychus pulled the stunt that had everyone talking for the next week, he alone was unsurprised.

There was one place called The Silver Belle. It was one of the more respectable "female dancer" venues in Deadman's Port—which was to say it was cleaner than most and the alcohol was pretty good. The girls, too, were cleaner than most, and also pretty good. They had a genuine show, with an actual script and something approaching decent acting. There were three shows that they cycled through regularly.

This one was some sort of romantic tragedy. It vaguely reminded Jim of one of the classics . . . if the classics had simulated sex scenes and reasons for the characters' clothes to conveniently become torn, damaged, or removed in some other fashion.

They had shown up halfway into the first scene—which was fine, as they'd seen it before—and Tychus immediately went to use the facilities. Five minutes later Jim, who had been relaxing in his seat, sat bolt upright.

Tychus Findlay stood on the stage, playing the lead male character. He wore a huge grin, and very little else. Jim groaned and placed his head in his hands. Over to the side, the manager looked slightly sick, but he was also holding an enormous sack of credits.

Jim had to admit that Tychus wasn't half bad. He knew the script—well, mostly. And when he didn't, the other actors ad-libbed or shed their clothes for no particular reason, and the crowd seemed to approve. Jim found lots of reasons to get up and leave during particularly, uh, *dramatic* scenes.

There was a party afterward, and later Jim was sorry that he had gotten so drunk that he remembered very little of it.

Despite the giddiness of their new, elevated status, Jim found himself more subdued than one might have expected. Tychus, knowing Jim as long as he had, picked up on it and commented with his usual subtle, caring understanding as they watched a floor show.

"You look like you've been drinking piss instead of fine booze," he said.

Jim, who had in fact been drinking quite a lot of fine booze, nodded somewhat unsteadily. "Yeah," he said, "I reckon I do. Things don't feel good, Tychus."

Tychus leaned back in the chair, watching the nearly naked women gyrating about two feet from them. He puffed one of Scutter's cigars—a handful of which he had accepted from O'Banon before Randall had shown them out. Jim thought that Scutter had looked surprised and was fairly certain he had been offering only one or two, but was also fairly certain it was no skin off his nose to acquire more.

"What don't feel good about this?" Tychus lifted his arms expansively to include the view, the booze, and essentially the entire joint.

Jim opened his mouth to tell him about the message Myles had sent, but thought better of it, at least for the moment. Instead he said, "I keep seein' Ryk in my head. With his neck squeezed by Daun."

Tychus's grin faded. "Yeah. I seen a lot in battle, Jimmy. And I seen a lot just bein' me. But that . . ." He shook his head and was quiet for a long moment. "Jimmy, I don't think it makes me any less of a man to tell you that Ezekiel Daun scares the shit out of me."

"Me too," Jim said. "I think he'd scare the shit out of any sane human being. Kydd was a good one. Better'n you and me, Tychus. He had a chance to go back to the sort of life we're scrambling to find, and he didn't." Jim was surprised to feel tears stinging his eyes. He blamed it on the booze and the extreme agitation Daun had caused.

"Yeah," Tychus agreed quietly. "He didn't never let anyone down. Not ever."

"When they came for him, and he coulda gotten his old life back. . . . Turning away from that chance was a noble thing, Tychus. A noble thing. He stayed because he wanted to make sure his friends stayed alive."

Tychus nodded, blowing a stream of smoke into the air. "That it was. I ain't seen a lot of noble things in my life, but I seen that."

"We didn't do that much with him afterward," Jim muttered, knocking back a drink and pouring himself another with an unsteady hand.

"Don't you go blaming yourself, Jimmy," Tychus said, his voice slightly sharp. "We didn't ditch him or nothing. We just kinda went our separate ways."

"Yeah? And what kind of way did *he* take? We didn't even bother to ask."

"Ryk was a sniper. Stands to reason he'd use the skills he had."

"Yeah, but . . . you know how he looked at it." Jim fumbled for words. "Ryk used his talents to keep us safe. He was . . . protective. But I'm thinking that maybe he just went and hired himself out as an assassin."

"Again, I say that complicated word: 'so'?"

"That ain't right. Killin' ain't just killin', and you know it. Not for him, at least, it wasn't. For him it was about helping his friends stay alive. About doing something good. Maybe if we'd stuck together, he wouldn't have had to go hire himself out like a common killer. Take that gift and just use it for money."

"Maybe if we'd stuck together, Daun would have had three at once."

"Maybe not. Maybe we could have stopped the bastard."

"You know, Jimmy, 'maybe' is a fine word, but it don't get you drunk, rich, or laid," drawled Tychus.

Jim allowed as how Tychus had a point. "Still," he said, "we'll never know, because we didn't do a noble thing. And I wish to God we had."

"Hell, Jimmy, I ain't any more capable of doing something noble than of jumping off the roof and flying," Tychus said.

"On that we are agreed," Jim said, smiling a little. He lifted his glass. "Here's to Hobarth, who had the guts to crawl out of a prison camp with enough wits left to bring it down. To Feek, who saved our lives more than once. And to our buddy Ryk. Noble people all, and I aim to never forget them."

"I'll drink to that," Tychus said, and began to back up his words with action, adding, "Course, I'll drink to just about anything."

* * *

As they stumbled down the troughs between ruined ships that served as streets, Jim's mood grew darker and darker, and his thoughts turned to what Scutter O'Banon did. Jim didn't mind exotic dancers who did a little more on the side. He didn't mind getting drunk. He didn't mind "liberating" credits.

He minded selling people. He minded running drugs known to be dangerous or far, far too addictive—substances that turned people into zombies. And he very, very much minded torture. He did not like Scutter O'Banon: did not like what the man did, did not like that the deal had changed now that Ezekiel Daun was on their tail—did not like that Daun was on their tail, period—and did not like that he had had to hightail it out of New Sydney space before finding out what the *hell* Myles had wanted with him.

So, while Tychus wanted to pop his head into every crevice that promised "Girls," "Booze," or "Gambling," Jim, despite the fuzziness of his head, found himself looking for other, tamer distractions. He did not find them, and so he was in a surly mood when he found himself at a bar, both hands wrapped around a beer, talking to the bartender who, while not Misty, actually looked like she gave a damn.

"Just . . . you know, wanna make sure she's okay," Jim was slurring as the dark-skinned girl nodded sympathetically. Her brown eyes were kind as she set another bottle down in front of him.

"Been a long time since you've seen your momma?" she asked.

"Yep. Too long."

She dried a glass. "I've not seen my momma and daddy for a long time myself." She smiled a little. "Not by my choice, though. Guess that being a bartender in a place called Deadman's Port isn't exactly the future they envisioned for their little girl."

Jim winced. Her words had struck too close to home for his comfort. A few meters away, Tychus cried, "Come to Papa!" and presumably either was hauling in his winnings at the gambling table or hauling an attractive girl onto his lap.

"I got a friend might be able to link you up— for a fee," the bartender continued.

"What do you mean, 'link me up'?"

"He could get a message through to your momma."

Jim started so violently, he almost spilled his beer but, with the reflexes of several years spent drinking, caught it just in time. "I don't wanna talk to my mom."

The girl seemed puzzled. "Well, all right, then. Anything else I can get you, hon?"

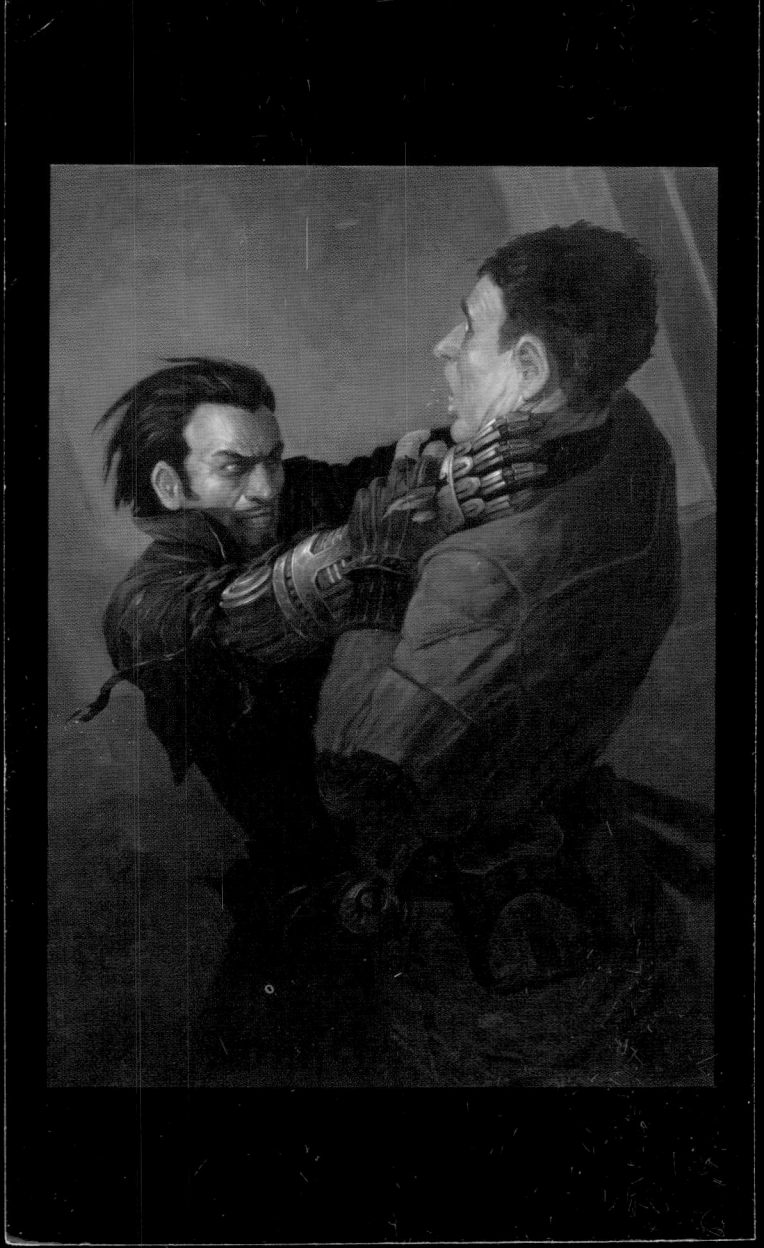

"Wait." He hesitated. "Your friend. I want to talk to him."

"He'll find you," she said, and winked.

Jim was even further in his cups when a man of medium build and nondescript appearance sat down beside him as he watched the show. The girls had barely started their routine and most of their clothes were still on. Jim didn't even notice the man until he spoke—quietly—yet somehow managed to be heard over the whooping of appreciative customers and blaring music.

"I understand you need a message delivered," the man said.

Jim turned. The man was completely forgettable, although being drunk probably didn't help Jim's powers of observation. It took him a couple of seconds, then his eyes widened. "Bartender's friend," he said.

"Exactly. Now, how can I help you?"

Jim told him. The man listened, nodding now and then. "Yes, I believe I can assist you. Shiloh is rather out of the way and a bit of a backwater, so I'm afraid I'll have to charge extra."

"Don't care." Jim didn't.

"Wish more customers were like you, Mr. Raynor." The man smiled. "I receive messages at this address." He slipped Jim a data card. It was too dark and Jim was too drunk to read it anyway, so he merely nodded. "If you don't hear from me, feel free to stop by," the man suggested. "Quietly. With a little bit of luck, you'll be hearing from one Mr. Myles Hammond of Shiloh very soon."

He named his fee; Jim paid it; they shook hands; and Jim returned his attention to the dancers. His heart felt somewhat eased, and he realized just how much this had been weighing on him. He even felt better about the deal they had struck with Scutter O'Banon. At least it would keep the walking nightmare that was Ezekiel Daun at bay.

He ordered another beer, stretched out his long legs, and smiled at the buxom beauty gyrating near him. She responded by closing one heavily made-up eye in an inviting wink.

The sun was merciless and cruel, and when the door to the room Jim had reserved for the night opened and the men who entered pulled the shades, Raynor was hard-pressed not to yelp in agony even as he reached for his gun and trained it on the intruders. He blinked, lowering the gun as he recognized Cadaver.

"Baines? What the hell are you doing here?"

The girl beside Jim, significantly less lovely in

the harsh morning light, muttered and ducked her head back under the covers.

"Mr. O'Banon has just learned that you have received an encrypted message from Shiloh."

Jim was so muzzy-headed it took him a few seconds to catch up with Cadaver's words. From Shiloh? Already? Damn, that . . . whatshisname was good.

"That was fast," he said, moving as quickly as his protesting head would let him. "Would you boys mind closing the shades?"

"Mr. O'Banon is not pleased that anyone is contacting you on secure channels."

That irritated Jim. He swung his feet over the bed and pulled on his trousers, not caring about his unexpected audience. That was what they got for barging in on someone.

"Well, apparently it didn't get by his sniffer dogs, did it? Or else you wouldn't be here with your panties in a bunch."

They exchanged glances, frowning. "Mr. O'Banon requests that you come with us to—"

"I'll be there as soon as I can. Thank you kindly for delivering the message so promptly. I'm going to go get my message, on my secure channel, and you can tell your boss to . . . wait."

He threw on his shirt and vest, tugged on his boots, and was buckling his gun belt as he strode out the door, leaving some rather stunned people behind.

"You boys gonna pay for my services for him?" he heard the girl saying as the door closed behind him.

The site that Mr. Mystery gave was deceptive—the name wasn't even on the card, just a code that, when keyed into Jim's fone, had given him an address. At first, it didn't even look like it was an actual address, and Jim had to double-check it. There it was, a narrow aperture between two other "storefronts," in a manner of speaking, and Jim slipped inside into the darkness.

It was very dark indeed, and his hand went to his pistol in anticipation of an ambush. It wouldn't be the first time something like that had happened. As his eyes adjusted, he saw that there was a dim glow up ahead at the end of the narrow corridor. Gun at the ready, Jim moved slowly, emerging into what had obviously once been the cargo area of a ship. The faint lighting revealed that small portable alcoves with individual partitions had been set up. Jim saw movement out of the corner of his eye, and he whirled around to see someone almost as nondescript as Mr. Mystery approaching.

"Do you have a card, sir?" he asked.

"Yeah," Jim said, handing it to him. "Name's

Jim Raynor. Was told there was a message for me from—"

"Yes," the man said, interrupting him smoothly. "Follow me, please." He led Jim through the maze of partitions, and Jim caught brief glimpses of other patrons here to receive messages. Some of them were quietly sobbing; some had smiles on their faces. All had small earbuds and were watching holograms.

"Here you are, sir. Your payment permits you to watch it three times. If you wish to watch it again, there will be an additional fee. Please insert the earbuds to ensure privacy. To activate your message, press this button here."

"Gotcha," Jim said. He was already seated and reaching for the earbuds. The man slipped away quietly.

Jim hesitated for a minute. He hadn't been sure what to expect. Realizing that he was nervous, he scowled at himself and pushed the glowing red button with unnecessary vigor.

The image of Myles Hammond appeared, a mere third of a meter high. He looked much older than he had when Jim had seen him last, even though it hadn't been that long. Grayer, more stooped, the lines around his eyes captured by the surprisingly high-quality hologram.

"Jim. I was worried when I didn't hear from you. I . . . listen. I understand that what I'm about to ask is dangerous, and a risk. I wouldn't ask it if . . . well. There's just no easy way to say this."

Jim's gut clenched as the holographic Myles took a deep breath.

"Your mother's dying, Jim. She's been sick for a long time, but she's recently taken a turn for the worse. Doctor reckons she don't have much more than a couple of weeks, maybe a month at the outside. I know you couldn't be here when your daddy died, but you didn't have no warning then. This time you do. If you want to see her before she passes, you better find a way to get out here soon. You let me know when you're coming, and I'll find a safe spot for you to land and have clothes and transportation ready for you." His voice broke on the last word, and he cleared his throat. "Take care, Jim."

The image froze. After a second or two, it reset and began to play again. Jim paused it and stared blankly at nothing.

Was this some kind of trick? Had Myles sold him out? Was this a way to get him to come to Shiloh, by lying about his mother so that . . . what? Jim buried his face in his hands for a moment.

Myles Hammond had been a fixture in Jim Raynor's life since he could remember. Hammond had been a Raynor family friend, at dinner two, three nights a week, and had attended all of Jim's derbies. Jim had been grateful that Myles had been there for his family after he had left, and even more glad that the man had been there when Karol Raynor had suddenly become a widow after an accident on the farm. It was the years of living on the edge that made him suspect anything ill of that man.

Now she was dying. Dying of what? How? Would money help? Could he talk her into going to a doctor who—

No. She wasn't taking the money he'd sent already. She would have had plenty to get off planet, go to some specialist. And she obviously hadn't done so. Anger welled up in him. It would serve her right, he thought bitterly. She didn't want to see him. She didn't want his money or anything to do with him. Why should he risk his life trying to get back to Shiloh, away from the protection of Scutter O'Banon? Hell, maybe he'd lost it already, pissing off O'Banon just by making contact with Myles.

No. No way he'd go back, giving Daun a chance for easy pickings, just to see a woman who . . .

Jim closed his eyes, but not before hot liquid had begun to seep from them.

He emerged, sober and resolute, blinking into what passed for sunlight in Deadman's Port. He wasn't sure where to go or what to do, so he headed back to the place where he'd struck up the conversation with the bartender. She wasn't there at this hour, of course; she had the night shift, and the large tattooed man who was clearly polite only because he had to be did not invite conversation. Jim was nursing a shot of whiskey when a large shape filled the doorway.

"There you are," said Tychus. "Been huntin' all over for you."

"All you needed to do was ask Cadaver and his goons where I was," Jim muttered.

"Which is precisely what I did," Tychus said mildly as he sat down next to Jim at the bar, ordered a beer, and turned to his friend. "Scutter O'Banon ain't altogether happy with you right now."

"Ask me if I care," Jim said.

"Someone got out of bed on the wrong side this morning."

"Someone got rousted out of a warm bed with a warm girl by a man who looks like a walking corpse." Jim downed the shot and gestured for a refill.

"Well, this'll make you happier. We got our first job, and it's a sweet and simple one."

"Like getting the logs from a scrap yard?"

Tychus frowned as the bartender plunked a sweating beer bottle down in front of him. "I don't like your attitude, Jimmy. We're sitting on a fine deal here and you keep acting like you're doing O'Banon a favor by breathin' the air on this planet."

Who says I ain't? The retort came to Jim's lips but he choked it back. Tychus was right: Jim might not like O'Banon, but it wasn't the man's fault that his mother was dying, or that a sicko who liked to make holographic recordings of his victims had been hired to kill them.

"Go on," he said instead.

"Simple retrieval and smuggling mission on Halcyon. Get something, get back with it. Cake." Tychus took a long pull of the beer.

Jim nodded. "Okay. But I gotta make a stop first."

"What?"

"I gotta go to Shiloh."

"What the hell you wanna go back *there* for?"

"I don't want to talk about it."

Tychus regarded him for a long moment. His eyes had narrowed and gone cold, like chips of ice. "If you ain't willing to tell me why you want to make a stop, we ain't making one. We got a job to do."

"I don't have to explain myself to you!" Jim snapped.

Tychus rose slowly, still holding the bottle. Jim was reminded of just how big the man was. "I give you a lotta slack, boy. I put up with things

I wouldn't take from any other man alive. But there are some things I ain't taking. Your whole attitude stinks, Jim Raynor. It has from the minute I brought up O'Banon's name, and I'm getting mighty tired of the stench."

"I'm getting mighty tired of your attitude, too, Tychus," Jim said. He slid off his chair as well. He was not as big as Tychus—few were—but he was no small man, either, and the life he had been leading for the last few years had made him tough with muscle. Besides, he was royally pissed. "It's *my* life, *my* business, and I am going to make a stop before we do anything else!"

Tychus took a long swig of his beer. He wiped his mouth with the back of his free hand, seemed about to say something, and then swore violently as he hurled the bottle angrily at Jim. It flew past Raynor, spewing frothy amber liquid as it turned end over end to crack against the wall.

Jim's mouth dropped open.

"You son of a—"

"Hold it right there!" snapped a voice. Hands came out of nowhere and closed on both men's arms.

It was a very big mistake.

Tychus let out an enraged bellow and whirled with a clenched fist. At the last second he recognized the man as Cadaver, but that didn't slow him down one bit, and his mammoth hand

connected quite audibly with Cadaver's face.
Cadaver let out a yelp and staggered backward,
blood pouring from his shattered nose. Four
others sprang from the shadows and leaped on
Tychus, trying to bring him down like a bull at a
livestock show. But this bull was having none of
it. Tychus shook off two of them almost casually,
whirling and slamming the other two into the
bar. One of them swung before impact, getting
off a lucky punch that caught Tychus's jaw.

Raynor, meanwhile, found himself staring at
one of the men who had barged into his room
that morning. He made a fist, putting all of his
fear, anger, helplessness, and righteous fury into
the punch as he swung. He felt the gratifying sensation of cartilage crumpling beneath his knuckles. Then he was doubled over as another one of
O'Banon's goons kidney-punched him. Grunting
in pain, he turned, reached out with both hands,
grasped his attacker's head, and head-butted him
as hard as he possibly could.

Someone sprang on him from behind, pinning Jim's arms to his sides and making him
lurch off balance. The arms were like steel bands.
Jim struggled, swearing, but to no avail. . . .

Then abruptly the weight was gone. Jim
stumbled forward, whirling to see Tychus throwing Jim's attacker clear across the room like he
weighed nothing at all.

Their eyes met, and Jim grinned.

Then they turned their backs to each other and began slugging it out for real against O'Banon's boys. Approximately five minutes later, the area around the bar was in shambles and there were ten men in various stages of pain, trauma, and semiconsciousness.

Cadaver stared at them, shaking with dissipating adrenaline and rising fury. He was holding a cloth to his nose.

"You hab just bade a serious biscalculation," Cadaver said, his voice muffled by the cloth, which was turning bright red.

"No. We did exactly what you knew we would do," Tychus growled. "You jumped us with no warning, so we beat you to a pulp." He nudged one of the bodies on the floor. The man groaned weakly. "You'd best be getting these boys to a doctor's care if you want to reuse them. Jimmy and I were about to depart on O'Banon's business. I suggest you leave us to it."

Jim tensed slightly at the words but said nothing as Cadaver and his cronies limped, lurched, stumbled, or were carried out, some of them casting hate-filled glances behind them as they left. Tychus turned to the surly bartender, who also looked at him with contempt.

"Looks like we made a right mess here," Tychus said, counting out credits. "This should cover repairs. And this is a little something to cleanse your lily-white innocent mind of this terrible scene you were forced to witness."

The man looked at the amount and brightened considerably. "Mr. Findlay, you and Mr. Raynor are welcome to trash my joint any time you want."

He plunked two bottles of ice-cold beer in front of them and they all grinned. Jim picked up the bottle and took a swig.

"Tychus, I still want to—"

"I know, Jimmy. Whatever is going on, I can see it's important to you. I'm thinking I'll enjoy letting O'Banon stew awhile after this bullshit he just pulled on us anyway. I'll drop you off on Shiloh and give you a day to conduct your business. But then no slacking. Deal?"

Jim grinned. The gesture hurt like hell as he realized he'd gotten at least one good punch in the face, but he couldn't stop smiling. He clinked his bottle against Tychus's.

"Deal," he said.

CHAPTER THIRTEEN

CENTERVILLE, SHILOH

It was early fall, and the heat was searing.

Jim squinted in the bright sun as the dust devils swirled about him, kicking up little puffs as he walked. He had sent a reply back to Myles, and true to his word, Myles had found a good spot. Jim had had Tychus drop him off in the prearranged site, a field that struck a good balance between "in the middle of nowhere" and "driving distance to town."

This field should have been bursting with triticale-wheat ready to be harvested. Instead, it was sere and dry. The dust would make for a spectacular sunset, Jim remembered, and as luck would have it, Centerville lay to the west.

He wore nondescript farmer's clothes that had been left for him at the drop point along with an older-model pickup truck. Jim knew that he was a wanted man, but he also knew Shiloh, and people on this planet tended to mind their own business. He clapped the hat on his head to complete the disguise, climbed into the truck, and took off.

He barely recognized the place. The town itself had sprawled past the limits he remembered as a youth, but many of the buildings had been built, inhabited, and then closed down—an entire life cycle in the period in which he had been away. The main street had several FOR SALE signs on places that Jim had never seen.

It was early evening, and the sun was only beginning its glorious red-hazed descent, so most of the remaining businesses were closed for the day. That made it safer for him. As he passed a small park on the right, something caught his eye. He slowed, made a U-turn, and stopped.

It was a large rectangular wall made of the tan stone quarried in Shiloh. The stone had been cut and highly polished, and there were some kind of drawings etched in it, and a plaque. Curious, Jim climbed out of the truck.

As he drew closer, he realized that it was a memorial for the Guild Wars. A small flame flickered in front of it, and at the little fire's feet were the words WE WILL NEVER FORGET. The drawings were of farmers on one side, armored Confederate marines on the other. All struck poses so heroic, it would have made a recruitment officer weep.

He walked around to the other side. It was almost completely covered by a huge plaque. Jim realized with a jolt that it was a list of those sons and daughters of Shiloh who had fallen in the wars.

It was a hell of a long list.

Slowly, he reached out and touched the raised names, trailing his fingers downward through the alphabet. Too many to read each one, but those he recognized jumped out at him: Phillip Andrews, Jacob Cavanaugh, Roger Gregson, Henry "Hank" Harnack . . .

Harnack. Hard to believe he and Jim had grown up as bitter enemies, and become friends, brothers in arms, when they both had joined Heaven's Devils. Hank's death . . . had not been a good one.

Felicia Karlson, Vincent Lamont . . .

"Thomas Omer," he said quietly. He and Tom Omer had grown up together. They had signed up together. He'd watched his friend receive the wound that would take his life. Jim allowed his fingers to linger on the name for a moment, remembering.

He didn't belong here. Not anymore. He turned, got back in the truck, and sped on his way.

The offices of the mayor were small and out of date. A fan whirred, laboriously trying to cool the receiving room, succeeding only in feebly blowing the hot air around. The mayor returned from a quick dinner break, briefcase in hand, to file some papers and sighed as he realized the room was not noticeably cooler than it had been several hours earlier. He loosened his tie and removed it; it was, after all, after office hours.

He removed his hat, hung it up, and headed down the narrow corridor to his private office. He opened the door—

And closed it behind him quickly, staring at the man who sat in his chair.

"Well, hello, Myles," Jim Raynor said. "You know, all this time, when you told me in the messages that you'd become mayor, I thought you had lost it. But you really *are* the mayor, you old son of a gun!"

Myles Hammond laughed. "Some days I wish I was crazy and imagining this, let me tell you," he said, chuckling. He regarded Jim with kind eyes, and the smile faded. "Now . . . what in blazes are you doing here? I left the clothes and the truck specifically so you wouldn't have to come into town."

"I wanted to see you," Jim said, rising. He stuck his hand out. Myles clasped it warmly, then pulled the younger man into an awkward but affectionate embrace.

"I'm glad to hear that from you, Jimmy, I am, but you are a wanted man. This was a dangerous little stunt."

He unlocked the briefcase he'd been carrying, reached into it, and pulled out a piece of paper. Jim found himself staring at his own face with the word WANTED written over it in large capital letters.

"Huh," he said jokingly, "I thought I was better-looking than that."

"This ain't a laughing matter," Myles said. "I assume you were too smart to let anybody see you."

"People see what they expect to see," Raynor said. "I look like a farmer in these clothes, and that's what anyone who noticed me at all saw. I promise."

Myles relaxed slightly, nodding. "Good, good. That poster was at the post office. I just came from there. I took down all I could find. Still—hardly a hero's welcome. Cup of coffee?"

"If you still call that swill you brew coffee,

sure," Jim said. Myles smiled again and prepared a fresh pot. He locked the door, pulled down the shades, and turned to Jim.

"So," Jim said, sitting on the edge of the desk, "tell me about Mom."

"You know all I know, Jim," Myles said.

"I mean about the money. I've been sending you a goodly amount of money from my"—he was about to say "heists" but caught himself—"*business profits* for several years now. What's been happening to it?"

Myles sighed and rubbed at his eyes. "I been trying to tell you, Jim, she won't take it. Not her, not your father before her."

"None of it? It's tens of thousands by this point."

"Not a single credit," Myles said firmly.

Jim swore. "She always was stubborn."

"Her and your father. Salt of the earth."

"She's okay, though?"

"Well enough. Farm Aid's been a real blessing to the people of Shiloh. A lot of families here have been able to have roofs over their heads and food on the table because of it. Your mom's one of those."

Jim nodded. Myles had mentioned Farm Aid before. He was glad to know that hadn't stopped for some reason.

"Since you're here . . ."

Myles went to the wall behind the desk and removed a painting of Creek Canyon at sunset. Behind the painting was a safe. Myles keyed in a code, and the door swung open. "You might as well take your money back," he said, removing several sacks that made a distinctive clinking sound. Myles also took out a small data chip.

He placed the sacks and the data chip on the desk and went to pour their coffees. Jim looked at the sacks for a moment, pushed the data chip out of the way, then opened the sacks and dumped their contents on the table. It made for a large, messy pile.

Jim started counting. "Nothing personal, Myles, I'm just used to counting my money before I walk away from a deal."

Myles stiffened slightly, but then nodded and finished pouring. "I reckon you would be, considering the line of work you're in. Count away."

Several moments later, Jim was both disappointed and angry. "You're short, Hammond."

"Yes, I most certainly am."

"What's going on?"

Hammond plunked down a steaming cup of coffee in front of Jim and pointed to the small data chip Jim had ignored. Jim looked at him, puzzled. Myles picked up the data chip and slid it into the computer on his desk. A file came up.

"Take a look. Jim, we both know that what you're doing ain't on the right side of things by anyone's reckoning. We also know your parents needed that money. I couldn't get them to take it, but I did what I could. It's all there. I took a small percentage of what you sent me each time. I routed it through various channels and was able to directly pay off the liens that were put against the Raynor farm without your mom catching on. It wasn't what I wanted to do, but sometimes you just have to do the best you can with what you've got.

"I also invested some funds into research—compiling some statistics on your family compared with others on Shiloh. It was pretty persuasive stuff. Your parents, being your parents, insisted that others were in worse shape than they were, so they declined any kind of help other than the most basic survival assistance. I talked to some people at Farm Aid, showed them the statistics, and was able to quietly get your parents some better-quality food and supplies than they thought they were getting. It was what they rightfully deserved."

"I saw a lot of empty fields," Raynor said quietly. He was still staring at the documents on the screen. Everything corroborated Myles's words.

"You'd be seeing a hell of a lot more empty

fields here if it weren't for Farm Aid. That program is the only thing keeping a lot of people
afloat here. It sure helped your parents."

Jim leaned back slowly, still looking at the
screen.

"I owe you an apology, Myles," he said quietly. "I jumped to a conclusion. I—I guess I've
been dealing with con artists and crooks for so
damn long I forgot what it's like to do business
with decent men."

Miles sipped his coffee. "You were a decent
man once, Jim," he said bluntly. Jim's eye
twitched at the words, but other than that he
gave no reaction. "Your father always thought
you'd turn out like him, and why shouldn't he?
He was a man of strong principles. He—"

"Thanks for looking out for them," Jim said
abruptly. "I appreciate that. But I don't need no
lecture. Just set up the meeting with my mother,
and I'll be out of here."

He started to pick up the sacks of credits. They
were heavy and awkward. Myles wordlessly
pointed under his desk. Jim looked down and
saw a large satchel. He plunked the satchel on
the desk, opened it, and filled it with the sacks.

Myles took another sip of coffee. "I ain't lec-
turing, Jim. I understand that things aren't so
black-and-white all the time. Why do you think I
decided to run for office?"

"Hell, I don't know. Free checking account?"

"Because I thought I could make a difference. The Confederacy has become more corrupt than ever, and there was a little while when I was able to do a little good for people. But not anymore. Not here. They've got too good a grip on things here. Maybe things would be different somewhere else. I've been thinking about going to a settlement on Mar Sara."

"Mar Sara?" Jim laughed. "Remind me never to go on vacation with you. That planet is a hellhole."

Myles chuckled. "Maybe. But I ain't going there for the climate. There's good people out there, Jim. People just trying to make a decent living and lead decent lives. I've been offered an opportunity to become a local magistrate." He'd been looking off in the distance, his gaze unfocused, but now it snapped sharply back to Raynor. "If I go . . . why don't you come with me?"

"What? No, thanks. I got better things to do with my time."

"Sure you do." Myles's voice dripped sarcasm. "Just remember, the offer's there if you should change your mind."

"I won't, but . . . thanks."

"Anything for a Raynor. You know that." He cleared his throat. "Well, come on. I'll take you to see your momma."

* * *

Jim stood for a long moment in front of his boy-hood home. It was exactly how he remembered it. Most of it was located underground, keeping it safe from both blowing snow and sand and the annual temperature fluctuations. The roof was a dome covered by a semitransparent membrane that collected heat during the day to be stored in the farm's power cells. At night, the membrane was retracted. He used to lie back in a lounge chair and look up at the stars, wondering what was out there.

Now he knew, and he realized he'd give an awful lot to be that boy again, working hard dur-ing the day, gazing up at the stars at night and wondering, and then sleeping the sleep of the exhausted innocent.

He swallowed hard past the unexpected knot in his throat and had to make a determined ef-fort to get his feet to move down the ramp.

Habit saw him removing his boots in the entryway so as not to track dust all over the house. In his stocking feet, he slowly went through the living room, with its old furniture and steadily ticking chrono, into the kitchen, which had been the heart of the home.

His mother was there, as he knew she would be. Her back was to him as he entered. He took it all in: the wooden table and chairs, the tiny counters still scrupulously clean. She was busy making a meal for herself. No more large roasts from the local ranchers, served with potatoes and homemade bread, for a hardworking farmer husband and a growing young son. Just simple vegetables for a salad. She was standing, but there was a cane within easy reach, and she moved very slowly as she chopped the bright yellow farra roots and round, purple sur fruit. A box sat on the counter with FARM AID SUPPLIES emblazoned upon it.

Suddenly she went very still and straightened, and it was only then that Jim realized just how stooped she was.

"Jim," she said, the word a statement, not a question.

"Hello, Mom," Jim said, his voice thick.

Still with her back to him, Karol Raynor carefully put down the knife, reached out for her cane with a trembling hand, and turned to face her only child.

Jim had known his mother was ill. Had known she didn't have long to live. But that knowledge had not prepared him for the sight of what a handful of years and the ravages of sickness had done to a formerly robust and hearty woman. Once-ebony hair was almost completely white now, and thin, as if it had started to fall out in places. Her green eyes were sunken and dull, and what Jim remembered as a few wrinkles had deepened to crevices. Her cheeks were hollow, and he realized that she had lost a great deal of weight. But the most immediate, most visible thing about her was the look of pure joy on her face.

Tears blurred Jim's vision. He stumbled forward three steps and caught her up, so fragile, so breakable, in his arms and hugged her.

Twenty minutes later he was seated in the living room, having made iced tea for both of them. Both glasses sat untouched. Karol Raynor leaned back against the sofa, seeming to need it to support her fragile weight. She looked as if a good puff of wind would blow her away. He could see the fine bones in her hands and arms.

"He was with us for a day and a half before he succumbed to the injuries," she was saying of his father. Jim had heard about it through Myles right after it had happened. The ancient robo-harvester had malfunctioned, stalling out in the middle of a field. Trace Raynor had been attempting to make repairs when the machine had unexpectedly roared to life, crushing him beneath it.

"The doctors wanted to put him on all sorts of

painkillers, but he wouldn't let them. 'Just treat the injuries,' he said. 'Let me stay for as long as I can.'"

Jim winced and reached for the bony hand, holding it gently in his own. It was like holding fine china.

"So . . . he was in pain the whole time?"

"It was his choice, Jim," Karol said gently. "We all knew he wouldn't make it. He just . . . wanted to be present for the last few hours of his life."

Tears stung Jim's eyes, and he blinked them back.

She patted his hand. "There was nothing you could have done, even if you'd been here."

Except say good-bye, Jim thought bitterly, but he said instead, "The money could have helped."

She smiled slightly, the gesture lighting up her haggard face. "Now, how do you reckon that? Wouldn't have made the surgeons any more skilled; they did the best they could with what they had. Shiloh doesn't have a lot of the high-tech medical equipment that other planets do. Even if we'd taken your money, Jim, we couldn't have gotten your father to a proper facility in time for all that technology to be of use. It was just his time, son. Money wouldn't have done a thing."

"Might have bought a new robo-harvester."

She looked at him with deep compassion.

"I love you, Jim. But you know we couldn't take money that was earned through criminal activity."

"It's not from that."

Karol squeezed his hand, and her smile deepened. "Ah, now you're a criminal *and* a liar."

Jim couldn't help it: he laughed at that. She joined him. "Stubborn woman. Always too smart for your own good."

They chuckled together for a moment, enjoying the release of tension in the room, and then Karol's laugh turned into a violent coughing spell. She turned away quickly, hacking into a handkerchief, but not fast enough so Jim didn't catch the sight of blood on the white linen.

"Mom," he said quietly, "Myles said you were dyin'."

She wiped her mouth and leaned back. The fit had clearly exhausted her. "Myles is right," she said resignedly. "Which is why I am so glad to see you."

"What is it, Mom?" He reached again for her fragile hand.

"Some kind of cancer. Doctors don't rightly know. It's something new, and we don't have the testing equipment here to do research on it. There are several of us with the same symptoms, though."

"So . . . something caused this?"

She nodded weakly. "Looks like. They think it might have something to do with the material the old canned rations came in. We stopped using those once Farm Aid stepped in, but—"

"Rations?" Jim stared at her, aghast. "During the Guild Wars?" He had joined up with the sole intention of getting money to send back home. "Mom, you didn't use the money I sent you to buy food?"

She smiled at him again, but there was a trace of irony in it. "We used the money to pay down the debt, Jimmy. We didn't need food. The Confederacy was providing it."

"Damn it!" Jim sprang up from the couch, stalking about the small room like a caged tiger. He wanted to break something, but everything he saw had a newly found value to him, as a relic of his childhood and youth. As something his late father and his dying mother had touched, cleaned, cherished. His hands clenched with anger that had no outlet. "And no one's saying anything about this? That the Confederacy's decision to cut corners is killing people?"

She didn't answer and he knew why. Ever since Korhal IV, people were scared. No one would dare speak out now.

"You know," his mother said, breaking the

uncomfortable silence, "your father always believed you'd come back one day. When he was in that hospital room, broken and dying, he knew he wasn't going to live long enough to see that day, but he knew it would come."

Jim was standing with his back to her, one hand gripping the mantelpiece hard. He was glad he had come, but at the same time the emotions that were racing through him were ripping him to shreds, and he just wanted them to stop.

"Myles helped us out, and your father made a holovid so he could say good-bye properly."

Jim was surprised. His family couldn't afford to make a holovid. Myles had helped again, indeed. His eyes fell on a small urn a few centimeters from where he grasped the mantel, and he felt a fresh wave of pain as he abruptly realized what it contained. Or, more accurately, who.

He had to get this over with, had to get out of here, into the comfortable, familiar world of violence and near escapes and theft, of drinking and women and forgetting.

"Well," he said, surprised at how steady his voice was, "that was right nice of Myles. Can't say as I'm surprised, though. Where is this holovid Dad wanted me to see?"

"Right there, beside his ashes," his mother

said, confirming what he already knew. He looked over and, sure enough, there was a small, personal-sized holoprojector and a disk. It was an older model, clunky and unrefined, but it would get the job done.

"I keep it there so I can see him now and then," his mother said. "The recording was for you, not me, but . . . well, I'm sure you wouldn't mind if your old mother got a little comfort from seeing her husband sometimes."

The lump that suddenly filled Jim's throat rendered speech impossible. He turned his head and gave her a faint, strained smile. She nodded, reaching for her iced tea.

"Go on, play it, Jim. I've wanted to watch this with you for a long time now."

He turned back, inserted the disk, and pressed the button.

His father appeared. He was in a hospital bed, and the camera was jumpy: probably the ever-reliable Myles had filmed it himself. Jim could barely see his dad through all the things that were hooked up to him. He seemed almost lost in a jungle of tubes and hanging bags. He looked terrible, and his voice was faint.

"Hello, son," he said, managing a smile. "I sure wish I could be looking better for my only holovid recording, but these damn doctors say I need all these things. Won't for too much longer, at any rate. And that's why I'm making this for you, Jim. Because I know in my heart that, one day, you're going to come back to Shiloh. I'm just sorry I won't be around to tell you this in person when you do.

"I love you, Jim. You're my son, and I always will love you. I used to think I could also say, 'I'll always be proud of you.' But I can't honestly say that anymore."

Jim looked down, hot shame and grief filling him, but continued to listen.

"You're walking down a dark path, Jim. A path I never could have foreseen for you, and one I simply cannot respect. We love you, but we can't take your money. That's blood money, Son, and that's not how you were raised."

There was a rustling. Jim looked up again to see his father struggling to sit up and lean forward, peering earnestly into the recorder.

"Do you remember what I used to tell you, son? A man is what he chooses to be. It's not how he's born, or how he's raised, that makes the man. It's his choices. Right now, you're choosing to walk this dark path I can't condone. But a man can turn his life around with a single thought, a single decision. You can always choose to be something new. Never forget that."

He eased back down, the effort clearly having

exhausted what little strength he had. His face was pale and he was trembling, probably from pain. "I love you, son."

The recording ended.

For a long moment Jim simply stood, breathing hard, trying to process what he had just witnessed. He took a steadying breath and turned to face his mother.

She sat where he had left her. The iced tea had spilled in her lap, the empty glass lying on the upholstery beside her. Her face looked less drawn, and her eyes were closed. There was a slight smile on her lips.

"Mom," Jim said, tears filling his eyes. He went to her, gathered her in his arms, and sat with her for a long, long time.

Myles knew what had happened the moment Jim opened the door. The older man's face fell, and he seemed to be fighting back tears himself.

"Your mother's gone," he said quietly. Jim nodded. "I'll take care of everything; don't you worry. It's a blessing she hung on long enough to see you, and that's a fact, though it might have been sheer stubbornness. She always knew you'd come home. And with the pain she was in, and what she had to look forward to as this Confederate-cursed disease advanced . . . well, it's a blessing she's with your father now too."

He squeezed Jim's arm. Jim stared at him with haunted eyes.

"A blessing," he said in a hollow voice. "Maybe you're right."

The thought was a bitter one.

"You'd best be off. Leave the clothes in the truck; I'll get them after dark. Right now I'm going to attend to your mother. And, Jimmy . . . don't forget what I said about Mar Sara. You'd be right welcome there."

Nearly an hour later, Jim Raynor sat in the copilot's seat of a system runner. He stared as the ship lifted off, soaring upward. The brown earth dropped away, becoming not fields as far as the eye could see but merely patchworks the size of a hand. He had worked those patches, had walked those now-tiny streets. Had napped beneath trees that, from this height, looked only as large as thumbnails. He closed his eyes for a second, then focused on the vessel's control panel as he and Tychus flew up past the clouds, into the atmosphere, and then among the stars.

"You're mighty quiet, Jimmy," Tychus said.

Jim didn't answer. His thoughts were elsewhere: in his mind he was sitting in the living room with his mother, watching the holovid of his dead father. . . . And wondering why the thought of a night with Evangelina—complete with all the booze he could drink—didn't sound as appealing as it once had.

TARSONIS

The room was filled with the noises that never ceased: the whooshing of Vanderspool's forced breathing, the whir of machinery, the click-click of the elaborate machines that made billions of calculations a minute. Other than that, it was silent.

The door opened. One of Vanderspool's resocs entered and approached the giant metal coffin.

"They'll be dead in two days."

CHAPTER FOURTEEN

SKYWAY STARPORT, HALCYON

They met, far too early for either man's taste, at the Skyway Starport at 0600. Jim had tried to grab some shut-eye at the hotel, making full use of the credits O'Banon had given them for lodging, but Tychus looked as if he'd simply stayed up all night. Jim was so tired he felt almost drunk, and Tychus looked the same. It was not the optimal way to begin an extremely important assignment.

They headed off in groggy silence in the attractive, sleek little system runner that was waiting for them. Once they had cleared the atmosphere of Halcyon, Jim reached under the seat for the packet he had been told would be there. He broke the seal, stifling a yawn as he did so.

Tychus raised an eyebrow. "Mighty cloak-and-dagger fancy," he said.

"Yeah," Jim said. In the packet were a small, old-fashioned key, falsified IDs, a notification that they had outfits awaiting them in the back, and a data chip, which he inserted into the ship's drive.

Jim read through it quickly. His eyes widened; he looked at the key and then summarized for the benefit of Tychus, who was entering their route.

"Our heist . . . well, half of it, anyway . . . is a person. Who is apparently eagerly anticipating us."

"What?"

"There is someone named Andrew Forrest. He's . . . a pharmacologist."

Tychus snorted. "'Hello, Dr. Forrest, I need something for this *pain in the ass* I'm experiencing.' Why the hell are we picking up a pharmacologist? I thought Scutter wanted us to steal something useful. Like credits."

Jim started to shake his head, then he figured it out. "Drugs. O'Banon is also a drug runner."

"Then steal the drugs, don't steal the . . ." And then Tychus figured it out too. "*Do* steal the guy who created the drug! Scutter, I take it back: you are one smart bastard."

Jim nodded. "I'll bet you anything this Dr. Forrest is one of a handful of people who know how to replicate the formula for something that's currently very popular and very lucrative. He may even have been the one who initiated the contact with Scutter."

Neither, for all their myriad other vices, was heavily into the illegal stuff. While they'd had the chance to snort, swallow, or smear on an impressive variety of pharmaceuticals at various times over the years, alcohol was still their drug of choice. It was cheap and easily obtainable in vast quantities, which was how both of them liked it.

Tychus had once said that he didn't want to be beholden to anyone or anything—up to and including women and addictive drugs. Jim just never saw the appeal.

Too, the recent encounters with sicko Daun had started to stir up memories they'd tried their best to forget. It had been a long time since either of them had thought about Lisa Cassidy, once known as "Doc." Doc had been hooked on a substance called crab. The despised Vanderspool had played on her addiction in order to get her to betray not just Tychus, whom she had hooked up with, but also the rest of Heaven's Devils. It had worked, too: eventually she had become a willing informant, with the lure of the drug to keep her going. In the end, Doc had died of a battle wound in front of Tychus, assuring him that her deception "wasn't personal." Both Tychus and Jim had known it wasn't: there was nothing personal about what a highly addictive drug could do to you, nor the torment another human being could put you through when you desperately needed the stuff.

"What do you think it is?" Jim wondered aloud. With Doc in his mind, he couldn't help but wonder if it was crab. Almost at once, though, he dismissed the thought. Crab was once hard to come by, but these days it was becoming more and more common. No, whatever O'Banon was after, it had to be something out of the ordinary. Something rare, expensive, upscale—and probably more addictive than anything Jim had ever run across. That would be the only thing that would make it worth O'Banon's while.

"Don't know, don't care, just want my payment. Get in, get the guy, get done in time to get drunk and poke a pretty girl."

The words and images they conjured up were rough and tumble, crude, physical. Just what Jim needed so he could stop thinking about Doc— and, even closer to his heart, about Shiloh, and his mother, and that damned holovid.

"I like this plan," Jim said.

Halcyon was a fringe world that, right from its colonization, had opened its arms to corporate development, and probably half the big companies on Tarsonis and other worlds had branches here. It was a pleasant world: not quite nice enough to be a vacation destination but the sort of place where hardworking businessmen could be provided with fine facilities, earn excellent pay, and have decent places to raise the kids. The research and development branch of Besske-Vrain & Stalz Pharmaceutical Corporation looked like any other building on a fairly well-established fringe world. It was large and comfortably sprawling, with neatly manicured lawns and benches and fountains scattered here and there. The whole was encased in state-of-the-art security designed to be as unobtrusive as it was efficient. If you didn't know where to look and what to look for, you would miss the cameras, the heat sensors, the motion detectors, and the approximately sixteen other devices being employed. Jim and Tychus would have needed a security systems expert if they had had to break in.

Fortunately, they did not have to do it the hard way. They had badges proclaiming their identities. Jim was now a high-ranking faculty member of the Tarsonis University, City of Tarsonis campus. Tychus was the point man for an organization called Physicians for Results Now. According to the literature, the organization wanted to cut through the red tape to get "results now" for patients who were in the latter stages of diseases. In other words, they advocated legalizing and distributing medications that perhaps hadn't been tested enough to be proven safe.

"Yeah, I can see you pushing for results right now, damn it." Jim laughed.

"Can't see *you* as a doctor, though," Tychus shot back.

Their clearance level was extremely high. It would permit them access to the laboratory, private offices, and, as a special bonus, the executive bathroom.

They were greeted in the cavernous lobby by a meticulously well-groomed, bright-eyed young man who introduced himself as Jason Richfield. He seemed a touch suspicious of Tychus—probably because of the man's size and roughed-up appearance, even with a shower and haircut—but after checking out their clearance levels, he ushered them in graciously.

"I'll let Dr. Forrest know you're here," he said. Jim and Tychus waited patiently while listening to generic, non-threatening music piped in from somewhere, their large frames nearly swallowed by comfortable upholstery, until said Dr. Forrest appeared.

"Gentlemen, welcome to the research and development branch of Besske-Vrain & Stalz,"

Forrest said, smiling and extending a hand. He was in his later middle years, tanned, healthy-looking, and graying in a most distinguished manner. He had a firm handshake, soft, well-manicured hands, a crisp white coat, and a fine chin. Jim disliked him immediately. He couldn't put his finger on it. Maybe the handshake was too practiced, the voice too well modulated.

Or maybe it was because Forrest was going to come work for a man who'd pay him millions to get people hooked on something that would in all probability turn them into desperate slaves.

Jim knew it was not his place to pass judgment. But somehow everything had felt cleaner when he was robbing trains and stealing Confederate credits.

"Let me give you a tour of the lab area first, then we can break for lunch and attend the meeting at 1400," he said. "You'll like our cafeteria: our chef used to work for one of the top restaurants on Tarsonis. The food's both delicious and nutritious—not a mean feat!"

Jim and Tychus smiled and nodded, following him down the marble-floored corridor as they went to the elevators. The two took their cue from the scientist and chatted about inanities while they were in the elevator. So calm and unruffled was Forrest that Jim was starting to wonder if there had been some kind of mix-up and they were with the wrong guy.

The chitchat continued until they approached the lab. Two out-of-shape, bored-looking security guards stood on either side of a massive metal door. Forrest gave them a pleasant smile and swiped his ID. Jim and Tychus did likewise, and then the guards gave the IDs a cursory inspection. All went smoothly.

"Welcome to the research and development branch of Besske-Vrain & Stalz," one of the guards said mechanically as he keyed in a code. "Please follow all safety instructions given to you by the medical personnel inside the laboratory and enjoy your visit." Something clicked and whirred, and the door slowly slid open.

The lab was enormous. There were long tables and individual workstations. State-of-the-art equipment sat next to mundane single-flame gas burners upon which glass beakers bubbled. Scientists, clad in white coats and wearing gloves and face masks, moved about with deliberate speed, doing something that was repetitive but clearly required concentration. The air was cool and moist, obviously strictly temperature regulated, and there was the faint hum of hardworking machinery.

"Please put these on, gentlemen," Forrest said,

handing them each a face mask. Tychus and Jim obliged. "Now . . . this is where all the fun is." Forrest laughed. "I know that it certainly doesn't look like much fun to nonscientists. It looks a bit arcane and perplexing."

"Looks kinda boring more than anything, actually," Tychus drawled from behind his mask. Jim glanced at him, trying to shoot him a warning. That was hardly the sort of thing a representative of a physicians' organization that focused on medications would say. Tychus was not really cut out for this sort of thing, and Jim worried that his attitude might give them away before they'd gotten what they'd come for.

Forrest laughed easily. Listening to him made Jim dislike him even more.

"That too!" the doctor agreed. "But it's very exciting, actually, even if the steps become a little bit rote. We're searching for cures for all kinds of diseases here, as I'm certain you know."

Like the cancer caused by Confederate rations? Jim thought. He had to actually physically clench his teeth to not say it.

"Doctors such as yourselves will be able to administer medications that will stop the progression of deadly diseases right in its tracks. You'll be able to test for them before they've even begun to manifest, then begin preventative, lifelong treatment of your patients. These people you're looking at are not merely scientists: they're savers of lives. Heroes. They put in long hours simply because they want to do the right thing: help others."

The speech was practiced, easy, and the scientists pouring things into beakers and jotting down notes gave halfhearted waves to the onlookers. Jim wanted to spit. These people weren't here for altruistic purposes, not with the sort of pay they made. They were here for profit. Oh, the cures for diseases just might actually be discovered here, but not because the doctors were bleeding hearts who wanted to Do Good. It was because curing diseases—or, rather, developing medicines that people would need to take, preferably long-term—was highly profitable.

So was hooking people on drugs.

Jim and Tychus nodded politely. Forrest led them around to various stations, chatting away about what each chemical was, and what it did, and so on. The chrono moved to 1300, over halfway through Halcyon's twenty-five-hour day, and while no loud siren blared, the reaction of the scientists was as uniform as if one had. They put down data logs, removed masks, traded lab coats for regular ones, and left for lunch. The last to leave—a woman who appeared to be in her thirties, with black hair and blue eyes—paused and looked uncertainly at Forrest.

"Run along, Madeleine," Forrest said. "I'll finish up here and take them out for lunch in a little bit. There are just a few more things I'd like to show our guests."

Madeleine glanced over at Jim and Tychus. Tychus leered and Jim rolled his eyes. She turned back to Forrest and nodded.

"Of course, honey." She removed her mask, tugged his down and kissed him, smiled at Jim and Tychus, and left.

"My wife," Forrest explained. Jim stared at him as he and Tychus removed their own masks.

"She wasn't part of the deal," Tychus said. "We ain't taking two people."

"Of course you're not," Forrest said smoothly. He smiled. "I'm sure Mr. O'Banon can provide me with someone to assuage my grief at being forced to leave my darling bride. Now, we've got about fifteen minutes before I'm technically in violation of the rules. We've probably got about five more minutes after that; as I'm certain you've observed, enforcement is rather lax here. Watch the door."

Jim was taken aback at the man's callousness, but supposed that he should have expected it. After all, Forrest had cheerfully sold out to a notorious crime lord and intended to use his knowledge to help produce addictive drugs.

And I've sold out to a notorious crime lord to get

a bounty hunter off my back, and now I'm helping this scum to become a billionaire, he thought. *Who's worse?*

"I don't need no girl-handed doctor telling me my job," Tychus said. He seemed as irritated with Forrest as Jim was, but Jim wondered if it was for the same reasons.

Tychus went to the door to stand watch while Jim kept an eye on Forrest. The doctor quickly downloaded information from various sites, and then moved around the room, pocketing small items. At one point his sleeve fell back, and Jim saw what the small key that had been in their assignment packet was for. Fastened around the middle part of Forrest's lower arm was a small box.

"The formula?"

"And an extremely pure sample of Utopia," he said. "Hottest designer drug on the market. Everyone's scrambling to replicate it, and so far they haven't."

Utopia. No wonder this guy was such a hot item. Addiction was usually swift and hard to break. Something about how the drug altered the brain. Utopia apparently gave one of the highest highs ever, with a mild crash and few side effects—initially, at least. After a few hits, the highs didn't come as high. It took more and more of the drug to produce the same effect. In some cases, severe adverse reactions had occurred, with test subjects going into fatal convulsions. Jim didn't know much more and didn't want to.

"So you're the guy who made this?"

"Indeed." Forrest shot him a grin. "Started out as an attempt to make a really good painkiller."

"Sounds like you succeeded," Jim said. He was pretty sure he had managed to keep the contempt out of his voice.

"Ten minutes," Tychus growled.

"Almost done." A few more items went into sealed compartments in Forrest's pockets.

"Now, I can't help but wonder," Tychus drawled, "why we need you if we got the formula and a sample."

Forrest's silver head whipped up, and his blue eyes were like chips of ice. "Because the formula is missing something. Something that's here." He tapped his temple.

"My boss paid for you and the formula," Tychus said, turning away from the door. He had his gun out now, and lifted it slowly. "You ain't trying to cheat him, are you?"

"No," Forrest said dryly. "I'm trying to make sure I survive being smuggled off this planet by hired thugs like you."

Tychus clapped a hand to his chest. "Aw, now, Dr. Forrest, you done gone and hurt ol' Tychus Findlay's feelings."

A small, elegant pistol appeared from nowhere in Forrest's hand. "I'll hurt something else if you don't lower that weapon immediately."

"Oh, for Pete's sake," Jim said. "Let's all just get out of here, all right?"

It was then that the lights went out.

"What the hell?" Forrest's voice was high with alarm. "Tell me this is part of the plan."

"No, it ain't," said Jim. The lights had gone out, but there were still a few gas-lit burners going. He wondered why the doctors had left them on; probably they assumed that Forrest, as the last one to leave, would turn them off. The light was not enough to see much, but it was something. "Stay calm, Dr. Forrest. Do you have what you need?"

"Close enough." The voice was shaking. Jim smirked in the darkness. Jerk was probably pissing his pants.

"Shouldn't there be some emergency lights?" Jim asked. "I mean, this is a pretty significant and state-of-the-art research lab. Isn't there backup in case of a power outage?"

"I—I don't know," stammered Forrest. "There's never *been* a power outage. I think there should be, yes."

"I don't like this one damn bit," said Tychus. "Let's get out of here pronto."

Forrest suddenly pushed past Tychus, trying and failing to open the door.

"Damn it," muttered Forrest. He started banging on the door. "Hello? Guards! Help! The door won't open!"

Unease was prickling at the back of Jim's neck. Something wasn't right.

And then he knew. "Tychus, get away from the—"

Tychus had apparently been thinking along the same lines, because the second Jim called his name, he turned and flung himself as far away from the door as possible.

The door exploded with a deafening sound. Dr. Forrest, who had been pounding on it, begging to be let out, didn't stand a chance. His dismembered body and large chunks of hot, jagged metal flew into the room. Tychus and Jim dove for cover from the shattered glass as Forrest's head and a piece of the door landed on one of the large tables. They got to their feet and trained their weapons on the doorway.

The shape of a man loomed there, blocking the exit. They fired repeatedly, seeming to fill the figure with bullets, but it still stood. A laugh filled the room, and as the smoke cleared, the two men recognized the tall figure.

Ezekiel Daun.

CHAPTER FIFTEEN

Jim felt as if his muscles had turned to liquid as terror surged through him. At least two dozen bullets had gone right through the—

"Goddamned hologram!" Tychus bellowed. "Come on, Jimmy; let's not let this rat bastard have playtime with us again."

A hollow laugh filled the room, seeming to come from everywhere. "Well done, Mr. Findlay. Sharp eyes, squinty though they are."

"Jimmy!" Tychus's voice was sharp and brittle as glass. Jim knew his friend well enough to know that Findlay, too, was struggling against panic. "Get the stuff off of Forrest. *Now!*"

Having something specific to do helped Jim focus. He sprang into action, stymied only momentarily when he realized that Forrest was actually in several pieces, then spotted his torso lodged underneath a table. The small metal box was still attached to the right arm.

"Don't go to pieces like your friend did," came Daun's mocking voice, "even though you are trapped like rats. Rather appropriate, as you're about to die in a lab."

"Ain't about to die anywhere—not yet," snarled Tychus. Jim was fumbling with the key, and when he dropped it and it clattered away into the darkness, he gave up and drew out a knife he always kept in his boot. Grunting, he began to hack at the limb.

"You know . . . Feek said the same thing," mused Daun. "It was one of the last things he ever said. I found his voice irritating, so I cut out his tongue. He was still able to scream for some time after that. Do you want to know what it sounded like?"

Jim felt fresh sweat break out under his arms as he continued cutting through the dead arm. It was a grotesque endeavor, the brutality alleviated only by the fact that Forrest had been a despicable example of a human being. Jim was down to the bones now, trying to sever the hand from the wrist. His hands were warm and sticky, and the smell was turning his stomach. If Daun started playing the sounds of Feek's screaming,

Jim wasn't sure if he could keep it together.

Another smell was assaulting his nostrils. Something was burning. He poked his head cautiously out from under the table and looked up to see that one of Forrest's legs had fallen next to one of the gas burners: low flames were rippling along what remained of the fabric of his pants. And of course Daun had deactivated everything—including any automated fire prevention.

"Shit," he muttered, ducking back under the table. He hadn't gotten the box off Forrest's arm yet, but with all the chemicals in here, he had to stop the fire. He tore off his suit jacket, backed out slowly from under the table, and began trying to slap out the flames.

"It was amusing to discover you had gone crawling to Scutter O'Banon. One might say, 'Out of the frying pan into the fire.' I offer release; he offers slavery."

Jim ignored him. Tychus was silent as well, which told Jim he was utterly focused on finding Daun and taking him out. Jim was completely fine with that. He continued slapping out the fire, reaching to turn off the burner. As his fingers closed on the knob, he jostled it slightly, and something in the beaker atop the burner splashed out and landed on his jacket sleeve, burning a neat little hole in it, but it didn't seem to eat its way through to his arm.

He stared, and then his fear started to abate. The fire that had been consuming Forrest's pants leg now extinguished, Jim dropped to the floor and crawled underneath the table again. Calm now, he gave the wrist of the late Forrest one final chop, tugged the hand off, and slipped the small lockbox off the doctor's arm and into his pocket. Then he got a firm grip on the torso.

Suddenly, Jim began to sob loudly. "I can't take this anymore!" he cried. "I can't take living in fear!"

"Jimmy, what the hell you saying, you idiot?"

"I can't take it no more, Tychus! He's right: Scutter can't protect us. Nobody can. We're dead men, just as dead as Forrest!" He hoped that Tychus would pick up on what he was planning; he couldn't be any more obvious than he already was. Daun was as intelligent as he was terrifying.

"Why, Mr. Raynor, I'm surprised to hear you fibbing. Though it was quite a good performance. You might have missed your calling."

Shit. Daun was an empath. No actor in the world could have tricked him.

"Defiant to the end," Daun continued. "All the more fun for me, after the merry chase you've led me on."

Swearing, Raynor half-stood, swiftly raising Forrest's torso above him with one hand. Gunfire came from a corner of the room near the window, and despite what Daun had said about toying with Jim, bullets spattered Forrest's body. At the same moment, Jim reached out for the beaker on the burner, hissing as his hand closed on the hot glass, then threw it in the direction of the gunfire.

Daun screamed in agony. He stumbled forward, Jim and Tychus forgotten, clawing at his eyes. Jim realized with a jolt of cruel pleasure that the acid had struck the bastard full in the face. Jim heard gunfire behind him as Tychus took a few shots at their enemy, but Raynor was already heading for the window. The room wasn't that high up, if he recalled correctly, and it was safer than being in the lab with Daun and a whole mess of chemicals that might—

He and Tychus crashed through the window a scant three seconds before the laboratory in the research and development branch of Besske-Vrain & Stalz Pharmaceutical Corporation exploded in balls of black and orange hellfire. The heat was at their backs, and Jim and Tychus instinctively waved their arms and legs as if trying to swim away from it.

The fall seemed to take forever, but as they crashed into springy green bushes that some landscape designer had blessedly decided to plant along a walkway, they realized that (1) the fall was only about three stories and (2) they were alive.

Hurting, but alive. Jim was pretty sure something was broken in his already burned hand, and he felt as if he'd been shaken like a rat in the jaws of a lyote, but they were alive.

"Don't nap, Jimmy! Get your ass outta that bush!" Tychus growled. He pressed a hand to his ribs but seemed to be moving briskly enough. His face was scratched, and Jim tasted blood from his own split lip.

Jim clambered out of the lifesaving topiary. Sirens were already wailing, mixing with the sounds of people screaming. Tychus pointed at the crowd of people fleeing the building. Guards tried to instill some sense of calm, but it was useless: the terrified doctors, technicians, and office drones were not having any of it. "That's our cover," he said. "Let's go!"

Before Jim could object, Tychus was hightailing it toward the stream of terrified people, waving his hands in the air and screaming like a little girl. Jim shrugged mentally and joined the flow, shrieking and flailing, too, and the two let the crowd carry them out. The chaos was indeed perfect cover, and less than three minutes later Jim and Tychus had followed the stream of Besske-Vrain & Stalz employees all the way to the parking lot.

Many of the groundcars were beautiful, befitting their task of ferrying obscenely wealthy business executives. Others were a bit simpler. In the confusion, Tychus approached one of the executives just as he was about to get in his vehicle, knocked him unconscious with a well-landed punch, and hopped inside while Jim tumbled in the passenger side.

Jim's face split into a grin, despite the terrible pain of the gesture and the agony in his hand, as the long, sleek silver groundcar roared to life, and a few minutes later the panicky throngs, wailing ambulances, and plumes of smoke were fading in the rearview mirror.

"Tychus?" Jim said after they had made certain that they had indeed escaped undetected. "I . . . don't know if I can keep doing this."

"Doing what?" Tychus asked. He pressed a hand to his side briefly, then reached in the breast pocket of his suit coat and removed a smashed cigar. He sighed sadly at the waste.

"This. That bastard is a damned shadow. We can't shake him. The only reason we've been able to dodge him twice now is because we've been lucky. That's it. Not because we're smarter, or better, or sharper shooters—but because of blind, stupid, fickle *luck*. We got out last time using some poor bastard's body as a shield, and this time only because of a damned Bunsen burner and the beaker on top of it."

Tychus grunted. "Well, I won't argue that

we've been lucky. But I don't think Daun could have survived that." His lips curved around the cigar in a smile. "Was awful nice to hear him screaming. Nice touch, Jimmy."

Jim shook his head and cradled his injured hand. "I don't think he was killed. I don't know that he *can* be killed."

"Now, that's just scared speaking."

"He might have survived. I don't know how, but he might have. And if he has, he is going to come back after us with a vengeance. How the hell did he know to show up there, anyway? So much for O'Banon protecting us," Jim said in disgust.

"I said, I think Daun's crunchy on the outside."

"Tychus, we almost got killed! By all rights we should have been! Scutter was supposed to protect us!"

"Look. If somehow Daun did survive this, O'Banon will make a deal for us, Jimmy, and then that psycho will go away."

"A deal that will make us slaves to him. Tychus, there's nothing about this that doesn't stink to high heaven. Not a damned thing."

"*You* stink pretty bad," was Tychus's only comment.

* * *

"Gentlemen," said the image of Scutter O'Banon from a computer screen, "I have to say, you are failing, quite drastically, to live up to your reputations. You have been given exactly one mission, and it was a complete disaster." The voice was clipped, cool with barely concealed anger. O'Banon himself was off on business and not physically present, which was probably a good thing. A stone-faced Cadaver had collected the lockbox when Jim and Tychus had arrived at the mansion, and had left them alone in the receiving room with the computer.

Tychus blew out a breath. "Now, sir, I will remind you that we came under attack by a very zealous bounty hunter. We adjusted our percentage with you in order to be protected from this same asshole. And despite this, we survived and came home with the formula for and a sample of Utopia. Frankly, sir, Dr. Forrest was a dick, and I say we brought you the better end of the deal."

"Your job was to bring back both the lockbox and all it contained *and* Dr. Forrest. It seems the late doctor failed to include a very important part of the formula. It's going to take weeks to determine the missing element."

Tychus feigned shock. "Really? Why, that treacherous bastard! But that ain't our fault that he did that. You know, upon reflecting on the entire incident, I'd say that it was hardly a complete disaster. Looks like neither of us held up our ends of the bargain."

"I don't care if you were under fire from the entire Confederacy. You have failed."

Jim gritted his teeth, almost literally biting back words.

"I bet you we'd be a hell of a lot more efficient if we didn't have to worry about Daun nipping at our heels all the time. That was our deal, Scutter: we come work for you, you keep us safe while we're doing it."

"I don't know that you're worth trying to keep safe if you can't even manage a heist a toddler could handle."

Jim had had enough. "I'm outta here," he said, turning for the door.

Tychus muted the mic. "Jim, wait a—"

"Hell with waiting. I need a drink." He stalked off as Tychus resumed trying to placate the shark.

Tychus found Jim about an hour later. He was in a darkened corner of the bar in one of the comparatively quieter establishments. He'd ordered an entire bottle of Scotty Bolger's Old No. 8 and was well into it by the time Tychus's large shape loomed up in front of him.

"This place is utterly dead. What the hell you wanna come *here* and party for?" Tychus reached out a dinner plate–sized hand, grasped the bottle, and took a swig.

"I ain't come here to party," Jim said.

"I don't know what's going on with you, Jimmy, but you ain't been a lot of fun recently. And as nothing *else* has been a lot of fun, either, that kinda pisses me off."

Jim poured himself another shot and downed it. "You wanted to know what business I had on Shiloh?"

"Yep."

"My mother died."

There was silence. "Well, Jimmy, I am right sorry to hear that," Tychus said quietly, and Jim knew he was being sincere.

Slightly mollified, Jim nodded and asked, "What happened to your parents?"

"Don't know, don't care. Ran away from home at age twelve and ain't never looked back."

"You'd care if you heard they was dead."

"I don't know about that," Tychus said, again with total honesty. "But it's obvious you do. And like I said . . . I'm sorry."

Jim smiled a little. "Thanks. I just want to sit here for a bit and drink and think."

"Usually the former don't help with the latter, but sometimes it does. You do whatever you gotta, Jimmy. Me, I gotta get trashed and make little Tychus happy."

Jim laughed aloud at that. "You go take care of that."

"I'll come find you tomorrow."

"Bet I'll still be right here . . . except facedown and with a few more bottles around me."

"You should get that hand looked at," Tychus said.

"Yeah . . . I don't feel like asking Scutter for anything right now."

"There are places around here that'll fix you up, no questions asked, for enough credits."

Jim shrugged. "Scotty Bolger seems to be a pretty good doctor too. Ain't feeling much pain right this moment."

Tychus grinned, clapped his old friend on the back, and left.

Jim poured himself another shot but did not drink it immediately. Instead, he lifted the small, clear glass and idly looked at the amber liquid within. He remembered the first time that he had been introduced to the stuff. Tall, gangly Hank Harnack, a former enemy who had become a cherished if unpredictable brother in arms and fellow Heaven's Devil, had ordered Scotty Bolger's Old No. 8 for himself, Raynor, and Kydd, calling it "the good stuff." It had, of course, tasted like crap, but Harnack had assured Jim he'd get used to it. A fistfight had broken out, of course, and the three of them had escaped on a "borrowed" vulture hovercycle. Jim smiled at the recollection of the happy chaos of that evening.

So much had gone away in the last few years. Jim's unfamiliarity with drinking. The camaraderie of the unit. His parents, both of them. Ryk Kydd and Vanderspool both—the good and the bad. Hell, Jim thought with a self-deprecating smile, he could count his own naïveté among the casualties.

It had been unsettling, revisiting Shiloh. Even if his mother had been well, the trip would have been uncomfortable. Everything had changed, and nothing had changed. There was new building in progress, new hardships, but the land and the sunsets and the struggle were the same as what he had faced as a child growing up there. Except then he had had a family, a place. He had turned from that path, and he wasn't sure where he was anymore.

Jim had first turned from it when he had opted to go off world, dazzled by a recruiter offering a "generous" enlistment bonus, to become a Confederate marine and fight in the Guild Wars. That path had led him to witness acts both heroic and despicable, to trust and to have trust betrayed.

His eyes narrowed and he gulped the liquid, relishing the fire as it burned its way down to his gut.

Vanderspool.

Jim wasn't a man who hated easily; that kind of emotion had to be earned. But by God, Colonel Javier Vanderspool had earned it in spades.

He'd earned it because he was utterly corrupted—rotten to the core. Because he had been prepared to sacrifice the lives of—well, everyone under his command for money. Because he had installed kill switches in suits that were designed to save the lives of soldiers in battle. And because, in the end, he had given Jim Raynor a choice that was no real choice at all. Raynor had gone AWOL rather than face resocialization. That decision had forced him to turn his back on his parents, and both of them were now dead.

Fortunately, Vanderspool had met a fitting end. Jim Raynor himself had fired the gauss rifle spike into the man's chest.

When you broke it all down and analyzed it, he supposed it all made sense, each step of the journey. But when you just looked at now versus then . . .

Raynor poured himself another shot.

He was glad, fiercely glad, that he had had a few moments with his mother before her death. He wished he had had the same with his father. In a way he had, through the holovid. His mind went back to what his dad had said.

I love you, Jim. You're my son, and I always will love you. I used to think I could also say, "I'll always be proud of you." But I can't honestly say that anymore.

Jim grimaced and knocked back the shot.

We love you, but we can't take your money. That's blood money, Son, and that's not how you were raised. . . . Do you remember what I used to tell you, son? A man is what he chooses to be. . . . You can always choose to be something new. Never forget that.

Words. Nice-sounding ones. "Some things are easier to say than to do, Dad," Jim said softly.

Where he was right now was good. He knew it. Sure, there was Daun, but there was also Scutter, who would kick Daun's ass at some point; Tychus seemed certain of it. The money was good. They could buy the best booze, women, and parties with it. He hopped from high to high.

But in return for Scutter's help in defeating Daun—and whoever the hell had sent the bastard after them—O'Banon would own them. Their legacy would be not portraits hung in museums or colonial courtrooms, or names carved on memorials for the honored dead, but having their pictures on wanted posters. The money would run out; the women would betray them; the booze would make them sick. From high to high.

Jim didn't want to think anymore. He'd heard that answers were sometimes found at the bottom of a glass. He intended to find out.

CHAPTER SIXTEEN

DEADMAN'S PORT, DEADMAN'S ROCK

Tychus blinked awake to find Raynor staring down at him. "I'm getting mighty tired of people wakin' me up," he grumbled. The girls on either side of him muttered.

"I know. Me too. Come on. Let's get some food."

Ten minutes later, they were in a seedy diner chowing down on flapjacks, crispy fried skalet strips, eggs, toast, jam, and black coffee strong enough to stand a spoon up in. Jim was surprised to see so many people up at such an early hour; the place was bustling. He supposed that in a port like this, there was no "better" or "worse" time for activity, criminal or otherwise.

"Got your hand fixed, I see."

"Yeah. Booze wore off and it hurt like hell, so around three I found someone to do the job."

"Surprised you didn't end up with another tattoo." They grinned at the memory. Ages ago, it seemed now, the entirety of Heaven's Devils had trundled, absolutely blotto, into a tattoo parlor and gotten their emblem placed on various parts of their bodies. Jim remembered very, very little of it, so "memory" was perhaps not the most accurate term. Still, it made him smile.

"So, Jimmy, I know you. Spill. You didn't get me out of a sandwich just to go eat flapjacks."

Jim chewed the surprisingly delicious flapjacks under discussion, washed the bite down with a swig of thick coffee, and nodded.

"You're right. And because you know me, you may not like what I'm gonna say, but I bet you'll understand it."

Tychus scowled. "I better get more coffee in me if you're gonna start talking like that. Maybe with a shot of something."

Jim put down his fork. "Tychus . . . I been doing a lot of thinking. And I've made a choice."

Tychus looked at him expectantly, chewing.

"I want out."

"Aw, hell, Jimmy," Tychus groaned. But as Jim suspected, Tychus didn't look surprised. He forked another mouthful of eggs into his mouth and looked around with studied casualness. More quietly he said, "That ain't something you should be advertising in Deadman's Port. Be careful about that kinda talk, you hear me?"

"I hear you," Jim said. "That's why we're here. We're not as well known here as we are at the bars and gambling dens and whorehouses. Places I find I'm getting right sick of being in."

Tychus stared at his half-eaten breakfast, then pushed his plate away. "You don't just 'get out.'"

"*I* do. And you can too. Tychus, you're a bull, and it makes me sick to see anyone riding you."

"Anyone who's not a pretty female, anyway." Tychus leered.

Jim didn't bat an eye. "Scutter—"

Tychus made a keep-it-down motion with his hand. Jim continued more quietly but with equal vehemence. "Scutter O'Banon has got a ring through our noses, and yet he ain't done a damn thing for us. I know that's gotta sit bad with you."

Tychus nodded slowly. "We still can't just up and leave."

"Damn it, Tychus—"

"Shut up and listen to me, boy." Tychus's voice was serious. "We don't jump without a parachute. We don't ditch O'Banon without some way of taking care of ourselves. We can't say, 'Why, thank you, kind sir, but we'd like to go work for someone else.' If we're getting out, we need to get out and be able to *stay* out. Drop out completely, for good. Do you understand what I'm saying?"

Jim did. Tychus, as usual, was one step ahead of him. Jim knew that plenty of people underestimated Tychus Findlay. They saw how powerfully, almost impossibly built he was, and didn't think past the muscle. Big as he was, Tychus was extremely fit. He was also extremely intelligent. Jim knew he himself wasn't a slouch in the fitness or mental acumen department, but Tychus thought about things in a different way than he did. They complemented each other well.

"Sounds like you might already know of something," he said, taking another bite of flapjack.

"I listen," said Tychus bluntly. "Even when I'm doing other things. And people talk, even when *they're* doing other things. Scutter's boys are no exception. Now, Cadaver and that butler know how to keep their mouths shut, but some of the others . . . well, let's just say Scutter's got a big, big score coming up. One that could keep us set for a long time. A *long* time."

Jim was intrigued. "You know who we're robbing? Where the money's coming from?"

Tychus shook his head. "Nope. And it don't matter none, anyway, because by the end of it all, that money's going to be ours and no one else's." He grinned wickedly.

* * *

The man in the duster landed his small vessel at Deadman's Port. He emerged from the ship and looked about, fixing his one-eyed gaze on the "authorities" there. The other eye was covered by a patch. There was something in that single cold eye surrounded by scars that made the men avert their own. They took his credits, wished him good day, and were happy to see the back of him.

He strode through the channels between hulking vessels with the confidence of one who knew he would not be bothered, and he was not. Not by adults, anyway. One member of a gang of urchins made the mistake of reaching out a small hand to clutch the duster. The child found herself staring wide-eyed at a pistol an inch from her face.

Daun smiled at her fear. "You know who I am?"

Tears welled in the brown eyes, slipped down the tanned face. "N-no sir."

"I'm the bogeyman," Daun continued. He clicked off the safety, slowly, knowing it would be heard clearly in the frightened silence that had fallen on the cluster of children. He lowered his face to the little girl's, then lifted the eye patch. The girl shrieked. Beneath the black fabric was a patchwork of scar tissue. A glowing red orb sat in the black, acid-scarred socket. The orb seemed to dilate and constrict, making a slight whirring noise as it did so.

"I'm going to come at night, and crawl into your head, and haunt your dreams as I stare at you with my red, red eye. And then tomorrow I'll be following you. *Watching* you. Do you know what I want to see with my red, red eye?"

She was fighting back sobs now, her whole body trembling. Her terror was intoxicating. It was a pity his line of work didn't bring him into contact with children more often. Their fear was so . . . *pure*.

"No, sir," she whispered. "What do you want to see?"

"I want to see you looking over your shoulder, wondering where I am. Will you do that for me?"

She nodded, screwing her eyes shut. Mucus ran from her nose.

"Good. Maybe I won't come back in your head after that. Or maybe I will. Run along now."

She and her little group fled, scattering like roaches when someone turns on the light. Daun grinned and replaced the eye patch, straightening.

He always had liked Deadman's Port.

He had a lead on whom he was looking for, and where he might be found. There was a small opening off to the side that denoted either a very secretive establishment or a very seedy one. His intel told him that this would be a good starting place to look, and if his quarry was not here, he would flush the rabbit elsewhere.

Daun slipped inside, pistol at the ready. No one challenged him. The building opened up as he went farther in, and strains of . . . singing? . . . reached his ears. The soft voice of a woman, not shouting obscene lyrics, nor fighting to be heard over blaring, raucous music. She was softly singing, with only a few instruments as background noise, an old, old song about love found and lost.

Daun frowned and moved fully into the room. The environment was calm, one might even say placid, even though there were a surprising number of customers sitting at small tables lit only by a few candles. The décor was subdued, almost spartan. The singer was on a stage illuminated by a single spotlight. She was attractive, but older and a little overweight, and her clothing actually left something to the imagination.

He shook his head at the strangeness of the place—no wonder the clientele was so secretive: in a place like Deadman's Port things like this were shameful, he thought—and looked around for his target.

The man was sitting alone, sipping something out of a small glass and watching the singer with a half smile on his face. Disgusted with the mellow feel of this place, Daun slipped beside him and pointed the gun at the base of his skull. The man's sudden spike of fear was most rewarding.

"You're Edward Baines, aren't you?"

The man started to nod, felt the muzzle at the back of his neck, and stopped the motion. "Yes," he said, with calmness that was both admirable and annoying. "And you must be Ezekiel Daun."

Surprise flitted through Daun. "I could be a two-bit thug."

"Unlikely," Baines continued. The man was thin and as gaunt as a corpse. Daun disliked him, not least because Baines was quickly mastering his fear. "A two-bit thug wouldn't have the connections or the funds to pull the sort of strings it takes to learn about this place, let alone be able to sneak up on me."

"Don't flatter yourself," Daun snorted, lowering the gun. Baines turned around to face him, regarding him with calm, watery eyes.

"So. What do you want from me, Mr. Daun?"

"I need the dog to take a message to his master," Daun said, smiling a little. "You tell that comfortable bastard who plays all sides that I'll respect his little duchy here. I won't make a play on Findlay and Raynor while I'm in town. Bad for business . . . his *and* mine."

Baines nodded. "I will tell him. I'm sure he will appreciate your business acumen."

"But," Daun said, reaching over and picking

up Baines's drink, "that only lasts while I'm here and they're here. I'm not interested in any kind of deal that makes me renege on a bounty. I don't care how much someone pays. Besides, it's gotten personal now. I want those two. And I'll have them." He swirled the drink, sniffed it, and raised an approving eyebrow before gulping it down and setting the glass back on the table with an exaggerated thump.

"Once Raynor and Findlay leave Deadman's Port, they become fair game."

Baines nodded. "I will tell him. Anything else? Perhaps about how long you expect to be in town?"

Daun chuckled. "I only came down to find you to deliver the message. I'm not interested in any of the other entertainment Deadman's Port provides."

It wasn't quite true, of course. He still had to get back to his ship. There were a lot of places a man could visit while retracing his steps. But once he had reached his vessel, he would simply stay in orbit, a spider watching his web very, very carefully.

"That might be best for all involved, sir."

Daun rose, patted Baines on his bony shoulder, regarded the singer with a thin smile of contempt, and left as quietly as he had come.

*   *   *

"How the hell did you even hear about this heist?" Scutter O'Banon was saying.

He, Jim, and Tychus were at O'Banon's mansion. Tychus had insisted on meeting there, due to the extremely private nature of the information. "You don't want this to be overheard," Tychus had warned, and had been quite correct in the assumption. Even so, they were no longer being feted with lavish food and drink. The dapper Randall was conspicuously absent, and they were meeting in a small room off the front hall rather than in the parlor. There were no chairs. Scutter was saying without words that the business would be conducted quickly.

"I ain't gonna name names, but people do talk, especially when they're liquored up," Tychus said.

"It would be worth your while to name names, Mr. Findlay," O'Banon said. "Especially considering the trouble you and Mr. Raynor here keep causing me."

Tychus shook his head. "Naw. You'd know I'd rat someone out then, and the next person I ratted out might be you."

Scutter sighed. Tychus had raised a good point. Still, he frowned. "You two are starting to become more effort than you are worth."

Jim felt a chill. Words like that were never pleasant to hear. If Scutter felt they had exceeded their value to him, no one would ever find their bodies. Not that anyone would miss them, he mused darkly.

"Your hound showed up on my planet today," Scutter said.

Jim's stomach dropped into his shoes. Daun! He was alive after all. Jim had dared to hope— but it was hard to kill someone like him. Hard as hell.

O'Banon walked over to a hutch, opened a humidor, fished out one of his thin cigars, and began to trim it as he spoke. He did not offer one to Jim or Tychus. "Told me that he was going to play nice and not cause any trouble in my sandbox." O'Banon almost spat the words. "Mighty gracious of him, don't you think?" He lit the cigar and turned back to them. "So you're safe here. But once you leave, he'll be after you. I'll do what I can."

"Oh, that's just great—" Jim started to sputter, but Tychus held up a hand.

"See, and that's another reason we should go on this heist. Your boys might talk, but they ain't stupid. Might have figured Jimmy and I already knew about it. Point is, nobody else does. Including Daun."

O'Banon's eyes narrowed. "True," he said. "And you two do have certain . . . *expertise* that could enhance things."

"Damn straight we do."

"Very well. I'll let you come along."

"'Come along'?"

Scutter smiled with his very pursed, very red mouth. "You couldn't possibly imagine that I'd send you two off alone with something of this magnitude. . . . Hell, boys, you're lucky it's Randall's day off, or you'd be bleeding on the floor right now."

"Now wait a—" Jim began. Again Tychus held up a hand, though the strain was starting to show on his face.

"We'll do it. But we want an equal cut."

Scutter chuckled. "You pull this off, you'll get an equal cut. My word on it."

"I knew we could come to an agreement that would be of mutual benefit," Tychus said. He ambled over to the sideboard and helped himself to a cigar. Scutter's eye twitched, but he said nothing as Tychus prepped the cigar and began to smoke it. "So. Here we are. Fill us in."

"I'm sure you boys are familiar with Bacchus Moon," Scutter said.

"Hell yeah," Tychus replied. "Gambler's paradise. The Koprulu sector's high rollers go there. Lots of entertainment too." He looked at Jim and waggled his eyebrows.

"Entertainment of that sort, certainly," agreed O'Banon, "and other types of shows and performances for those with more discerning tastes. Incredibly fine hotels, famous restaurants. Fantasy fulfillment on all levels, for the right price. The place caters to gamblers, as you say, but also hosts conventions. A very great number of people are moving through there at any given minute."

"Good place for crime," Jim said.

"Less than you would think," Scutter said, in a *this is why I'm the boss and you are the henchmen* tone of voice. "Security is a going commodity, and people can pay for the best. Especially," he emphasized, "the banks."

Jim's heart sank. He had hoped that they would have a specific mark, or that they would pull off a sting or fleece some gamblers. He didn't know a lot about Bacchus Moon, but he knew the things that everybody knew, and one of the things that everybody knew was that if your money was in a bank safe on Bacchus Moon, the operative word in that sentence was "safe." Nobody was going to touch it.

He began to wonder if he and Tychus were being set up for a suicide mission, just as a way for Scutter to punish them. Then he realized that all Scutter needed to do was let Daun have a crack at them. In the end, that would be more efficient.

Even Tychus's body language changed. "I

see," was all he said, though, as he thoughtfully blew out smoke.

"It has come to my attention that the Covington Bank will be the location of a massive stockpile of Confederate credits for exactly thirty-seven hours before the credits are dispersed."

"Define 'massive,'" said Jim.

Scutter eyed him. "Seven hundred million, thirty-six thousand, four hundred and twenty."

Jim wasn't sure, but he thought he made a small choking sound. Even Tychus coughed a little as he inhaled the smoke from his cigar.

"For thirty-seven hours," Tychus confirmed.

"At the Covington Bank."

"Well, now, I must say, Scutter, that's a right tidy sum."

"I thought so. And since it's so bountiful, and the job so tricky, I'm inclined to be generous with the men who get it for me."

"There's the rub, isn't it?" said Tychus. "Gettin' those seven-hundred-plus-million credits. What's the current plan?"

"One cannot simply march in and ask for the money, so my man Ash Thompson has been doing some research into what's below the bank. There was a cave-in about six years ago that severely damaged the sewer system. Costs to dig it out and rebuild it to meet safety regulations were prohibitive, so they simply let it stay caved in. Now, we don't care about how good a sewer system it is; we just need to get access to the vault. Ash believes that—"

"Nope. That plan is total shit."

O'Banon blinked. "'Shit'?"

Tychus shook his head. "Too risky, from a lot of standpoints. Too time-consuming and uses too much manpower."

A slow flush began to creep up Scutter's face. "You have a superior plan?"

"I think I do," drawled Tychus. "And you will recall, it was our reputation that got you interested in us."

"I agree with Tychus," Jim said. "We need to get in, get the credits, get out. The longer we're digging in the dirt, the greater the chance someone will find us."

Scutter took a puff of his skinny cigar and narrowed his eyes, thinking. "You know," he said at last, "I did not get to the current position I so happily occupy by doing the dirty work myself." He smiled thinly—at least, as thinly as was possible with his full lips. "Both you and Ash know your jobs. I think I'll leave you three to figure it out. May the best man win, eh?"

He retrieved a piece of paper and a gold pen from the desk, jotted down an address, and handed it to Tychus. "Be there in three hours. I will expect to hear what you come up with in five."

CHAPTER SEVENTEEN

DEADMAN'S PORT, DEADMAN'S ROCK
JACK'S SPOT

Jim and Tychus knew the place well. Scutter owned it, as he did many—most, actually—of the businesses in Deadman's Port. It was a place called Jack's Spot, with a gambling theme to play along with the pun, and was run-down enough to be inconspicuous and clean enough not to be a cesspool.

They arrived early and ordered food. "I don't plot bank robberies on an empty stomach," Tychus said. He ordered two sandwiches, chips, and beer, which for him was essentially little more than a midday snack. Jim poked disinterestedly at Tychus's basket of chips and nursed his own beer. He was growing less and less excited at the prospect of what they were about to embark upon with every passing moment, and was beginning to wish he had just left and not let Tychus talk him into one final big heist.

At exactly one minute to the appointed time, three men approached them and slid into the booth.

"I like it when my team is punctual," Tychus said.

Jim evaluated the men who had just joined them. They looked exactly as he had expected them to look. Hardened, calculating, wary, and yet confident. Just like Scutter O'Banon's boys *should* look.

He wondered how *he* looked to *them*.

The one sitting beside Tychus—a man in his thirties, about Jim's size and build, with dirty blond hair and a pale scar down one cheek—narrowed his eyes at the comment.

"The name is Ash Thompson. And *I* am the leader of this . . . team. I was told to listen to your plan and, if I found it sound, to bring you in on the job."

Tychus took an enormous bite of his second sandwich, chewed, and swallowed. "Well, maybe we can learn a lesson from the playground and share the ball, then, Ass." He feigned mortification. "Sorry . . . *Ash*."

The man seated next to Jim and across from

Tychus growled. "This guy is starting to piss me off, Ash. I already don't like what I'm hearing. Let's end this now."

The third man stayed silent. He was small, thin, and dark-haired. Jim didn't like his silence and glared at all of them.

"Now, now, Rafe, settle down. Let's hear the man out before we cut his throat."

Jim actually rolled his eyes. "Ash, I gotta tell you, if this clichéd routine you three have going is any indication, *we're* the ones who want out."

Ash's mouth slowly stretched into a smile. It was thin, and cold, and dangerous. "The quiet one speaks."

"Hell, he ain't quiet," Tychus said. "You'll find that out soon enough."

"I'm just enjoying the potato chips," said Jim, munching another one. "And I want to listen before I speak."

Ash nodded approvingly. "Let's get down to business, then. I understand that you said my plan was crap."

Tychus shook his head, swallowing a bite of the sandwich. "Nope. I said it was shit. There's a difference."

Jim smothered a chuckle as Ash's face darkened. "I doubt you will come up with anything better. But Scutter told me to listen and decide which of us is right. I like to obey the man who pays me. Let's start with an overview before we get to specifics."

He took out a pocket-sized holoemitter and placed it on the table. At the touch of a button, the Covington Bank building appeared, then proceeded to slice itself into sections like a three-dimensional blueprint.

Jim started, spilling his beer. "What the fekk, man, do you want everyone in the sector to know about this?"

Ash laughed. "Scutter owns this place, right down to the dirt on the floor. I could bang a senator's wife right here on the table and no one would bat an eyelash."

Jim threw up his hands in surrender. "Don't mind me. I just like to be smart sometimes."

Ash ignored him. "The Covington Bank is one of the sector's most secure. It has state-of-the-art security systems, walls thicker than a man is high, and a reputation that discourages all but the most die-hard." He flashed a grin. "That's us. Now—the creds are only going to be inside the bank where we can get at 'em for thirty-seven hours. It's a narrow window, but we have a few days before the chrono starts ticking. We have something working for us, and something that *seems* to be working against us but really isn't. First off, we have an ace in the hole." He pointed to the fourteenth story of the massive building. "The bank itself occupies the entire lower level, but there are other businesses here, and from the tenth story up, it's luxury penthouse apartments."

"Don't tell me," said Jim. "Scutter O'Banon owns one of them."

"Not so you'd ever find out, but yes," he said. "For the last few years, he's had an inside man who's been operating from here. This is going to help us out in all kinds of pleasant ways."

Tychus allowed that it certainly would. "What's the thing that seems bad but isn't?" Jim asked.

"Well"—Ash half-smiled—"it seems that during our narrow thirty-seven-hour window, the Interstellar Marshals Convention is in town. Over a thousand law enforcement officials are going to be running around the place."

Tychus grunted. "Shit, Ash—how the hell could that possibly be anything but bad?" He finished off his sandwich with a single bite and fished out a cigar.

"Think about it," Ash said, his voice a trifle condescending. "Sure, they're marshals—when they're on duty. You think lawyers at a convention are going to be working on their cases? Hell no. They're going to be attending seminars during the day, conveniently all holed up in one lavish hotel. After the speeches and seminars and boring lunches, they're going to be drinking, gambling, eating, watching strip shows, patronizing prostitutes, throwing up, and passing out, just like everyone else does after hours at a convention on Bacchus Moon."

Jim nodded.

"Our inside guy sees this convention every year, and that's exactly what he reports. Listen—they're going to be in town, but the last thing on their minds will be enforcing the law. It's party time, and this is Bacchus Moon."

"The town *and* the bank are going to be lulled into a false sense of security," Jim said before Ash could continue. "The bank's going to think, Hey, we've got the safest money in the sector right now—there's a thousand law officers right down the street. Who's gonna try anything with *them* in town?"

Ash nodded. "And *that*, my dust-kicking friend, is why it seems to be a liability but actually is a plus."

Tychus nodded, lighting the cigar. "Makes sense. Regardless, ain't a thing we can do about it."

"Go on," Jim said.

Ash leaned forward slightly. "I said I would follow my boss's orders. I'm going to listen to your plan with an open mind, because I want to do this successfully. But I will tell you this: I've been breaking into banks for six years. Places that are so beyond your abilities you can't even have wet dreams about them. Rafe and Win here have been with me for most of them. We know what can and can't be done a lot better than two low-life dirt-pushers like you."

"Aw, now, that done gone and hurt my feelings," Tychus said, blowing smoke right into Ash's face. "Why don't you just hear me out and use your own best judgment like you said you was gonna do?"

Slowly, Ash sat back in the booth and nodded. "Sure, sure. Let's see what the guy with the neck that's thicker than his head can come up with."

Tychus smiled around the cigar. Jim smothered a grin of his own. Both men loved it when people thought Tychus was stupid. It was such a kick to prove them wrong.

"When Scutter O'Banon sent Cadaver—"

"'Cadaver'?" asked Rafe, frowning.

"Guy who looks like a walking corpse," Jim supplied helpfully. Rafe made an "Ah" of recognition and nodded.

"—to ask me and Jimmy here to work for him, it was because of our reputation. We ain't the sort of men who come up through the ground. We come in through the front door, during business hours. In broad daylight. And we get out the same way."

Ash stared for a long moment. "You're a fek-king lunatic, Tychus Findlay."

"Now, now, your momma shoulda taught you to watch your language, son," Tychus said. "Let me tell you what I can do if you give me three days' lead time and enough credits."

Edward Baines had the night off, and he was planning on celebrating. Any day that got Tychus Findlay and James Raynor out of Deadman's Port was a good one, and they should be gone for a while. With a little luck, permanently.

He slipped in through the narrow doorway, hearing the soft sounds of a quartet, and felt his heart lift.

This place was an oasis for him. Baines didn't get to come here often enough, and he was already looking forward to a glass of something pleasant and an evening of soft, soothing music. Tonight his favorite singer, Tanya, was scheduled to perform.

His eyes adjusted to the dim room, lit only by candles, and he eased into his favorite seat close to the stage. The quartet finished up and their leader stepped up to the mic.

"Thank you, thanks very much. Now, we know that most of you came here expecting to hear the magnificent Tanya, but she won't be able to join us this evening. Instead, we have a special guest here to sing for you tonight. I hope you'll enjoy her performance."

Baines sat down, a bit disappointed. He loved hearing Tanya, but it was also nice to hear new talent as well. He gave his drink order to the waiter, then settled in.

The quartet packed up, and for a few moments the stage was empty. The crowd began to murmur, although they were genteel murmurs. Baines's drink, scotch and soda, came, and he sipped it, frowning slightly.

Then the spotlight came on. There was a lone microphone stand. "Ladies and gentlemen, please welcome . . . *Kyttyn!*"

Baines's eyes widened.

The young woman—he could not imagine calling her a "young lady"—who came onstage was dressed in tiny striped scraps of clothing. She wore large fake cat ears and a tail sewed onto the rear of the microbikini that covered—well, not very much at all. Her body was toned, tight, and in-your-face.

"Hey, everyone!" Kyttyn said cheerily. Her pert little nose was painted black, and three whiskers adorned her cheeks on either side. "Tonight, I'm doing a special performance for one very lucky Mr. Edward Baines."

Another spotlight practically blasted Baines's retinas as it glared down at him.

"Mr. Baines . . . or should I say Cadaver . . . this is just for you, from Jim and Tychus."

And she launched into something loud, and raucous, and screaming, peppered with words that would make a marine blush to hear.

The spotlight stayed on Edward Baines for the duration.

There was no green on Bacchus Moon.

Jim had been looking at images of the place, and it was wall-to-wall plascrete and neosteel. The only areas where living things seemed to grow were on the grounds of the acres-wide luxury hotels. The rest was solid city. It had once been a verdant and pleasant world, he learned, with the sort of land that his parents would have tilled with care and from which they would have reaped bountiful crops. But because of its convenient location, its destiny had been determined early on.

He, Tychus, Ash, Win, and Rafe were approaching at night, and the only spaces where there were not bright lights were the oceans, dark and black and open. Every single landmass was glowing from coast to coast, crowded with people, glitz, and glamour.

It was beautiful, after a fashion, but Jim found himself thinking about it in a way he hadn't before. He had grown up on Shiloh, where every bit of energy was carefully safeguarded and used as efficiently as possible. The amount of energy required to run the capital city of Semele, where they were headed, was likely enough to power all of Shiloh. He'd liked the glitz and the glamour and the high life, but now its waste and crassness were spread out before him, starkly and almost lewdly, and Jim realized that even the things he used to enjoy now had a pall cast over them.

He settled back, mentally counting the hours until this was all done. Having made his decision, he was ready—more than ready—to turn his back on this life.

Their destination approached rapidly as they made their descent. Jim shook his head quietly as the lights of the city seemed to surge to meet them, and they docked in the starport that Jim just knew would have jingling slot machines available the second they disembarked.

"I don't like how you're looking, Raynor," said Ash. Jim started from his reverie.

"I don't like big cities," he said. "Especially garish ones."

"That's fine," Tychus interrupted as he was directed in for docking. "With the money we'll get from this haul, you can buy yourself your very own planet and decorate it just how you like it, Jimmy."

That brought a chuckle from everyone but

Ash, who continued regarding Jim thought-fully. Jim and Tychus had discussed what would happen after they made off with several million credits. Jim would receive his share and be quietly dropped off somewhere on the way back to Deadman's Port. They hadn't chosen to inform Ash and the rest of Scutter's boys of this change in plans. Ash disliked them enough as it was.

They had rooms in one of the more middle-of-the-road hotels, neither too ritzy nor too much of a dump. They would check in, then Ash and his boys would begin reconnaissance while Jim and Tychus hooked up with Tychus's contacts.

The sooner they did, the sooner it would all be over, and the better Jim would like it.

A vessel designed for only one person without much cargo also was vectored in for docking at the Semele port. The ship had been following the vessel bearing Jim, Tychus, Ash, Rafe, and Win ever since it had departed Deadman's Port. The man piloting it reached out with a gleaming metal hand to press a button.

"Acknowledged," said Ezekiel Daun.

The place was every bit as high-intensity, bright, obnoxious, and loud as Jim had expected it to be. Hovercars and -bikes whizzed past their taxi as it ferried them to their hotel, the Bellissima Grande Hotel and Casino, and Jim worried that the driver might have a heart attack, considering how loudly he yelled and how vigorously he gestured at other drivers.

The streets were crowded and bright as day, even at this hour, and attractive women called out to them as they made their way the short distance from the street to the hotel's entrance. Tychus whistled and said a few lewd things, but Jim just kept his head down. Inside, it was gaudy and crowded and thick with smoke. The constant sound of bells and whistles and the shouting of players as they won—or lost—bombarded his ears, and when at last he and Tychus settled into their own musty rooms, Jim leaned against the door for a moment.

Even here, the world of high-stakes gambling and partying intruded. The walls were thin, and he was treated to the sounds of just how much his neighbors were enjoying their bedrooms. He headed into the sonic shower, threw on some clean clothes, and met Tychus in the lobby.

Tychus looked surprisingly good. His suit, like Jim's, was understated but well tailored and fit perfectly across his broad shoulders. He had a fine cigar clenched in his teeth, and his eyes gleamed with delight as Jim walked up to him.

"I like this place," he said. "Lots of distractions. For the marks while I work, and for me when I'm done."

"It's all yours," Jim said. "Where do we go first?"

"Don't tell me you ain't gonna even try to enjoy your last big fling," Tychus chided.

"That's exactly what I'm telling you."

Tychus slipped an arm around his friend's shoulder in a mock-paternal gesture. "Jimmy, I'm going to make you have fun if it's the last thing I do. Fortunately, our meeting with my contact takes place in one of the most popular hotels on this whole glitzy moon. Come on."

Twenty minutes later, Jim felt as if he had stepped out into an entirely new world. The little bar called the Blue Note, in the Rapture Hotel and Casino, was so far removed from the almost frantic energy and neon colors of every place else Jim had seen as to be almost disconcerting. The décor was comprised of stepped forms and sweeping curves, and there were freestanding pieces of art made of inlaid wood and steel in repeating patterns of chevrons and sunbursts, as well as paintings adorning the wall. Soft jazz came from somewhere; the leather seats were incredibly comfortable; and the waitress spoke in a soft voice and had something approaching a genuine smile as she brought Tychus and Jim their drinks.

A few moments later, there was a soft rustle of satin. A tall, gorgeous woman, clad in a floor-length red dress and carrying a shopping bag from one of the finest stores in the city, slipped into the seat across from them.

"Jennifer," Tychus said, "damn, the years like you, honey."

She smiled, and Jim saw what he hadn't observed at first, thanks to the soft lighting. This woman, despite her jet-black hair and slender figure, was actually much older than they were. But Tychus was right: she didn't need flattering lighting to be breathtaking. There was an elegance to her movements, and her face was finely boned. She'd be a beauty in torn clothes and sitting in the mud, Jim thought.

Jennifer smiled. "Tychus Findlay," she said. "Long time no see. This must be Mr. Raynor." She extended a slender, well-manicured hand. Jim found himself struggling against the urge to kiss it and instead shook it awkwardly.

"How d'you do, ma'am?"

Jennifer's lovely smile widened. "Much better manners than you, Tychus. I like this boy."

"Don't get too fond of him," Tychus said. "He's going straight soon, or so he tells me."

Jennifer's brow furrowed in sympathy. "Really?

That's too bad," she said, as if Tychus had just pronounced dreadful news.

"Jennifer and her husband, Gustav, are from Umoja," Tychus explained. "Can't wait to see what she's got for me."

"I love it when I hear from you," she said. "You always give Gustav and me such interesting things to design."

If she hadn't had Jim's utter attention before, which she pretty much had, she had it now. With a small government and a lucrative economy, Umojans were known for cutting-edge technology. Jim, too, now leaned eagerly forward as Jennifer removed a gift-wrapped box from the shopping bag and handed it to Tychus. Tychus grinned and opened it.

Inside was a beautiful patterned vest. The main color was black. There were small diamond shapes cut into the bottom of the vest, and in each nook sparkled a green or red gem. The colors alternated in a complex pattern all around the front and, Jim saw, even the back. It was beautiful, and elegant, and utterly not Tychus.

Then Jennifer turned the vest and opened four cleverly concealed flaps. Jim realized that they were holsters, and that definitely was utterly Tychus.

"My, my, ain't that pretty?" Tychus said. "Jennifer, you do outstanding work."

"Ah, but such a nice waistcoat demands the right accessory," Jennifer continued. She handed him another, smaller package.

"I feel like this is my birthday," Tychus chuckled. He opened the box to reveal an exquisite antique pocket watch. Jim whistled softly.

"Gustav wanted to put your initials on it, but I recommended he refrain," Jennifer said. "Here . . . let me show you how to set the time and wind it."

She removed it carefully from the box. "To set the time, pull this little notched knob called the winding crown straight up, like so. Set the hands to the time you wish, then push it back down. To wind it, turn the winding crown clockwise until you cannot wind further. Very simple."

"Very simple indeed, but effective." Tychus grinned at her. "I'll be sure to take very good care of it."

"These"—and she handed him a final box—"are for all your friends. Also watches, but not quite as nice as yours. You must make sure they wear them, or at least have them on their person in some fashion."

"I will, darlin'. You and Gustav are too good to me."

Jennifer's smile widened, became mischievous. "You've admired them enough, Tychus. You can investigate them a little more closely when you're in your room. But for now . . . why don't you take them, and me, for a spin? There's dancing right next door."

"Hell, honey, you know I can't dance. I'll step on those dainty feet of yours."

She laughed throatily. "I know. But it's a practical test. . . . I just want to see how you'll be able to move in the vest, see if I need to make any adjustments. Come on."

Tychus sighed in resignation. "You coming with us, Jimmy?" Tychus asked.

Jim grinned. "Think I'll stay here. You two crazy kids have fun."

Tychus shrugged, removed his coat jacket, and put on the vest. He placed the watch securely in the slit pocket in the front. Jennifer gracefully slipped Tychus's arm through hers, gave Jim a smile that melted him, and led Tychus off to the dance floor. Jim had to admit as he watched them go that Tychus looked positively dashing in his new vest.

Pity he wasn't going to have it long.

Tychus had not lied to Jennifer and Jim: he couldn't dance. He was large, and while he was agile, he was not graceful, and he knew nothing—less than nothing—about ballroom dancing.

While he stumbled more than a bit awkwardly around the ballroom floor, Jennifer lifted her lips to his ear and whispered. Not sweet nothings, no— she was whispering key information about the vest. He nodded, taking everything in, then whispered back comments about how it felt as he moved in it.

So far, all seemed to be perfect. Tychus felt good enough to execute a twirl, which Jennifer, as a gracious dance partner, spun through so easily, she made him look good. By now he was confident enough to glance around the room slightly as he pulled her back to him, even dipped her, and the dance ended.

He placed his hand on the small of her back and guided her to the refreshment table, continuing to look around as unobtrusively as possible. At first the crowd seemed to be typical for such a place: middle-aged men with red-rimmed eyes; women showing too much cleavage for their figures; some nice dresses and suits, most of them off the rack. It was—

They locked eyes.

Tychus stared at a man with a thick head of glossy black hair, piercing blue eyes, and a glorious mustache.

"Aw, shit," Tychus Findlay muttered as he recognized Marshal Wilkes Butler.

CHAPTER EIGHTEEN

Jim was on his second beer when Tychus burst into the Blue Note and jerked his head toward the exit commandingly. Immediately Jim sprang up and followed, quickly tossing a few credits on the table.

"What is it?" he asked as they hastened outside and tried to flag a cab.

"What kind of convention is being held here?" Tychus asked suddenly. He seemed torn between anger and humor.

"Marshals Con—Oh, you're shitting me."

"Nope."

"Wilkes is here?"

"In the flesh."

"He see you?"

"That he did."

Jim swore. They tumbled into a cab, and Tychus directed the driver not back to the hotel but to another casino. "Gotta throw him off our trail," he explained.

"So, what do we do? We gonna tell Ash?"

Tychus shook his head. "Nope. They're already looking for any excuse to cut us out of this. Butler's not an idiot, but he'd have to act way too fast."

"What if he tells the whole damn convention?"

"He won't, not unless he has to. That ain't his style. You know grabbin' us has always been a personal thing with him. He'll try to get us first on his own."

"I cannot believe it," Jim fumed. "Out of all the people in that place—what, a couple hundred? More?—you happen to catch his eye across a crowded room."

"Almost sounds romantic, don't it?" said Tychus, and finally gave in to the humor of the situation. He threw back his head and let out a loud guffaw. Jim stared at him furiously for a moment, then his lips twitched, and a few seconds later he, too, was laughing at the absurdity of it all.

Tychus wiped his eyes. "Well, I guess it woulda

been too easy without a few more wrinkles to complicate matters," he said. "Can't have boring on our last heist, now, can we?"

"That woman! After her!" ordered Wilkes Butler. Rett immediately took off after the tall, attractive woman who a second ago had been at Tychus Findlay's side. Butler went after Tychus. The crowd was thick, and it took too long for Wilkes Butler to push through it. He realized even as he tried that he would be too late to spot Raynor and Findlay leaving. He always was.

He emerged on the street, glancing around. There was no clue where they might have gone, and there wasn't any indication that they had come out here. They could have doubled back into the hotel, taken the elevator to any one of the multiple stories, or ducked into the restroom. Maybe even all of those things. The marshals had been permitted to carry weapons with them to the event, but Butler had opted to leave his in his room, laboring under the mistaken impression that he might actually be able to relax for four days.

Rett came up behind him. "Did my best, but she vanished."

Butler grunted. "Likely simply an expensive hooker." Such women were paid to be discreet; her disappearing act probably was one of the reasons she was so expensive. Even so, any information, even from a high-class prostitute, would've been useful, and he was disappointed they'd lost her. Still, he did not rebuke Rett; his deputy had doubtless done his best.

"What now?"

What, indeed. "Well, he may have caught us off guard, but I don't think he planned for that. He certainly looked surprised enough to see me. That could work to our advantage. I need to do some research first. Keep this quiet until we know what we're dealing with. I'll let you know as soon as I know what our next step is."

Rett nodded. "Yes, sir," he said.

"Go back in and keep socializing. Don't want to raise any alarms just yet."

Butler sighed as Rett returned to the party. He mulled over his options, and the things he needed to find out, as he stepped back inside and returned to his room.

He had no misconceptions about his strengths and weaknesses. He well knew that he was not a lightning-fast, brilliant thinker. But he also knew he wasn't stupid. He was careful, and methodical, and usually very successful. It was mainly for this reason that Findlay and Raynor had gotten under his skin as badly as they had. They were the two men he'd been chasing the longest without ever catching.

And he badly, badly wanted to catch them.

He closed the door, loosened his tie, and fired up his computer. He chafed at even the brief delay of the fingerprint scan required for him to access the most sensitive case files back on New Sydney.

First, he had to decide if he wanted to bring everyone in on this. There were certainly more dangerous criminals out there, but most of the people he'd attended seminars with over the last two days would know of Raynor and Findlay, and would hanker for the glory of being the one to bring them to justice. That didn't sit well with Butler. Most of the crimes they had committed over the years had taken place on one of his planets, had wronged his people, and he wanted to be the one to have the satisfaction of saying the happiest of phrases: "You're under arrest." The feeling was a bit selfish, and he told himself that if he couldn't figure things out quickly, he would enlist some aid. But for now, he wanted to see what he could come up with.

So . . . what sort of things were Tychus and Jim likely to be engaged in on Bacchus Moon? They had never been hired assassins, nor did they tend to harm innocent bystanders. Most of the people who got injured during their robberies were professional guards, and even then—and Wilkes admitted this grudgingly—Findlay and Raynor usually managed to disable the guards without killing them. So it wasn't likely that they were here to kill anyone.

Second, they liked money. They liked to take it and they liked to spend it. Normally, that would mean Butler would focus on where they might acquire credits, and where they might spend them. Unfortunately, there were far too many places here where they could do both of those things.

He ordered a sandwich and a pot of coffee from room service and removed his tie altogether, tossing it on the bed with a sigh as he unbuttoned his collar.

It was going to be a long night.

The very audacity of the whole thing was why it was going to work, Jim thought. As Tychus had said somewhat more crudely, "This robbery has balls."

They had gone over the plan several times. They had it scheduled down to the minute. All their information was completely up-to-date. They had checked and double-checked equipment, schedules, weapons, and blueprints, and now all that remained was to actually do the thing.

It was 1256 when the five of them entered the bank and stood in line for what Tychus called a "dry run." It would give them a chance to familiarize themselves with the bank's interior, tellers, patterns, and so on. They had decided to proceed exactly as they would tomorrow. So they had arrived in the hovercar they would be using, which was now pulled up close to the bank's carefully manicured lawn. They wore what they would be wearing this time tomorrow, and they had brought their weapons just in case something went wrong.

Tychus was looking a bit flamboyant: in addition to the natty vest Jennifer had made for him, his suit coat pocket sported a silk handkerchief, his hands were encased in fine leather gloves, and every inch of him was creased, ironed, and spit-polished. The vest was, of necessity, so distinctive, they'd figured the rest of him should be as well. After all, Tychus was always memorable by virtue of his sheer size. The others, except for Jim, were clean-shaven and sported haircuts and tailored suits, but still managed to be nondescript and would likely not be recalled too clearly by witnesses.

The bank screamed respectability at every turn, from the conservative yet high-quality furniture, to the original paintings on the walls, to the polished gleam of the red-brown tile. Tasteful, luxurious, unobtrusive. Jim shifted his weight as he stood in line, feigning boredom and looking around. There was the entrance to the vault room; inside was the vault itself, where the money would be kept. Over there were meeting rooms. Down the corridor were staff offices, restrooms, custodians' closets. Just as the blueprints had said there would be.

Casually, Tychus drew his pocket watch out and frowned. He glanced up at the large chrono on the wall. It ticked placidly, revealing that the time was now 1259.

Tychus shook his head at the pocket watch as if he were disappointed in it, pulled up the winding crown, mimed setting the time, then pushed the crown back down.

"Oh, dear," came a voice.

Jim and Tychus recognized that voice. Their heads whipped around and they stared, mouths open, at a slender man in a business suit with a badge that proclaimed him as an agent of the Confederate Bureau of Protection of Monies and Valuable Items. His eyes were wide, and there was a look of resigned terror on his face. Jim was suddenly transported back to the train robbery, with this same shaking man standing in front of them, forbidding them access to the train's safe.

"George Woodcock," Tychus murmured.

"Woodley," Raynor corrected in a hollow voice.

"Mr. Raynor, Mr. Findlay, I am so sorry to have to do this. . . ." He reached for a comm unit on his black belt.

"Tychus"—it was Ash, his voice a yelp—"what the hell—"

"So much for a dry run," Tychus muttered. He threw off his coat and twisted the winding crown of the watch counterclockwise twice.

Two things happened simultaneously.

First, the lights went out. The lobby suddenly went dim but not dark, thanks to the large windows.

Second, the small, glittering gems set into the diamond-shaped cavities of his vest sprang forward. The "jewels" fell to the floor, sprouted legs, and scuttled away with astonishing speed. Each was about as large as a thumbnail and about as thick, its dozens of tiny legs propelling it toward the now-screaming crowd. Even before the little things had hit the floor, Tychus had a gun in each hand.

"Ladies and gentlemen," Tychus said, pitching his voice loud, "listen very, very carefully to what I am about to say, and do not make the slightest move. Your lives will depend upon it."

The crowd fell silent, save for the sound of quickened breathing and the occasional whimper.

"First, outside in the trunk of our vehicle is a large device that generates an electromagnetic pulse. It was just switched on from a signal from this charming, deceptively antiquated-seeming little Umojan device. Said EMP has deactivated every electrical system and high-tech micro-circuit in this building and for several blocks around, so trying to flip any alarm would be quite futile. It would also be quite deadly. Deadly because, secondly, I direct your attention to those small spidery things that are currently right at your feet," he said. "They got a long and fancy name, but I'm just gonna call 'em spiders. They are programmed to go toward any heat source between 96 and 102 degrees and stay there until they are deactivated by yours truly. They are also programmed to climb up your leg and inject a lethal toxin at the sign of any movement sharper or more sudden than normal breathing or facial expressions. Which means that, yes, you can blink."

He was clearly enjoying himself. While he was speaking, Jim had his gun out, just in case something went wrong. Ash was already at the safe, and his men hastened to close the blinds and lock the door. Win turned the CLOSED sign to face out, then he and Rafe went to join Ash. Jim looked around the room and, reassured that the spiders were having their desired effect, asked, "Who is the highest-ranking bank employee present?"

There was a silence, then an elderly woman quavered, "I am."

Jim went up to her and pointed the gun at her with one hand. "I know you have simple keys for the safety deposit boxes," he said quietly. "Just for situations like this. Tell me where I can find them."

"Over behind the main desk," the woman whispered. "In the second drawer down."

"Thank you kindly," Jim said, and retrieved the keys. Sometimes, he mused, simple was better.

For having to act on the fly, they were doing well. The first level of security had been disabled by the EMP. The human factor had been disabled by the spiders and "closing" the bank. The door to the main vault room was unlocked, as it always was during business hours. All that remained to do was to employ extremely low-level but highly efficient technology and quite literally blow the door off the vault itself. Ash stood by, his eyes flickering from Rafe and Win—they were affixing the explosives and working up the wiring— to Tychus. A frown was deepening on Ash's face.

"This is too risky, damn it," he muttered.

Jim stepped over to him. He and the others could move freely without fear of spider repercussion. Each man either wore or had stashed in a pocket one of Jennifer and Gustav's stylish-looking watches that emitted a signal that made the spiders regard them as "friendly." The Umojan couple was proving to be an amazing team; Tychus had told Jim the spiders, as well as the vest, were Jennifer's creations, whereas Gustav had crafted both the pocket watch and its ability to trigger an EMP.

"None of us wanted to go early," Jim said. "Everything else is in place, isn't it? Our end of it is going perfectly."

"Yeah, yeah, it's all in place. Our guy won't be there to help us haul the creds, but things should be set up at the suite." Ash wiped his damp face.

"Well, then, nothing to worry about. Just have to make a couple extra trips to get it all up there. We got time." They had a full hour before the spiders self-destructed. That was one of the things Tychus and Jim had insisted on. Ash had wanted them to just kill everyone immediately rather than hold them hostage.

"No witnesses," he had said as they sat plotting in Jack's Spot. "Nice and clean."

"Yeah, no witnesses, but a couple dozen bodies and a couple dozen counts of first-degree murder," Jim had said. "And that certainly ain't clean."

"No one's gonna find us," Ash had retorted.

"Maybe not. But we still ain't doing it. My source who makes the spiders don't work that way," Tychus had replied. "Besides, if the spiders self-destruct, they can't be traced. And that, my friend, is operating clean."

Ash had rolled his eyes, muttered something about "soft," but had agreed. He'd really had no choice.

"I'd prefer to use that time to get out of here," Ash said, bringing Jim back to the present, "but we gotta run with this."

Rafe and Win rose and nodded. "All set," they said. They hurried out of the vault room and closed the door so that they would all be protected from the blast within.

A few seconds later, there was a huge but muffled boom. The five men exchanged grins despite the tension of the situation.

"That never gets old," Tychus said.

"Let's go, let's go!" Ash ordered, his grin fading as he became all business again. The vault lock had been well and properly blown, and they pulled open the door.

Inside were dozens of safety deposit boxes, each containing hundreds of thousand-credit coins. It was an almost overwhelming moment, and it was fully three seconds before Jim stepped forward and quickly began manually unlocking the boxes. Ash's men sprang into action as soon as the boxes were open. Tucked into the lining of their jackets were several bags made of material thin enough to fold easily and strong enough to support the weight of all those liberated credits. Jim followed, removing his own sacks and starting to fill them. A smile curved his lips as he did so.

Tychus had been right. The gamblers whose money this doubtless was would never miss it. However, it would give him the fresh new start he found himself yearning for more with every passing day.

"I have to say, Mr. Raynor," came Woodley's voice, "I'm right disappointed in you and Mr. Findlay."

Ash sneered and reached for his weapon. Jim put a firm hand on his arm and shook his head. "Don't. We don't need to add murder to this."

The blond man grimaced but lowered his weapon, impaling George Woodley with an angry stare.

"You should probably be quiet, Mr. Woodley," Jim said.

"Well, I'm afraid I do have to say it. I'm mighty disappointed in you. I wasn't mad at you when I was reassigned after you robbed that train. I was happy to get a new job here. I understand you need to, uh, do what you do and all, but from Farm Aid? I thought you was a better class of criminal than that."

Jim froze.

Then, deliberately, he moved over to where Woodley stood stock-still, his hand still halfway to his comm, his eyes fixed on the tiny mechanical spider at his feet.

"What did you say?"

"I said I am surprised you would be stealing money from Farm Aid. That money goes to help people who need it. It doesn't belong to wealthy gamblers or Old Families. Well, it did—I mean, they were the ones who donated it—but it goes to—"

"I know who it goes to," Jim growled, turning to look at Tychus. "I just didn't know where it came from. But *you* did, didn't you, Tychus?"

"Jimmy, just listen up a moment . . . ," said Tychus, lifting a hand in a placating manner.

"Fekk that. You *knew*! And you didn't tell me because you knew I wouldn't go along with it! That money *helps* people. *My* people."

"It's a goddamned tax break for folks who have way too much money—that's what it is," Tychus retorted. "Jimmy, the only reason this Farm Aid was even created was to help the rich out. Help them feel good about themselves and their empty but very wealthy lives. Come on, I know you know that!"

"That doesn't matter! That money lets people stay in their homes, Tychus. It means they got enough to eat. It means their *kids* got enough to eat. And you didn't tell me!"

"That's because sometimes you're too stubborn and stupid for your own good," Tychus said, his brows drawing together. "Shut up and take the damned credits, Jim. Then you can be a rich big baby and indulge your morals all you want to. So help me, if we get out of this alive, I'm gonna kick your ass so hard—"

There came a sudden high-pitched whine. Out of the corner of his eye, Jim saw movement. Faster than he would have believed possible, he whirled and brought his foot crashing down on the tiny spider that was scuttling toward Woodley's feet, smashing it to bits before it could inject its venom into the terrified agent.

"Th-thank you kindly, Mr. Raynor," Woodley managed in a weak voice.

"Aw, shit," Tychus muttered. "Why the fekk did you have to go and do that, Ash?"

Jim looked around, aghast at what he saw.

Dead. They were all dead. The tellers, the guards, the poor saps who had done nothing but come into a bank to make a deposit or withdraw some cash—they lay slumped where they had fallen. At least they didn't look like it had hurt. While he could imagine the lovely Jennifer putting a lethal toxin into the spiders for emergency purposes, he couldn't see her choosing one that would cause undue pain.

He turned slowly around to face Ash. "You activated the spiders, you son of a bitch. These people did nothing. Why did you do that?"

"To get you to shut up and focus," Ash said.

"Get your ass in here and get back to loading up the money. At least we don't have a stupid hour time limit now."

Something snapped, cold and final, inside of Raynor. He looked down at the two sacks of creds he held, then opened his hands. They dropped to the floor, spilling their contents. Jim lifted his gaze.

"I'm done," was all he said. He turned around and strode to the door.

"Don't you touch that door," snarled Ash. "Raynor! *Raynor!*"

Jim kept moving.

And the bullet ripped through him.

CHAPTER NINETEEN

Jim grunted as the bullet seared his right shoulder and heard Tychus bellow in fury. Jim whirled, gun in hand, to face Ash. But Tychus had beaten him to it.

Tychus hadn't bothered with a weapon. He *was* one.

He grasped Ash by the lapels as if the other man weighed nothing at all and slammed him hard into the wall. Ash went limp as a puppet when the strings were cut. Tychus dropped him at once. Ash lay where he had fallen, his head at an impossible angle.

Rafe and Win had been so surprised by the speed of this turn of events that they were only now just drawing their own weapons. Jim, gritting his teeth against the pain of his wounded shoulder, lifted his gun and fired. His arm was unsteady due to the injury and wavered slightly. The bullet took Win in the upper chest instead of the head, and the man grunted and dropped his weapon.

Jim started to fire again, but Tychus was there. He had Rafe's throat in one powerful hand and crunched down hard even as he sprang onto the wounded Win.

"You . . . don't . . . shoot . . . my . . . *friend*!" he grunted, punctuating each word with a solid punch into Win's thin, ratty-looking face. By the time he had reached the word "shoot" Win's face was a bloody mess, and by the time he reached "friend," it was obvious the man was dead.

But Rafe wasn't. He was still struggling. Jim lifted his gun, steadied his arm with his other hand, and fired into Rafe's chest.

There was silence in the bank as Jim and Tychus caught their breath. Tychus was spattered in blood. He turned to Jim with a large grin.

"It stopped bein' about the money," was all he said. "Let's take a look at that shoulder."

They had gotten very good at field medicine, and within a few moments Tychus had packed the wound with antibiotics from a small kit he'd brought with him and bound it tightly. "You're a lucky son of a bitch. Bullet went clean through."

"Search Ash," Jim said. "Make sure we got everything we need."

Tychus went to the broken body and quickly went through Ash's pockets. "Good call," he said. "He's got the key to the penthouse." He relieved the corpse of everything else of value as well.

A thin whimper reached their ears. "Woodley," Jim said remorsefully. He'd forgotten all about the man. "Don't worry. If we weren't gonna shoot you on the train, we sure as hell ain't gonna shoot you now. But I'm afraid we gotta disable you for a bit."

Woodley looked relieved. "Of course you do," he said. "I certainly understand. Are you gonna, um, knock me out?"

Jim glanced around. His eye fell on the lifeless bodies of their former cohorts. "Nah. Just going to truss you up a bit. Tychus, get their ties?"

Three minutes later, George Woodley beamed up at them as Tychus bound Woodley's hands and feet with Ash's and Rafe's ties. Tychus let a big hand fall almost affectionately on Woodley's head.

"You are one lucky devil, George Woodley. You should write your memoirs: *How I Survived Two Robberies by Tychus Findlay and James Raynor.*"

"Be kind to us in the retelling, will ya?" Jim said, grinning.

"Of course, sirs, you know I will!"

"I believe you," Jim said, and he did. "And . . . I'm glad you told me where the money came from."

Woodley gave him an oddly sweet smile. "You're mighty welcome, Mr. Raynor. I knew something had to be wrong. You just wasn't the type to steal from poor people who needed that money so bad."

A lump rose in Jim's throat. "No. No, I ain't. Thanks for stopping me from doing that."

"I hate to break up this sweet scene, but time is ticking by, and we did announce our presence by blowing a safe and firing weapons," Tychus said. "Let's get a move on."

The elevator had been one of the casualties of the EMP, and they didn't dare risk the stairs. Tychus had been right: once the safe had been blown, the residents and employees of various businesses located in the Covington Bank building had been tipped off to something more than just a pesky power outage. The luxury suite was fourteen stories up. In their planning, they had intended to make sure that the elevator car would be on the same floor as the bank when the EMP hit. It was there now, too—either that's where it spent most of its time, or they had just been lucky. Tychus quickly popped open the hatch on the roof and stuck his head up.

"My arm's pretty bad, Tychus," Jim said. "I don't know if I can climb this."

"Well, Jimmy, I sure as hell ain't leaving you to the authorities," Tychus said, hauling himself up to sit on the roof of the car, "so you'd better try."

It was a hot day, and the vehicle that Wilkes Butler had rented was not the most comfortable, but he bore it stoically. Because he was certain that his vigil would bear fruit.

He had been up all night, but it had been worth it. His research efforts had turned up what Butler was almost certain was the reason Jim Raynor and Tychus Findlay were on Bacchus Moon at this particular point in time.

One, he knew they would have done their research, and would likely not have scheduled a "visit" during an Interstellar Marshals Convention if their little caper could have been done at any other point in time. For instance, if they'd had some kind of gambling gig in place, they could have waited four days.

No, they were here because they *had* to be here. Which meant that something specific was going on.

Further research and calling in a few favors had revealed the likely target: the Covington Bank was going to be the repository of several million credits for a period of thirty-seven hours. And that sounded exactly like the sort of thing that would interest Findlay and Raynor.

Butler had alerted the bank to increase their security, even giving them descriptions of Raynor and Findlay, and had been rather snippily told that "The Covington Bank, sir, *always* operates under the highest level of security available. I'm sure your tip will be appreciated, but I am also sure it is unnecessary."

That had not been motivation for him to press the matter. He almost thought that such arrogance deserved what it got, but he was a lawman, and he badly wanted to collar these two. So he had had stakeouts operating from the moment he figured out what was going on, and now it was his shift from 0800 to 1600.

He had sat up when he saw the two approaching shortly before 1300. He almost didn't recognize them; they were certainly nattily dressed. But that was not what surprised him the most. There were three other men entering the bank with them, equally well dressed. Five total, then. Odd: usually Raynor and Findlay worked alone. Butler didn't like this. He didn't want to make a move without knowing the identity of these new comrades. Quickly, Butler vidsnapped a few pictures before the other three went in and transmitted them to his office with instructions to "find out who these three are."

The reply came back fairly quickly. Two were unidentifiable; the third, a fair-haired man, had a list of aliases as long as Wilkes's arm. The names didn't concern him. What did was the information tacked on at the end: "believed to have been or still be in the employ of Scutter O'Banon."

O'Banon was bad news. It surprised Butler that "his" criminals, as he thought of them, had fallen in with such bad company. This changed the game. He would need backup, and that would take at least a few minutes. He would not be able to collar them quietly now. To further complicate matters, once backup did arrive, a family, two parents and three children clearly playing tourist, had decided to stop for a rest on the green lawn in front of the bank and feed the birds. Wilkes fumed quietly. Time was ticking by.

In fact . . . he checked his chrono and frowned. It seemed to have stopped. His gaze fell on his dashboard: it was dark. Butler returned his attention to the bank. They had been in there a mighty long time. His instincts told him that something was very wrong indeed. He got out of the vehicle, his hand dropping to his weapon.

At that point he heard an explosion—muffled but unmistakable—from inside the bank. Butler seized his comm unit and found that it was dead. He swore. He turned and waved to one of his men, who had parked a distance away, and pointed at the bank. The man nodded and tried to comm in for backup . . . then Wilkes saw his face fall as he realized his equipment, too, had somehow been shorted out.

Damn them. He pulled out his weapon and raced toward the bank. Help would be coming eventually, but not immediately. For the moment, Wilkes Butler was on his own.

The climb up the elevator shaft was difficult.

Actually, the climb up the elevator shaft was pretty much hell. What seemed like kilometers of shiny metal loomed above them. Four stories would have been challenging; fourteen seemed impossible. There were, thankfully, service ladders attached to the sides at various points. No doubt those who paid the exorbitant costs of a luxury penthouse demanded that if there was any problem getting in and out of said penthouse, it would be attended to immediately.

Tychus pulled Jim up out of the elevator car and glanced up—and up—at the ladders. "Can you hang on to me, Jimmy?" he asked.

"I don't know," Jim answered honestly. "I'll try."

Tychus muttered and undid his belt. "Ain't good enough." Quickly, he made a loop with his belt and strapped it around Jim's shoulder, crossing it diagonally over his chest on the side opposite the injury. "Hang on to me as best you can, and I'll hang on to this."

With a curse, Tychus tied the bags containing the credits to the bottom rung of the first ladder, patting them fondly. "Soon as I get you up to the suite, Jimmy, I'm coming back for this. Love you like a brother, man, but you ain't about to cost me my retirement."

Jim managed a grin. He wrapped his arms around Tychus and clung for dear life. Tychus gripped the belt holding Jim with his left arm and used the right to climb, jerkily and one-handed, up the ladders. At one point, though, Jim's worry turned out to be completely justified. His arms gave way, and he dropped about a foot. Tychus grunted as his arm was nearly yanked out of its socket. His hand missed one bar, and they both dropped. At the last second, Tychus's powerful hand grabbed a rung, bringing them both to an abrupt halt so painful that Jim blacked out for an instant.

The last several ladders were a blur of pain to Jim. Later, he would dimly recall Tychus muttering and shoving and positioning him, sometimes ungently, but never, ever letting him give up. Jim knew, even in the red haze of agony, that no other man could have done this but Tychus Findlay.

For one thing, no other man would have been so stubborn.

Finally, they made it. Jim crawled out into

the dark corridor of the fourteenth story and lay panting. The pain was unspeakably bad; worse, it was starting to render his right arm almost useless. He was utterly dependent on Tychus, and they both knew it.

"On the left," Jim murmured, trying to get to his feet. Tychus saved him the effort by grasping his good arm and hauling him up. Jim nearly blacked out, but he fought to stay conscious.

There were only two penthouses on this level. O'Banon said he would "take care" of the residents in the one across the hall to ensure they would not be disturbed. The door had recently been fitted with an old-fashioned lock and key in addition to the extremely complicated alarm system that was now completely useless. Jim had to grin as he watched Tychus fumble for the key, so small in his massive hands, and open the door.

Still holding Jim by his good arm, Tychus swung it open.

"Holy shit," Tychus said.

They had apparently opened the door to one of the deeper levels of Hell.

For the first horrified instant, as the primal parts of their brains registered only what they saw and not the source of it, they simply stared at the multiple scenes of torture and carnage displayed before them.

Ezekiel Daun was everywhere. Right in front

of them, laughing at a woman who was bleeding from dozens of stab wounds but who was yet far from the mercy of death. Over by the fireplace, cutting off the head of Ryk Kydd. In the doorway to another room, collecting fingers from someone who begged him to stop. And there, and there, and *there*—

And the sounds. They had begun the second the door had opened, and the cacophony was overwhelming. The begging, the pleading: *"No, please, what is it you want? I'll tell you anything!"* *"Please stop . . . please . . . oh, God, just kill me!"* *"Who are you? Who the hell* are *you?"* And Daun's voice, promising more pain and suffering, and sometimes just . . . laughing.

"Beautiful, isn't it?" his voice came to them. "I can smell your fear. It's like perfume. Luck has been on your side, but not anymore. Which way do you want to go? Strangled? Stabbed? Mr. Raynor already has one gunshot wound. I can give him matching ones."

This couldn't be happening. After all the tension of planning the heist, finding out about the source of the money—the fight—Jim was already near breaking. This threatened to put him over the brink.

Daun. Always Daun. They couldn't escape him, no matter how they tried.

Then suddenly Tychus's lips were near his

ear, and the bigger man hissed, "Stay strong, Jimmy: the bastard loves to gloat. Let's keep him gloating."

Shaking, hanging on by a thread, Jim nodded. Tychus was right: Daun did love to gloat; he loved to scare them, and even though they had somehow managed to elude the bounty hunter twice—which had to be some sort of record, he thought wildly—Daun wasn't about to just shoot them and be done with it.

Tychus had already drawn his weapon, and now Jim did likewise, his wounded hand slowing him. He tried to remember what the escape plan had been. Things were fuzzy now, and he realized he had lost a lot of blood. Focus, damn it, Jim, focus. . . .

They had to get out of here, away from the fourteenth story. What was the escape plan? Ash had told them; why couldn't he remember—

"You son of a bitch," Tychus said, "you think you've got us? Well, remember what happened the last time. We rubbed your face in it, you sick bastard. I'm going to give you a one-fingered salute when we give you the slip this time."

He was pointing his gun in various directions, ready to shoot but not until he had a certain clear shot. He let go of Jim, and Jim nodded, indicating he could stand on his own. Tychus pointed to one side of the room and then began to move slowly toward the other. Daun's laughter came from somewhere.

"I'm almost tempted to let you live, you know. Keep you for my own amusement. I've not had so enjoyable a chase in a long, long time. But alas, I am a businessman, and I have a contract to fulfill."

Climb down? Jim thought frantically. No, that wasn't it. Jump. Something about jumping down and running away too fast to be followed. But that was crazy talk. It was impossible; no one could jump from this height and hit the ground running fast enough to elude their would-be captors—

He began to move, slowly and unsteadily, around the penthouse, using the light given off by the holograms and the fire burning so incongruously cheerily in the fireplace. Ash had said that the resident had—

Jim found one of the penthouse residents, almost falling over him, as he had suspected he would. Frustration and despair threatened to consume him. How many had Daun killed now, trying to get him and Tychus? How many had died down in that bank lobby? This had to end. Had to.

But it wouldn't. They couldn't beat him. It was too hard, just too hard. All the dead, whirling around him like ghosts, crying out for vengeance. He couldn't give it to them.

I'm sorry, Ryk. I'm sorry, Hiram, and Clair, and all you poor sons of bitches down in that lobby. I'm so sorry.

"Contract," drawled Tychus.

"You sound like you've got fine business ethics there, Daun. Too bad you don't have any other kind," snarled Jim. He stared at the corpse in front of him, scarcely visible in the faint light. It looked like a dummy rather than what had once been a living, breathing human being.

"Morals are such slippery things, ain't they, Jim Raynor?" said Daun. "They're so flexible. So adaptable. How are *your* morals doing now?"

A dummy . . . Jim turned his head and did a double take at what looked like another figure looming over him, this one strangely bulky and ominous but, like the body on the floor, one that didn't move. And then he remembered how they were planning to get out. Or at least, *had* been planning to get out before Daun had appeared like some sort of unstoppable Grim Reaper.

"Since you're gonna kill us," Tychus continued, moving with surprisingly slow grace in the room, attempting to locate their hunter, "why don't you just tell us who put the contract out on us? It'd be right gentlemanly of you to send us to our graves with that particular question answered."

"If I had more time, I don't think I would

answer that. At least, not right away . . . ," Daun said. He had been in several places, thanks to the holograms, but as Jim kept moving slowly, he caught a glimpse of something in a mirror. A small red dot that moved.

For an instant, he thought it was a targeting device that Daun was using, but that didn't make sense. If it were such a device, it would be focused on him or Tychus. Then, somehow, his muzzy brain understood with brilliant clarity.

So this was how Daun could see them so clearly. Jim wasn't seeing a red dot that indicated a targeting laser. He was seeing Daun's new eye. The bounty hunter already had a cybernetic arm. Thanks to Jim's attack the last time they had met—in the lab—he now had an ocular implant.

Despite the direness of the situation, Jim found himself smiling. Daun no doubt thought he had a leg up on them. He didn't realize that he was revealing his location. Judging from the way the mirror was positioned, Daun would be standing right about . . .

Jim lifted his wounded arm, biting back a shriek of agony, and pointed the pistol. He didn't dare say anything to Tychus, and could only hope his friend was paying attention to his movements.

". . . No, I'd string you along for a bit," Daun continued. The arrogant bastard wasn't even aiming his pistol. Though Jim could barely see

Daun in the dark, he could have sworn the man was grinning, as happy as a pig in mud. "But alas, our time together, gentlemen, is running out. So I think I will do as you request, Tychus Findlay. I will enlighten you."

Jim had a clear shot at Daun now, but he didn't take it. His arm quivered from the strain, red-hot pain becoming white-hot with every second he delayed, but he couldn't kill Daun. Not until he knew who had been responsible for siccing this bastard on them.

"My employer for this particular assignment is one Javier Vanderspool."

Jim staggered. Vanderspool? His vision swirled, becoming gray around the edges. Impossible. That evil . . . *thing* . . . was dead. Jim had seen to it himself. He felt his gorge rise. It couldn't be. This had to be a lie . . . one of Daun's sick little games.

"That ain't right," Tychus said. "Jim done put that mad dog down a while ago."

"You're wrong." In the center of the room, another hologram sprang to life. Jim lowered his weapon, staring. The hologram depicted a sort of giant mechanical coffin. A man was encased in it, all of him except his head. It was a dark location, and strain as Jim might, he couldn't identify the man.

And then he spoke.

"Ezekiel Daun."

Vanderspool. Dear God. It was true. He *was* alive . . . if you could call that living. . . .

Blood thundered in his ears. The words were garbled; they made no sense as Daun and Vanderspool spoke. Jim and Tychus watched as Daun drew something out of a bag.

It was Ryk Kydd's head.

Casually, Daun tossed it toward the man in the iron coffin.

Jim's stomach heaved, but with a will he hadn't realized he had, he refused to betray himself. Something had awakened deep inside him and was clawing its way upward, past the despair and the fear.

"It's a start, Mr. Daun. I believe you have two more left, don't you? Don't come back until your satchel bulges with two other trophies: Tychus Findlay and James Raynor."

"Don't worry, old man. They're next," came Daun's voice from the hologram. The image froze.

"And I'm afraid," Daun said with mock resignation, "that you are indeed next. Good-bye, Mr. Findlay, Mr. Raynor."

Jim fired about a foot below the glowing ocular implant.

The red dot vanished as Daun went down.

"Got you, you son of a bitch," Jim murmured. He swayed and then fell to the floor.

*   *   *

He awoke presumably a very short while later to find himself face-to-face with what looked like a hardskin. There was a loud banging that he suspected came from his own head.

"There you are, Jimmy," Tychus said. "Thought I'd lost you for a minute."

"Daun?"

"Ain't had time for an autopsy, but looks like you nailed him good. He won't be bothering us no more. Now, get into this thing and let's get out of here."

Jim now realized that the banging did not come from his head but from outside the penthouse suite. And the hardskin was not one of the standard-issue suits he and Tychus were familiar with from their days as marines; it was something much more advanced.

O'Banon had promised them five prototypes of a new, superior suit in order to make their escape. Equipped with grenade launchers on the arms, able to do everything the standard suits could and then some, the hardskins would enable the men to blast their way through the wall, jump easily to the street, thanks to a slow-fall modification, and race off, demolishing anyone attempting to stop them, until they reached the rendezvous point.

"Supposed to be five," Jim muttered. There

was only one, which Tychus was holding out to him now.

"I know," Tychus said. "Son of a bitch O'Bastard never intended for anyone but his pet Ass to survive this. That's why he was so generous in his terms with us. He was gonna leave you and me and the other two behind."

"Somehow I ain't surprised," Jim said.

"You ain't got time for I-told-you-so's, Jimmy," Tychus said. With one hand, he hauled Raynor to his feet and began to help him into the suit. Jim hissed as his arm was maneuvered into position. "This thing'll keep you alive long enough to get out."

The banging increased. Now there was a wail of sirens from somewhere.

Suddenly Tychus's words registered. "Tychus, you can't stay here!" Jim exclaimed.

Tychus didn't look at him as he snapped shut multiple clasps, sealing Jim inside the armored suit. "Jimmy, we got only one suit. And I know you wouldn't have been part of this thing if you'd known what the money was for. I lied to you, and that weren't right. You got a chance to get clear of all this. You're gonna even if I have to knock you out and set this thing on autopilot."

There was, of course, no way to set the suit on autopilot. Jim stared at his friend. "You can't hold them off by yourself," he said quietly.

"You insulting my masculinity, boy?" Tychus said bluffly. "Hell, I can handle these guys, no problem. And by the way, since you're too good to take the money, it's all mine."

"Tychus—"

With a hiss, the helmet sealed shut. "Go, damn it."

Jim turned, moving toward one of the windows, the suit feeling both familiar and strange to him. He lifted one of the arms, experimentally pressed something, and blinked as an enormous chunk of wall was suddenly blown out. Jim paused, then turned back to Tychus.

Tychus had his back to him. He had shucked the fine dress shirt along with the vest that had once housed the deadly mechanical spiders, and now stood only in an undershirt, suit trousers, and boots. He had a weapon in each massive hand and was facing the door, ready for when it would give way—which it would at any moment.

"I can't do this," Jim said.

Tychus whirled. His face was hard, set in the expression he wore right before he dealt death and destruction on a scale that was almost not human. But there was a look in his eyes that Jim had never seen there before.

"James Raynor," Tychus Findlay said in a calm, quiet voice that nonetheless somehow carried over the cacophony of pounding, shouting, and wailing sirens. "You once agreed with me when I said I'd never done a noble thing in my life. That I never could, that I just wasn't capable of it. I thought you was right, but you ain't. Go on, now. Get out, get clean, and do something with your life. You got the chance to do that. Don't take that away from me—not here, not now."

He turned back to the door. Jim stared at Tychus, wanting to find some parting words to sum up everything he felt for this unlikely friend. How much he appreciated the laughter, the skin-of-their-teeth escapes, the rowdiness of their partnership, the trust they'd developed over the years. But they couldn't get past the lump in his throat. Tychus nodded briefly, then turned to meet his fate.

Hell, Jimmy, I ain't any more capable of doing something noble than of jumping off the roof and flying.

He wasn't going to walk away from this. Jim Raynor knew he was watching Tychus Findlay's last stand. Then the words came of their own volition.

"I know you didn't cheat me, Tychus."

Tychus didn't turn around, but he seemed to straighten slightly. "No, Jimmy, I never did. And I know you didn't, neither."

It was enough.

Raynor turned and faced the glaring light of

the sunny day that bombarded the darkness of the room. For a moment he stood on the edge of the gaping hole he had blown into the wall. Below was green grass, and streets, and freedom.

Below was a second chance to become the sort of man his parents had raised him to be. To walk in that sunlight without looking over his shoulder.

Slowly, James Raynor lifted his arms, jumped out the window, and flew.

They were not fighting a man, Wilkes Butler thought wildly as the door gave way and they poured into the room. They were fighting a monster.

Holograms, too many to count quickly, were playing, each a danse macabre. The central figure in each one of the brutal scenarios was a man who seemed to have a cybernetic arm. Members of the local lawmen whom Butler had rounded up came to a full halt for several seconds on witnessing the bizarre scene, trying to figure out what was real and what wasn't. That sudden, shocked pause cost some of them their lives as the real adversary used that to his advantage.

Tychus Findlay was alone in the room. He had a gun in each hand and was firing away, screaming as he did so. Butler dove for a pillar in the vast penthouse and kept trying to get a clear shot, but

Findlay was surrounded by wave after wave of law officers, who injured themselves more than him in the cross fire. Bullets and iron spikes embedded themselves in the walls and the furniture, pinging chips off the marble behind which Butler had taken cover. And all the while that nerve-shattering bellow, the war cry of a trapped animal determined to take as many with him as possible when he went down, filled the room.

Butler kept his head and took stock of the situation quickly. Findlay had two weapons but apparently no spare magazines. There were two bodies on the floor that were not law officers. Neither of them was Raynor. Raynor's body was also not among those found in the lobby, and the single surviving witness had said both Raynor and Findlay had escaped.

Conclusion: Raynor had escaped, and Findlay was taking the fall.

Tychus Findlay therefore had nothing to lose. Butler swallowed hard.

He leaned over, took aim, and fired. Findlay grunted as a bullet embedded itself in his arm. His head snapped around, and his eyes locked with Butler's. A grin curved his mouth as he brought one of the guns around and pointed it right at the marshal.

It clicked. Empty.

Findlay didn't even slow down. He charged

toward Butler, who stepped out from behind the protection of the pillar. Butler took slow and careful aim—

Four of the armored cops jumped on Tychus. He shook them off as if they were so many flies, but they kept coming. Three more sprang on him, including Wilkes Butler. Even now Tychus Findlay tried to rise, but he had been wounded in the fight, and at last they had him pinned.

Butler snapped a pair of handcuffs on the bull of a man and stood over him, panting. Paramedics were already swarming over the wounded. He did a quick count: almost twenty. Some of them were far too still. He turned his gaze back to the man who lay before him, blood flowing from at least half a dozen places.

"Marshal Butler," came a voice, "this one's still alive."

Butler glanced away to see one of the paramedics tending to one of the bodies that had been in the penthouse before they had broken in. His eyes widened. The man had a cybernetic arm . . . and an ocular implant. Butler glanced up at the still-playing holograms, then back at the man on the floor.

"Hell's bells," he said. "That's Ezekiel Daun."

"Aw, for fekk's sake," muttered Findlay, "won't that bastard just die already?" His voice was strangely thick, and as Butler turned to regard him, Findlay spat out a great deal of blood and a few teeth.

"Patch Daun up and arrest him," he told his deputy. He thought about the bounty hunter's reputation. "That's someone who really needs to be behind bars."

"This the best you could do, Butler?" drawled Findlay. "Just the sort of pansy-ass takedown attempt I'd expect from someone dillydallying at a convention. Couldn't even kill me."

Butler's nostrils flared with anger. For so, so long, he had been chasing Raynor and Findlay. Findlay had gotten away every time, often with some scathing insult. But now the tables had turned. Tychus Findlay had finally been caught—by Marshal Wilkes Butler. He yearned desperately to find fitting words to humiliate this man, who had led him on such a merry chase— something memorable to quote as he told the story again and again over the years.

Tychus's grin widened, though it had to be a painful gesture. The seconds ticked by.

"Well?" said Tychus Findlay.

"You're under arrest," was all Marshal Wilkes Butler could say.

Tychus laughed.

CHAPTER TWENTY

MAR SARA

There was, mused Myles Hammond, about the same amount of papers to push here as on Shiloh. And there was red tape—because there was *always* red tape. But the furniture and supplies in his office were newer, and there was a lot less dust.

Best of all, when he pushed the papers and cut through the red tape, papers stayed pushed, and tape stayed cut. Things . . . got done. There were no veiled offers of bribes, no looking the other way. No trying to get something taken care of, only to find unexpected obstacles. He was now Magistrate Myles Hammond, and he was making a difference.

So it was that despite the pile of work on his

desk, he was whistling as he brewed a fresh pot of coffee and his door swung open.

He did a double take and started to grin. "Well, if it ain't Jim Raynor."

"Magistrate Myles Hammond," Jim said, walking up to his old friend and shaking his hand. He looked around. "Bigger office. Nicer title."

"Better chance of actually doing something useful," Myles said, handing Jim a cup of coffee.

Jim nodded his thanks and took a sip. "Better coffee here too. So . . . this is your little slice of perfection."

Myles chuckled and took a sip. "No, it ain't perfect. But it beats Shiloh, that's for sure. At least there's some decency here. Some damned honesty. People look out for one another instead of just themselves. They help. And my hands aren't tied here, so I can help too." He gave Jim a fond, proud look. "Welcome home, Jim."

"Whoa, whoa," Jim said, "I didn't say I was staying. Came to take a look-see is all. And I'm still looking."

"I think you'll like what you see," Myles said. "These parts . . . well, like I said, there's decency here. But you know as well as I do—hell, maybe better than I do—that when there are decent folks, there's people looking to take advantage of them. Mar Sara still needs some law to make sure that decency doesn't vanish. A man who understands both sides of that situation could really make a fine marshal."

Jim chuckled and scratched his nose. "You gotta be out of your mind, Myles."

Myles raised an eyebrow. "I don't think you came all the way out here, sneaking the whole way, just to have a cup of coffee—mighty fine though it is."

Jim shrugged and turned away, sipping his coffee. Myles continued.

"There'd be something in it for you other than altruism," he said. Jim turned his head slightly, listening. "I can offer you clemency."

"It was just a job you were offering back on Shiloh," Jim said. "You can really give me clemency?"

"Absolutely. It's within my authority as magistrate here."

"What would I have to do?"

"Be my right hand," Myles said. "Be my marshal. Get out there and protect the good folks and catch the bad. You do that, and I can promise that clemency's yours."

Jim finished the coffee and set the cup down on the desk. "Well, Myles, I gotta say, you make some mighty fine coffee here." He moved toward the door. Myles grasped his arm.

"Jimmy—marshal's where I can use you the most. Where you'll be able to make the most difference and—clichéd as it's gonna sound—do the most good. But the offer stands for anything you want. Even if you're just working for me filing papers, you'll have clemency."

Jim paused at the door to put on his hat. He turned to Myles. "I won't lie to you, Myles. After all I've seen and done . . . it's mighty tempting. But before I can tell you yes or no, there's something I need to put to bed first."

Something in his voice made Myles's eyes narrow, but he nodded. "You go on and do what you gotta do. I respect that. Offer's always on the table. After all"—and he winked—"it's not like Mar Sara is going anywhere."

The moment had been long in coming.

Raynor had begun planning it as soon as he jumped out of the Covington Bank building. It had been forming in the back of his mind as the modified prototype hardskin took him through the city, fighting off pursuit, outrunning and outgunning it until he got far enough away to break into an abandoned building and shuck the suit. He continued to elude capture the next day, finally managing to sneak out on foot to where the ship was waiting for him. The poor pilot seemed confused to see Jim instead of Ash, but went along with it long enough to give Jim the chance to knock him out and commandeer the vessel.

Then the journey had begun. Researching. Digging up old contacts who owed him favors. Getting in good with the right people. Five years of criminal activity harnessed, sifted, and milked dry to find out what he needed to learn, to do, to become, in order to put the plan into action.

For seven months, Raynor had been investigating something that made the heists he and Tychus had pulled seem noble. There was a black market for a very specific type of commodity—hard to learn about, harder to locate. It involved not just trafficking in goods but in humans—and not just the selling of bodies but of souls, minds, and hearts.

Unlike Tychus, Jim had not spent all his money like water—well, not quite—and was able to grease more than a few palms. He had next to nothing, now, at least with regard to funds—but he had something more important. He had the ID, the cover, the codes . . .

. . . and the room location.

He had easily negotiated the labyrinthine building's twists and turns. While he had never physically been inside before, he had been here a thousand times via a hologram he had had privately constructed, based on expensively stolen blueprints. He stood dressed in the white uniform of the resocs who had access to this, the inner sanctum of what was the modern equivalent of a medieval fortress.

As if to confirm the analogy, the resocs called it "the master's quarters." The door before him was large, dark, sinister. Considering whom it housed, Jim thought that was quite apt.

He looked at the door, and thought that he and Tychus had blown safes that seemed less secure. The thought made him recall the train robbery, and Woodley, and the jukebox, and Wilkes Butler. Already, the memories had a nostalgic quality to them. The taste of something that had passed.

Soon he would feel the same way about the next few minutes.

He looked over at the security pad. The code was not a problem. It was triply secured: the correctly entered code, fingerprint identification, and a retinal scan were all required. As he had managed to get himself hired by forging a completely new and thoroughly verifiable identity, this should be easy.

His "new identity" was as a resoc.

Raynor noticed that his hand trembled slightly as he entered the code, and forced himself to be calm.

The massive barricade slid open. It was even more dimly lit inside than in the corridor. Jim hadn't been expecting this and closed his eyes as the door closed behind him, helping them adjust quicker despite the burning desire to behold his enemy.

In front of him was a metal contraption that looked like a large coffin. Jim's lips twitched in a bitter smile at the appropriateness of the image. Lights flickered along the outside in a running pattern, and various tubes went in and out through small apertures. Jim's eyes strained, but he could make out only the barest outline of a head extending from the end of the metal box. A short distance away, a large bellows worked slowly and methodically, emitting a dull thunking sound as it operated.

This was what Ezekiel Daun had showed him and Tychus when he had revealed who had hired him to kill them. This room, this metal box . . . this shell of a man inside it.

Jim forced himself to turn his attention to the resoc standing off to the side in front of a screen, carefully examining rolling statistics. His hand dropped to his pocket and closed about a syringe.

The resoc looked up at him. "You're new," he said, frowning slightly.

"Yes, I am. I just got started a few days ago. I'm so pleased to be here." Jim stuck his hand out and smiled cheerfully, receiving a handshake and smile in return.

"How is the master doing today?" Raynor asked, feigning interest in the scrolling statistics.

"His condition hasn't changed much. He—"

The resoc gasped in pain at the sudden sharp needle stab, turned confused eyes on Jim for a few seconds, and then crumpled. Jim checked to make sure the man was really out—and that he would be out for a while—then rose and turned to the coffin.

"What's going on over there?"

The voice was hollow, weary, querulous. But it still had that same cool arrogance, and Jim was surprised at the quick flash flood of hatred that washed through him.

Javier Vanderspool.

He heard that voice again dripping contempt, snarling in anger. Heard it issuing commands. Heard it pathetically begging.

Jim's hand slipped into the other pocket and closed on the handle of his Colt.

He didn't answer at once. Partly because he wanted the bastard to sweat. And partly because he didn't trust his voice.

He relaxed his grip on the revolver, though he kept his hand on it. He had not come here as a vengeful murderer. He had come here for something else entirely.

"Who is this?"

"A ghost from your past, Colonel. Just the past, coming back to haunt you."

There was silence. The thunking noise continued. "I know that voice. Come over to where I can see you!" Vanderspool barked.

"Of course, *sir.*"

He moved slowly to where the light seemed greatest. There was movement as Vanderspool craned his neck to look at him. Their eyes met.

"Raynor," Vanderspool said quietly.

"The same. You don't look so good, Colonel."

Silence.

"Your dog got caught. But not before he tipped us off as to who was holding the leash."

"You always were so damn smug," snarled Vanderspool. "You and Tychus. Well, Tychus isn't going to be seeing sunlight anytime soon. I will be content with that. And I've spent quite a lot of money making sure my facility is secure. You might have gotten in, but any second now you'll be stopped. I'll have you. I always get what I want in the end."

"You got the others," Jim agreed. He drew out the Colt, as always admiring the craftsmanship. "Your sick dog filmed everything. You two probably watched the holograms together while he fed you popcorn. But you ain't getting *me*, Colonel. There's a balance in this universe. I knew that once, and then forgot it. But I've had a lot happen to me since then, and I remember it now. When I learned who was behind Daun, I wanted to kill you so bad, I could have ripped you apart with my teeth."

Despite his bluster, Vanderspool had to know that help wasn't coming. It would have been here by now. Why should it? Jim was a duly hired employee. He had access to this room. The weight of the gun was familiarly heavy in his hand.

"Yes, brave, noble outlaw James Raynor," drawled Vanderspool. "How tragically wronged you were. You rob from the rich, give to the poor, help little old ladies across streets, no doubt. It takes such courage to shoot a completely harmless man trapped in an iron lung."

Jim smiled in the dim light. "See, that's the whole point, Colonel. You ain't never gonna be harmless as long as you draw breath—even if you have to rely on a machine to draw that breath for you. Only reason you're even alive is that you're just too full of hate and twisted darkness to die properly the first time like you shoulda done. That's partly my fault. I was so damned angry, I couldn't see straight." The moment was as clear in his mind as if it had been one of Daun's holograms. Vanderspool, wounded, clutching his shoulder and sobbing. Begging for a medic. Offering to pay.

Pay. Like the soldiers he had tried to kill, control, or turn into resocialized zombies would accept money from him to tend his injury.

Vanderspool had first tried Tychus, then Kydd. Raynor had deliberately stepped on the man's hand as the bastard reached for a weapon, crunching the fine bones and relishing the screaming that resulted. He had fired a metal spike into Vanderspool's chest, watched him slump and, he thought, die. There had been a harsh pleasure—and then an ashy emptiness as he realized that he had become part of what he most loathed.

He had spent five years running since then. He thought he'd been running *to* something— but he'd been running *from* it. It was time to end the running.

It was time to end a lot of things—and to begin others.

"But I can see clearly now. And I know what has to be done."

"You can still get out of here alive," Vanderspool said. "Just walk out the way you came in. Tychus Findlay is going to rot in prison. I can afford to let you go."

Jim stared for a moment, completely taken aback by the sheer arrogance of the man. Then he laughed. It echoed in the large room.

"You still think you're in charge. Directing

the show, even if you can't act in it anymore. I used to hate you. Now I just feel sorry for you. And not because you're stuck in that contraption, neither. I feel sorry for you because all you got is hate, and control, and greed. I got more than that. But as long as you're alive, I'm stuck down here in the mud with you, Vanderspool. And I'm aiming to finally crawl out of the mud."

"I'll pay you."

"What?"

"Whatever you'd like. Enough for you to be comfortable the rest of your life. You don't have to do this. I'll leave you alone, I swear."

Jim shook his head, disgusted. He lifted the gun, as he had so many times before. With his thumb, he eased back the hammer, hearing the familiar and distinctive series of clicks. Vanderspool heard it, too, and actually whimpered.

"Please . . . look at the sort of life I'm consigned to, Raynor. Surely this is revenge enough!"

Incredulous, Raynor snorted, even more surprised by this tactic than Vanderspool's arrogance. "You're not helpless, and you fekking know it. You've done more harm from here than most people do in their whole lifetimes. From this damned coffin, you hired Daun. From here, you took delight in watching the Heaven's Devils fall, one by one. Because that's all you got, you sick shit. You're a rabid dog, Vanderspool.

You will continue to harm, and contaminate, and destroy as long as you are permitted to exist. Even if you did keep your word to let me alone, which we both know you won't, some other poor bastard is going to pay for some imaginary sin against you. You'll never stop. You'll think of another person, and another, and another. I once shot you in hate. I ain't doing that again."

"Your revenge—"

"Don't you get it?" Jim shouted. "This ain't about revenge. This is about justice. About restoring the balance. About taking something dark and ugly out of the galaxy once and for all, so that something—something decent and good—can grow instead."

He strode up to Vanderspool and gazed down at the remnants of the man. The face was pale, the eyes sunken. The being before him was so shriveled, so worn, that Jim almost hesitated. But then the lips thinned, the eyes flashed with hate.

No. Vanderspool's body might be crippled, but the essence of the man was as vile and as strong as ever. "This is for the Heaven's Devils," Jim said quietly. "For everyone who was their friend. And for everyone whose life you have ruined along your way to this moment."

He kept his gaze locked with Vanderspool's as he pulled the trigger.

The gunshot was shockingly loud and seemed to go on forever. Slowly, Jim lowered the gun, not flinching at the sight of the ruined face. This time there was no sick gnawing at his gut that he had become the thing he despised. Nor hot, glorious, righteous delight.

Just peace. Just quiet in his soul.

The rabid dog would never harm anyone, ever again.

The hologram that had been playing in his mind's eye shifted. It was no longer of him standing over Vanderspool and shooting him.

Instead, he saw his father, and heard words that echoed more loudly in his soul than that final gunshot in his ears.

Do you remember what I used to tell you, Son? A man is what he chooses to be . . . a man can turn his life around in a single thought, a single decision. You can always choose to be something new. Never forget that.

I won't forget, Dad. I won't. Maybe I'm not the man you thought I'd be . . . but that don't mean I'm not capable of being what I choose.

Jim looked at the gun for a long moment, remembering when his fingers had first closed about it; how it had fitted his hand perfectly; how he had felt at that instant that it had somehow been waiting for him—that it had been made just for him. And perhaps it had been: made for the man who was a thief and a criminal, who pointed it at innocent, frightened people. It still fit his hand, but it no longer fit *him*.

Slowly, James Raynor placed the antique Colt Single Action Army revolver on top of the metal coffin, turned, and walked out.

EPILOGUE

MAR SARA
JANINE'S

The bar was one of the smaller, friendlier ones Jim had run across. Cleaner, too, and brighter. Of course, he was here in the middle of the day, not at oh-dark-thirty like he usually was when he visited such establishments, so that probably made at least some difference.

He'd ordered a beer. One. Without Scotty Bolger's Old No. 8. And he'd been nursing it for the better part of an hour, settling his lanky frame into an old, comfortable chair and simply thinking and observing.

Oddly, he found his thoughts turning to Marshal Wilkes Butler. He and Tychus had made fun of the marshal's methodical, unimaginative pursuit of them. And yet . . . Jim found himself respecting the man. Tychus and he had been almost impossibly wily—half the time, because they never knew what they were going to do themselves. And yet, Butler had come after them time and time again, doggedly, doing everything by the book, until finally he'd gotten at least one of them. He'd not been seduced by Daisy's charms, nor used underhanded methods, nor ever employed greater force than was necessary. He'd been—and Jim was surprised to find himself thinking this—a decent man.

Janine's was more of a gathering spot than a watering hole. There were few hard drinkers here, and the food was actually pretty good. Standard stuff for a bar—skalet burgers and fries and such—but some fried range hen was also on the menu that the bar owner, the cheerfully hefty brunette Janine, made fresh herself every day. He was gnawing on a drumstick when the door opened.

"Afternoon, Liddy!" called Janine. "The usual?"

Still chewing the delicious range hen—Janine used some kind of spice that made it really zingy—Jim turned idly to see the newcomer.

She was slim and tanned and exuded that wholesome fresh-scrubbed appeal that women strove to attain through artfully messy hair and makeup carefully applied so as to not look applied at all. This woman didn't need to bother with artifice to look beautifully natural.

Her long blond hair, the color of the triticale-wheat his family used to harvest back on Shiloh, was tied in a careless braid and draped over her shoulder. Her eyes were sky blue and crinkled at the edges when she grinned. Her tanned face had just the faintest smattering of freckles.

"Heya, Janine. You bet: it's a hot one today." Her voice was as cheerful and warm as the rest of her.

Jim lifted an eyebrow as something sunny yellow was plunked down in front of the new-comer.

"Don't tell me that's lemonade," he said before he could stop himself. It wouldn't be made from actual lemons, of course. It was synthetic, but everyone had their own recipe, adjusted to their particulars.

"Best in the county," Janine said with pride.

"The county? Janine's range hen, potato salad, cobbler, and lemonade beat any other meal on the whole planet," asserted the incredibly gorgeous girl.

"Okay, you got me curious. I'll agree with you on the chicken, so, Janine, a lemonade here, too, please. And this lady's serving is on me."

The girl raised a golden eyebrow and toasted him with the beverage. A moment later Jim was drinking something cool, tangy-sweet, and utterly refreshing. He couldn't remember the last time he had had lemonade. It had to have been back on Shiloh, some hot summer's day when his mother had come out to the field with a cooler full of food and a vacuum flask of lemonade. Jim had been sweaty, exhausted, sunburned, and, he realized, probably happier than he had ever been since.

"Don't like it?" The voice of the wheat-haired angel brought him back to the present. He realized he'd just been sitting, holding the glass since he'd taken the first sip.

"Oh . . . yeah, love it, actually. Just . . . brought back memories. I grew up on a farm."

She looked at him for a moment, then slipped into the chair beside him. Sticking out a hand that looked calloused and strong, she said, "I'm Lidya. But everyone calls me Liddy."

Jim's fingers closed around her hand, and he shook it. She had a good grip—firm, friendly. "Nice to meet you, Liddy. That's a pretty name. I'm Jim Raynor."

"Nice to meet you, Jim Raynor." She tucked her legs up underneath her and leaned on the chair arm, chin on her hand, eyes bright with curiosity. "What do you do around these parts?"

Jim thought about Myles Hammond, his impassioned words about the decency of people on this world, and simply smiled.

STARCRAFT TIMELINE

c. 1500

A group of rogue protoss is exiled from the protoss homeworld of Aiur for refusing to join the Khala, a telepathic link shared by the entire race. These rogues, called the dark templar, ultimately settle on the planet of Shakuras. This split between the two protoss factions becomes known as the Discord.

(*StarCraft: Shadow Hunters*, book two of *The Dark Templar Saga* by Christie Golden)

(*StarCraft: Twilight*, book three of *The Dark Templar Saga* by Christie Golden)

1865

The dark templar Zeratul is born. He will later be instrumental in reconciling the severed halves of protoss society.

(*StarCraft: Twilight*, book three of *The Dark Templar Saga* by Christie Golden)

(*StarCraft: Queen of Blades* by Aaron Rosenberg)

2143

Tassadar is born. He will later be an executor of the Aiur protoss.

(*StarCraft: Twilight*, book three of *The Dark Templar Saga* by Christie Golden)

(*StarCraft: Queen of Blades* by Aaron Rosenberg)

c. 2259

Four supercarriers—the *Argo,* the *Sarengo,* the *Reagan,* and the *Nagglfar*—transporting convicts from Earth venture far beyond their intended destination and crash-land on planets in the Koprulu sector. The survivors settle on the planets Moria, Umoja, and Tarsonis and build new societies that grow to encompass other planets.

2323

Having established colonies on other planets, Tarsonis becomes the capital of the Terran Confederacy, a powerful but increasingly oppressive government.

2460

Arcturus Mengsk is born. He is a member of one of the Confederacy's elite Old Families.

(*StarCraft: I, Mengsk* by Graham McNeill)

(*StarCraft: Liberty's Crusade* by Jeff Grubb)

(*StarCraft: Uprising* by Micky Neilson)

2464

Tychus Findlay is born. He will later become good friends with Jim Raynor during the Guild Wars.

(*StarCraft: Heaven's Devils* by William C. Dietz)

2470

Jim Raynor is born. His parents are Trace and Karol Raynor, farmers on the fringe world of Shiloh.

(*StarCraft: Heaven's Devils* by William C. Dietz)

(*StarCraft: Liberty's Crusade* by Jeff Grubb)

(*StarCraft: Queen of Blades* by Aaron Rosenberg)

(*StarCraft: Frontline volume 4*, "Homecoming" by Chris Metzen and Hector Sevilla)

(*StarCraft* monthly comic #5-7 by Simon Furman and Federico Dallocchio)

2473

Sarah Kerrigan is born. She is a terran gifted with powerful psionic abilities.

(*StarCraft: Liberty's Crusade* by Jeff Grubb)

(*StarCraft: Uprising* by Micky Neilson)

(*StarCraft: Queen of Blades* by Aaron Rosenberg)

(*StarCraft: The Dark Templar Saga* by Christie Golden)

2478

Arcturus Mengsk graduates from the Styrling Academy and joins the Confederate Marine Corps against the wishes of his parents.

(*StarCraft: I, Mengsk* by Graham McNeill)

2485

Tensions rise between the Confederacy and the Kel-Morian Combine, a shady corporate partnership created by the Morian Mining Coalition and the Kelanis Shipping Guild to protect their mining interests from Confederate aggression. After the Kel-Morians ambush Confederate forces that are encroaching on the Noranda Glacier vespene mine, open warfare breaks out. This conflict comes to be known as the Guild Wars.

(*StarCraft: Heaven's Devils* by William C. Dietz)

(*StarCraft: I, Mengsk* by Graham McNeill)

2488–2489

Jim Raynor joins the Confederate Marine Corps and meets Tychus Findlay. In the later battles between the Confederacy and the Kel-Morian Combine, the 321st Colonial Rangers Battalion (whose membership includes Raynor and Findlay) comes to prominence for its expertise and bravado, earning it the nickname "Heaven's Devils." (*StarCraft: Heaven's Devils* by William C. Dietz)

Jim Raynor meets fellow Confederate soldier Cole Hickson in a Kel-Morian prison camp. During this encounter, Hickson teaches Raynor how to resist and survive the Kel-Morians' brutal torture methods. (*StarCraft: Heaven's Devils* by William C. Dietz) (*StarCraft* monthly comic #6 by Simon Furman and Federico Dallocchio)

Toward the end of the Guild Wars, Jim Raynor and Tychus Findlay go AWOL from the Confederate military.

Arcturus Mengsk resigns from the Confederate military after achieving the rank of colonel. He then becomes a successful prospector in the galactic rim. (*StarCraft: I, Mengsk* by Graham McNeill)

After nearly four years of war, the Confederacy "negotiates" peace with the Kel-Morian Combine, annexing almost all of the

Kel-Morians' supporting mining guilds. Despite this massive setback, the Kel-Morian Combine is allowed to continue its existence and retain its autonomy.

Arcturus Mengsk's father, Confederate senator Angus Mengsk, declares the independence of Korhal IV, a core world of the Confederacy that has long been at odds with the government. In response, three Confederate ghosts—covert terran operatives with superhuman psionic powers enhanced by cutting-edge technology—assassinate Angus, his wife, and their young daughter. Furious at the murder of his family, Arcturus takes command of the rebellion in Korhal and wages a guerilla war against the Confederacy.

(*StarCraft: I, Mengsk* by Graham McNeill)

2491

As a warning to other would-be separatists, the Confederacy unleashes a nuclear holocaust on Korhal IV, killing millions. In retaliation, Arcturus Mengsk names his rebel group the Sons of Korhal and intensifies his struggle against the Confederacy. During this time Arcturus liberates a Confederate ghost named

Sarah Kerrigan, who later becomes his second-in-command.
(*StarCraft: Uprising* by Micky Neilson)

2495

After living an indulgent, self-destructive lifestyle as outlaws, Jim Raynor and Tychus Findlay are cornered by authorities, and Raynor's criminal years come to an end. Although Tychus is apprehended, Raynor manages to escape. Raynor retires on the planet Mar Sara and marries Liddy. Their son, Johnny, is born shortly after.
(*StarCraft: Devils' Due* by Christie Golden)
(*StarCraft: Frontline volume 4*, "Homecoming" by Chris Metzen and Hector Sevilla)

2496

Jim Raynor becomes a marshal on Mar Sara.

2498

Despite Jim's reservations, Johnny Raynor is sent to the Ghost Academy on Tarsonis to develop his latent psionic potential. In the same year, Jim and Liddy receive a letter informing them of Johnny's death. Unable to cope with

her grief, Liddy wastes away and dies soon
afterward.

(*StarCraft: Frontline volume 4*, "Homecoming" by Chris Metzen and
Hector Sevilla)

2499–2500

Two alien threats appear in the Koprulu sector:
the ruthless, highly adaptable zerg and the
enigmatic protoss. In a seemingly unprovoked
attack, the protoss incinerate the terran planet
Chau Sara, drawing the ire of the Confederacy.
Unbeknownst to most terrans, Chau Sara had
become infested by the zerg, and the protoss had
carried out their attack in order to destroy the
infestation. Other worlds, including the nearby
planet Mar Sara, are also found to be infested by
the zerg.

(*StarCraft: Liberty's Crusade* by Jeff Grubb)
(*StarCraft: Twilight*, book three of *The Dark Templar Saga* by Christie
Golden)

On Mar Sara, the Confederacy imprisons Jim
Raynor for destroying Backwater Station, a
zerg-infested terran outpost. He is liberated
soon after by Mengsk's rebel group, the Sons of
Korhal.

(*StarCraft: Liberty's Crusade* by Jeff Grubb)

A Confederate marine named Ardo Melnikov finds himself embroiled in the conflict on Mar Sara. He suffers from painful memories of his former life on the planet Bountiful, but he soon discovers that there is a darker truth to his past.
(*StarCraft: Speed of Darkness* by Tracy Hickman)

Mar Sara suffers the same fate as Chau Sara and is incinerated by the protoss. Jim Raynor, Arcturus Mengsk, the Sons of Korhal, and some of the planet's residents manage to escape the destruction.
(*StarCraft: Liberty's Crusade* by Jeff Grubb)

Feeling betrayed by the Confederacy, Jim Raynor joins the Sons of Korhal and meets Sarah Kerrigan. A Universal News Network (UNN) reporter, Michael Liberty, accompanies the rebel group to report on the chaos and counteract Confederate propaganda.
(*StarCraft: Liberty's Crusade* by Jeff Grubb)

A Confederate politician named Tamsen Cauley tasks the War Pigs—a covert military unit created to take on the Confederacy's dirtiest jobs—with assassinating Arcturus Mengsk. The attempt on Mengsk's life fails.
(*StarCraft* monthly comic #1 by Simon Furman and Federico Dallocchio)

November "Nova" Terra, a daughter of one of the Confederacy's powerful Old Families on Tarsonis, unleashes her latent psionic abilities after she telepathically feels the murder of her parents and her brother. Once her terrifying power becomes known, the Confederacy hunts her down, intending to take advantage of her talents.
(*StarCraft: Ghost: Nova* by Keith R. A. DeCandido)

Arcturus Mengsk deploys a devastating weapon—the psi emitter—on the Confederate capital of Tarsonis. The device sends out amplified psionic signals and draws large numbers of zerg to the planet. Tarsonis falls soon after, and the loss of the capital proves to be a deathblow to the Confederacy.
(*StarCraft: Liberty's Crusade* by Jeff Grubb)

Arcturus Mengsk betrays Sarah Kerrigan and abandons her on Tarsonis as it is being overrun by zerg. Jim Raynor, who had developed a deep bond with Kerrigan, defects from the Sons of Korhal in fury and forms a rebel group that will come to be known as Raynor's Raiders. He soon discovers Kerrigan's true fate: instead of being killed by the zerg, she has been transformed into a powerful being known as the Queen of Blades.

(*StarCraft: Liberty's Crusade* by Jeff Grubb)
(*StarCraft: Queen of Blades* by Aaron Rosenberg)

Michael Liberty leaves the Sons of Korhal along with Raynor after witnessing Mengsk's ruthlessness. Unwilling to become a propaganda tool, the reporter begins transmitting rogue news broadcasts that expose Mengsk's oppressive tactics.
(*StarCraft: Liberty's Crusade* by Jeff Grubb)
(*StarCraft: Queen of Blades* by Aaron Rosenberg)

Arcturus Mengsk declares himself emperor of the Terran Dominion, a new government that takes power over many of the terran planets in the Koprulu sector.
(*StarCraft: I, Mengsk* by Graham McNeill)

Dominion senator Corbin Phash discovers that his young son, Colin, can attract hordes of deadly zerg with his psionic abilities—a talent that the Dominion sees as a useful weapon.
(*StarCraft: Frontline volume 1*, "Weapon of War" by Paul Benjamin, David Shramek, and Hector Sevilla)

The supreme ruler of the zerg, the Overmind, discovers the location of the protoss homeworld of Aiur and launches an invasion of the planet.

(*StarCraft: Frontline volume 3*, "Twilight Archon" by Ren Zatopek and Noel Rodriguez)

(*StarCraft: Queen of Blades* by Aaron Rosenberg)

(*StarCraft: Twilight*, book three of *The Dark Templar Saga* by Christie Golden)

Juras, the brilliant inventor of the protoss mothership, awakens from a centuries-long sleep to discover that Aiur is under threat from the zerg. Not knowing the zerg's true intentions or the reasons for their assault, the scientist struggles to decide whether or not to attack the strange aliens.

("Mothership" by Brian Kindregan at us.battle.net/sc2/en/game/lore/)

The heroic high templar Tassadar sacrifices himself to destroy the Overmind. However, much of Aiur is left in ruins. The remaining Aiur protoss flee through a warp gate created by the xel'naga—an ancient alien race that is thought to have influenced the evolution of the zerg and the protoss—and are transported to the dark templar planet Shakuras. For the first time since the dark templar were banished from Aiur, the two protoss societies are reunited.

(*StarCraft: Frontline volume 3*, "Twilight Archon" by Ren Zatopek and Noel Rodriguez)

(*StarCraft: Queen of Blades* by Aaron Rosenberg)

(*StarCraft: Twilight*, book three of *The Dark Templar Saga* by Christie Golden)

The zerg pursue the refugees from the planet Aiur through the warp gate to Shakuras. Jim Raynor and his forces, who had become allies with Tassadar and the dark templar Zeratul, stay behind on Aiur in order to shut down the warp gate. Meanwhile, Zeratul and the protoss executor Artanis utilize the powers of an ancient xel'naga temple on Shakuras to purge the zerg that have already invaded the planet.

On the fringe world of Bhekar Ro, two terran siblings named Octavia and Lars stumble upon a recently unearthed xel'naga artifact. Their investigation goes awry when the device absorbs Lars and fires a mysterious beam of light into space, attracting the attention of the protoss and the zerg. Before long, Bhekar Ro is engulfed in a brutal conflict among terran, protoss, and zerg forces as each fights to claim the strange artifact. (*StarCraft: Shadow of the Xel'Naga* by Gabriel Mesta)

The United Earth Directorate (UED), having observed the conflict among the terrans, the zerg, and the protoss, arrives in the Koprulu sector from Earth in order to take control. To accomplish its goal, the UED captures a fledgling Overmind on the zerg-occupied planet of Char. The Queen of Blades, Mengsk, Raynor, and the protoss put aside their differences and work together in order to defeat the UED and the new Overmind. These unlikely allies manage to succeed, and after the death of the second Overmind, the Queen of Blades attains control over all zerg in the Koprulu sector.

On an uncharted moon near Char, Zeratul encounters the terran Samir Duran, once an ally of the Queen of Blades. Zeratul discovers that Duran has successfully spliced together zerg and protoss DNA to forge a hybrid, a creation that Duran ominously prophesizes will change the universe forever.

Arcturus Mengsk exterminates half of his ghost operatives to ensure loyalty among the former Confederate agents who have been integrated into the Dominion ghost program. Additionally, he establishes a new Ghost Academy on Ursa, a moon orbiting Korhal IV.

(*StarCraft: Shadow Hunters*, book two of *The Dark Templar Saga* by Christie Golden)

Corbin Phash sends his son, Colin, into hiding from the Dominion, whose agents are hunting down the young boy to exploit his psionic abilities. Corbin flees to the Umojan Protectorate, a terran government independent of the Dominion.

(*StarCraft: Frontline volume 3*, "War-Torn" by Paul Benjamin, David Shramek, and Hector Sevilla)

The young Colin Phash is captured by the Dominion and sent to the Ghost Academy. Meanwhile, his father, Corbin, acts as a dissenting voice against the Dominion from the Umojan Protectorate. For his outspoken opposition, Corbin becomes the target of an assassination attempt.

(*StarCraft: Frontline volume 4*, "Orientation" by Paul Benjamin, David Shramek, and Mel Joy San Juan)

2501

Nova Terra, having escaped the destruction of her homeworld, Tarsonis, trains alongside other gifted terrans and hones her psionic talents at the Ghost Academy.

(*StarCraft: Ghost: Nova* by Keith R. A. DeCandido)

(*StarCraft: Ghost Academy volume 1* by Keith R. A. DeCandido and Fernando Heinz Furukawa)

Nova encounters Colin Phash, whom the academy is studying in an effort to harness his unique abilities. Meanwhile, four comrades from Nova's past desperately seek rescue from a zerg onslaught after they become stranded on the mining planet of Shi.

(*StarCraft: Ghost Academy volume 2* by David Gerrold and Fernando Heinz Furukawa)

During a training exercise in the Baker's Dozen system, Nova and her peers at the Ghost Academy discover that the planet of Shi has been overrun with zerg. Of even greater concern is the fact that several terrans—friends from Nova's youth on Tarsonis—are trapped on the planet.

(*StarCraft: Ghost Academy volume 3* by David Gerrold and Fernando Heinz Furukawa)

2502

Arcturus Mengsk reaches out to his son, Valerian, who had grown up in the relative absence of his father. Intending for Valerian to continue the Mengsk dynasty, Arcturus recalls his own progression from an apathetic teenager to an emperor.

(*StarCraft: I, Mengsk* by Graham McNeill)

Reporter Kate Lockwell is embedded with Dominion troops to deliver patriotic, pro-Dominion broadcasts to the Universal News Network. During her time with the soldiers, she encounters former UNN reporter Michael Liberty and discovers some of the darker truths beneath the Dominion's surface.

StarCraft: Frontline volume 2, "Newsworthy" by Grace Randolph and
Jam Kim)

Tamsen Cauley plans to kill off the War Pigs—
who are now disbanded—in order to cover up
his previous attempt to assassinate Arcturus
Mengsk. Before enacting his plan, Cauley
gathers the War Pigs for a mission to kill Jim
Raynor, an action that Cauley believes will
win Mengsk's favor. One of the War Pigs sent
on this mission, Cole Hickson, is the former
Confederate soldier who helped Raynor survive
the brutal Kel-Morian prison camp.
(*StarCraft* monthly comic #1 by Simon Furman and Federico
Dallocchio)

Fighters from all three of the Koprulu sector's
factions—terran, protoss, and zerg—vie for
control over an ancient xel'naga temple on
the planet Artika. Amid the violence, the
combatants come to realize the individual
motivations that have brought them to this
chaotic battlefield.
(*StarCraft: Frontline volume 1*, "Why We Fight" by Josh Elder and
Ramanda Kamarga)

The Kel-Morian crew of *The Generous Profit*
arrives on a desolate planet in hopes of finding
something worth salvaging. As they sort

through the ruins, the crew members discover the terrifying secret behind the planet's missing populace.
(*StarCraft: Frontline volume 2*, "A Ghost Story" by Kieron Gillen and Hector Sevilla)

A team of protoss scientists experiments on a sample of zerg creep, bio-matter that provides nourishment to zerg structures. However, the substance begins to affect the scientists strangely, eventually sending their minds spiraling downward into madness.
(*StarCraft: Frontline volume 2*, "Creep" by Simon Furman and Tomás Aira)

A psychotic viking pilot, Captain Jon Dyre, attacks the innocent colonists of Ursa during a weapon demonstration. His former pupil, Wes Carter, confronts Dyre in order to end his crazed killing spree.
(*StarCraft: Frontline volume 1*, "Heavy Armor, Part 1" by Simon Furman and Jesse Elliott)
(*StarCraft: Frontline volume 2*, "Heavy Armor, Part 2" by Simon Furman and Jesse Elliott)

Sandin Forst, a skilled Thor pilot with two loyal partners, braves the ruins of a terran installation on Mar Sara in order to infiltrate a hidden vault. After getting access to the facility, Forst realizes

that the treasures he expected to find were
never meant to be discovered.

(*StarCraft: Frontline volume 1*, "Thundergod" by Richard Knaak and
Naohiro Washio)

2503

When Private Maren Ayers, a Dominion
medic, and her platoon are attacked by zerg
on the barren mining world of Sorona, they
take refuge in a naturally fortified settlement
called Cask. Although the area proves to
be impenetrable to attackers, Ayers and her
comrades soon witness the zerg's frightening
adaptability when the aliens unleash an
explosive new mutation to overcome Cask's
defenses.

("Broken Wide" by Cameron Dayton at
us.battle.net/sc2/en/game/lore/)

Dominion scientists capture the praetor Muadun
and conduct experiments on him to better
understand the protoss' psionic gestalt—the
Khala. Led by the twisted Dr. Stanley Burgess,
these researchers violate every ethical code in
their search for power.

(*StarCraft: Frontline volume 3*, "Do No Harm" by Josh Elder and
Ramanda Kamarga)

Archaeologist Jake Ramsey investigates a xel'naga temple, but things quickly spiral out of control when a protoss mystic known as a preserver merges with his mind. Afterward Jake is flooded with memories spanning protoss history.
(*StarCraft: Firstborn*, book one of *The Dark Templar Saga* by Christie Golden)

Jake Ramsey's adventure continues on the planet Aiur. Under the instructions of the protoss preserver within his head, Jake explores the shadowy labyrinths beneath the planet's surface to locate a sacred crystal that might be instrumental in saving the universe.
(*StarCraft: Shadow Hunters*, book two of *The Dark Templar Saga* by Christie Golden)

Mysteriously, some of the Dominion's highly trained ghosts begin to disappear. Nova Terra, now a graduate of the Ghost Academy, investigates the fate of the missing operatives and discovers a terrible secret.
(*StarCraft: Ghost: Spectres* by Nate Kenyon)

Jake Ramsey is separated from his bodyguard, Rosemary Dahl, after they flee Aiur through a xel'naga warp gate. Rosemary ends up alongside other refugee protoss on Shakuras, but Jake is nowhere to be found. Alone and running out of time, Jake searches for a way to extricate the protoss preserver from his mind before they both die.

(*StarCraft: Twilight*, book three of *The Dark Templar Saga* by Christie Golden)

A mixed team of dark templar and Aiur protoss journeys to a remote asteroid in order to activate a dormant colossus—a towering robotic war machine created long ago by the protoss. En route to the asteroid, however, their ship comes under assault by the zerg, imperiling the entire mission.

("Colossus" by Valerie Watrous at us.battle.net/sc2/en/game/lore/)

In the closely guarded Simonson munitions facility on Korhal IV, the Dominion performs testing on its newest terror weapon: the Odin. Unbeknownst to the Dominion, one of the Umojan Protectorate's elite psionic spies—a shadowguard—has resolved to uncover the military's secret project at any cost.

("Collateral Damage" by Matt Burns at us.battle.net/sc2/en/game/lore/)

A team from the Moebius Foundation—a mysterious terran organization interested in alien artifacts—investigates a xel'naga structure in the far reaches of the Koprulu sector. During their research the scientists uncover a dark force lurking in the ancient ruins.

(*StarCraft: Frontline volume 4*, "Voice in the Darkness" by Josh Elder and Ramanda Kamarga)

Kern tries to start his life anew after a career as a Dominion reaper, a highly mobile shock trooper who had been chemically altered to be more aggressive. But his troubled past proves harder to escape than he thought when a former comrade unexpectedly arrives at Kern's home.

(*StarCraft: Frontline volume 4*, "Fear the Reaper" by David Gerrold and Ruben de Vela)

A nightclub singer named Starry Lace finds herself at the center of diplomatic intrigue among Dominion and Kel-Morian officials.

(*StarCraft: Frontline volume 3*, "Last Call" by Grace Randolph and Seung-hui Kye)

When a ragtag group of Dominion marines known as Zeta Squad patrols a mining outpost for signs of Kel-Morian terrorist activity, it comes under attack by an insidious zerg mutation that can take on the guise of terrans, blurring the line between friend and foe.

("Changeling" by James Waugh at us.battle.net/sc2/en/game/lore/)

2504

A world-weary Jim Raynor returns to Mar Sara and grapples with his own disillusionment.
(*StarCraft: Frontline volume 4*, "Homecoming" by Chris Metzen and Hector Sevilla)

Isaac White, one of the Dominion's heavily armored marauders, is ordered to save a group of Kel-Morian miners under attack from pirates. Yet White's task proves to be more than just a rescue mission: it becomes an opportunity for him to put to rest a terrible memory that has haunted him since his bomb technician years during the Guild Wars.
("Stealing Thunder" by Micky Neilson at us.battle.net/sc2/en/game/lore/)

After four years of relative silence, the Queen of Blades and her zerg Swarm unleash attacks throughout the Koprulu sector. Amid the onslaught, Jim Raynor continues his struggle against the oppressive Terran Dominion . . . and the restless ghosts of his past.